SUPER BLOOM

A Novel

MEGAN TADY

Zibby Books
New York

Library of Congress Control Number: 2022942886

ISBN: 978-1-958506-12-7
eBook ISBN: 979-8-9862418-9-0

Cover design by Allison Saltzman
Book design by Ursula Damm
www.zibbybooks.com

Printed in the United States of America
10 9 8 7 6 5 4 3 2 1

Praise for SUPER BLOOM

"*Super Bloom* is a true delight—hilarious, poignant, and as much of an escape as a spa day in the mountains of Vermont. Who could resist a novel about writers, romance, and the nuances of friendship? Not me! Take *Super Bloom* along on your next getaway."
—Amanda Eyre Ward, author of *The Jetsetters*

"A winning (and wickedly funny) debut about a massage therapist's second chance at life. Like a skilled therapist herself, Tady works all the right pressure points to leave the reader rejuvenated. I already can't wait to read what she writes next."
—Steven Rowley, author of *The Guncle*

"Fresh, funny, and told by a narrator whose voice I would follow anywhere, *Super Bloom* is a true delight. I absolutely adored this book."
—Annabel Monaghan, author of *Nora Goes Off Script*

"Absolutely delightful."
—Jenny Lawson, author of *Furiously Happy*

"*Super Bloom* is super fun! Like a great massage therapist, Tady's funny, feel-good debut will de-stress and delight."
—Georgia Clark, author of *It Had to Be You*

"*Super Bloom* is that rare sort of novel that's both a blast to read and leaves you thinking about the characters long after you've finished the last page. Set in a spa in Vermont (who doesn't

want to go there for a while?), Tady delivers a terrific satirical world in which our heroine—a down-and-out massage therapist mourning a lost love—has to fight her way back to happiness. Throw in some entitled clients and a narcissistic romance novelist with truly evil intentions, and you've got a sure hit from a wonderfully gifted new debut novelist. Can't wait to see what she writes next!"
—Katie Crouch, author of *Girls in Trucks*

"*Super Bloom* is such a fun read! Tady had me laughing out loud as I followed her quirky, broken-hearted heroine Joan as she bumbled her way through grief, loss, and the more typical hardships of a thirty something woman living in a small town. This life-affirming story (and a romance within a romance within a romance) is a tale of unexpected friendship, moving through grief, and never giving up on your dreams."
—Eileen Garvin, author of *The Music of Bees*

For Mom, may I never stop dreaming of you

SUPER BLOOM

Fall

ONE

I harbor a secret fantasy to go apeshit at work. Maybe today's the day.

My shift is over, and I'm waiting at the reception desk at the Apex Inn & Spa to get my bookings for tomorrow. It's been a doozy—one rude client took a phone call mid-massage, gabbing about who's getting the Hamptons house in her divorce; another client kept calling me "sweetheart."

Heather, the receptionist, is on the phone, forcing me to linger in the spa's tunnel of consumption: avocado lotions, chanting bowls, detox teas, ear candles. It's like Gandhi said: "Renounce and enjoy . . . all these products." An anger boils up in me that no amount of essential-oil sniffing can temper, and once again I think, *Apeshit?*

First, I'd upend the stacks of bright white towels that appear in my nightmares, a never-ending chore. Then I'd stand outside the Wellness Room and boo at all the yogis who practice a form of spiritual development that includes pretending to lose their complimentary slippers so they can bring home the extra pair.

All the while, I'd swing two strings of mala beads at anyone who tried to stop me, a pair of holistic nunchucks.

Heather says into the phone, "We don't offer Japanese cupping, but we do offer Chinese spooning." This is news to me.

Guess I'll learn the venerable (or brand-spanking-new) art of Chinese spooning any day now.

I narrow my eyes at the *gua sha* skin-scraping tool set—a recent bestseller. Clients go bananas for anything ancient—techniques, wisdom, modalities, grains. They want something time-tested and old, but they also demand the latest version, the current trend, which means we bodyworkers have to appear both cutting-edge *and* very, very wise.

The chestnut-brown mala beads are beckoning, but who am I kidding? I can't afford to get fired.

And anyway, it's not about the Apex. Yes, this place and *some* of my clients are beyond annoying, but I'm really raging against something else. Today is the two-year anniversary of Samuel's death.

I tried being mad at him for dying, but it doesn't work. Can't punch a ghost.

A firm tap on my shoulder makes me jump. It's Tara, the spa manager, her blond tresses spooling around her shoulders, sparking hair envy. She's exempted from our spa-issued (employee-purchased) black uniform with teal embossing, instead strutting around in a red calf-length sleeveless dress à la Olivia Pope. She's not smiling.

"We need to talk." Tara gestures for me to follow her, and a lump forms in my throat the size of a small chunk of rose quartz selling for twenty-five bucks.

The windows in Tara's office have a view of Mount Apex, the 2,500-foot peak for which the spa is named and one of the highest peaks in Vermont's Taconic Mountain range. Tara (pronounced "*Tare*-uh," and don't I forget it) motions for me to take a seat in a chair opposite her.

I eye a gold Buddha paperweight on Tara's desk. She folds her hands on her desk like a school dean. "I'll cut right to the point. You're on thin ice here."

"But I . . ." I was well behaved today, even with Phone Call Client and Sweetheart Client. A third person, Rip Van Winkle Client, fell asleep on my massage table and awoke with a start wondering where he was. To break up the day's monotony, I almost said, *You've been abducted by aliens.* But I didn't!

"I had a third complaint about you," Tara says. "From the client with the wig?"

"Oh, that woman," I say, rolling my eyes. *That woman,* a client in her late sixties, had removed her blond bob wig and hung it right over the mouth valve of my water bottle. C'mon, I *drink* from that.

"Joan, you called her out for it. She could be a cancer patient."

"Is she?" I didn't see that on her intake form.

"No. But that's not the point. You have a bad attitude. You mope around." Tara counts my indiscretions on her fingers. "A cloud of negativity hangs over you. Our clients come to the Apex for positive energy. We're a serotonin boost, but you're delivering the doldrums." It's a line she's obviously rehearsed.

Looking past Tara, I study a nature photograph on the wall, a tree stump with the rings miraculously forming the shape of a heart and words overlaid in bold type: "Love is all around you." The Apex is full of these tacky inspirational quotes, tempting me to pull a Banksy.

Tara mistakes my nonanswer for contemplation, and she softens her tone. "Joan, I know you faced some tough stuff when you first started here."

My stomach pinches. Is she referring to . . . no . . . not today, of all days.

"And we've given you a lot of grace. A *lot* of grace." Tara searches for eye contact, but I won't give her the satisfaction.

She *is* referring to Samuel. "I know he meant a lot to you, but you've been mourning him longer than you were together. We can't keep chalking up your bad behavior to heartbreak." I watch her eyes dart to a framed photo of her husband, and I imagine her mentally calculating the appropriate level of my grief. How bad could it still be? No kids, no in-laws, no house together, nothing that made it, well, harder.

I should be able to bounce back. This is what she's thinking. I know, because it's been implied before. I bite the inside of my cheek so viciously I nearly puncture the skin, and the look on my face must tell Tara to move on, because she does, clearing her throat as she shifts back into authoritarian mode.

"Anyway. This is your third strike. Technically, I should fire you."

"You're firing me?" Panic rises in my chest. I'm in serious debt from paying for massage school, and my list of bills is longer than a hypochondriac's pharmacy receipt. I've been playing a dangerous game at work, I know, but I can't seem to stop myself.

I *could* be a good massage therapist—I once had the drive and the curiosity—and even if I'm not exactly a "people person," I love that muscles speak their own language and that I can spend hours coaxing them to reveal themselves to me. But it's not like I've had a fair chance. Chronic sadness stripped my gears, and I've been careening ever since. I don't think I can survive being brokenhearted *and* broke. This job is the only thing I get up for, even if I'm sabotaging it.

"Actually—" Tara's computer chimes, and she leans over to type a few keystrokes, smiling to herself, leaving me to squirm. Is she *Google chatting* someone while giving me the ax?

As I wait to hear my fate, I fidget with the straps of my canvas tote bag. Inside is my journal, which was suggested as a grief tool by the therapist I saw only once. She instructed me to journal about the loss of Samuel, but that was too painful.

Instead, I imagine my clients' private lives and then write down the stories, envisioning their secrets and passions and hurts based on the slope of the lower back, the elasticity of skin, the rigidity of muscles. My hands pass over bodies as if I'm reading braille, and their worlds unfold.

The wig lady: her aching sciatica told me that she sits a lot, crossing her right leg over her left, and I pictured a dangling stiletto, four fluffy Pomeranians vying for her lap.

The sleepy client: his rounded shoulders, tight scalene muscles sloping down his neck, and general drowsiness suggested stressful computer work, and I saw him as an accountant cooking the books for a major corporation, doubts creeping in at night.

A woman yesterday: The masseter muscles in her jaw were extremely tight, meaning she clenches and grimaces throughout the day. People think the back muscles reveal stress, but I know that it's actually the face. In hers, I glimpsed a hidden life—an abusive marriage, perhaps—and I longed to give her extra time on the table, but I had another client waiting in the wings. It was her first massage, she'd said. A gift certificate. Not everyone who comes to the Apex is demanding. Some of my clients are lovely.

I'd likely never see her again, and I hoped I'd given her a small window of relief.

Of course, Tara doesn't know about this woman, or these moments. She hears only the complaints. She pries her eyes away from her computer and blinks. "Where were we?"

I drop the handles of my bag. "You were about to fire me?"

"Actually, I'm giving you one last chance. You have a celebrity client tomorrow."

"What?" I nearly choke. It's not uncommon for celebrities to zip up from New York City to recharge in anonymity. But they're never assigned to me. I'm the schmuck who gets the tourists with Groupons. "Who is it?"

Tara hesitates, twisting her long earring. "Carmen Bronze."

I frown. "Never heard of her."

"The famous romance novelist? She's quite the, um, force." Tara pretends to straighten a pile of papers on her desk.

Oh, no. No, no, no, no, no. This sounds like industry speak for "worst nightmare."

"And she can have some"—Tara drums her fingers on top of the pile—"creative requests. Not sexual, mind you."

"So far, she sounds intimidating."

"She's actually quite small. In stature."

"Uh—"

More paper shuffling as Tara avoids my eyes. "She has a 'bad-ish' reputation, but that doesn't make it all true."

"You're saddling me with the client everyone's afraid of?"

"Not everyone . . ."

"There's got to be someone else. Carlie?"

"She has a funeral tomorrow." Ugh, I curse Carlie for pulling the funeral card. I know she's driving to Burlington to get a new tattoo.

"Tree?"

"He's too sensitive. She'll flay him."

"Lou?"

"He's off celebrity clients since the whole Jenna Elfman thing."

"Damn."

"Joan." Tara sighs, her patience as thin as the cucumber rounds bobbing in the spa's water. "Trust me, I don't like this any more than you do. As you can see, I don't have other choices. I'm offering you a chance at redemption. You shouldn't *want* someone else to take it. Here's the deal: If you get a glowing review from Carmen Bronze, I'll wipe your slate clean. No more strikes. You start over."

A clean slate. Maybe I *could* start over, find my way back to what I loved about massage, become engrossed in anatomy books again, be kinder to people. To myself. Samuel would want that. He wouldn't like this version of me. *I* don't like this version of me.

"I need Carmen to go home happy, or she could be a big headache for me." Tara rubs her temples. "Her online reviews are *legendary*. She decimated Banyon Ridge over their detox herbal wraps, and business hasn't been the same since. And we can't afford a bad review from Carmen Bronze." Tara sits up straight in her chair, suppressing a shudder. "Not after Jenna."

A gentle knock at Tara's door interrupts us, and Tony, head of maintenance, nudges it open, struggling under the weight of a large framed print under one arm and a stepladder under the other.

"Ah, Mr. Fix-It is here," Tara says, without offering to help. "Can you lean the artwork over there and come back in five?" She answers her phone and turns away from us.

I flinch at how Tara's reduced Tony to the guy who does all of the odd jobs. I stand up, taking the ladder.

"Thank you," he says.

"These god-awful prints will be the death of us," I whisper. Tony chuckles easily, as if a laugh has been waiting to happen all morning. The first genuine smile of the day springs to my lips.

"You got that right," he responds, smiling, too, the skin around his eyes folding like the ribs of a seashell. He starts to say something else, but the walkie-talkie on his belt interrupts: "We got a problem in the pool." He groans, but he doesn't seem annoyed to go deal with what's likely a floating turd. Reaching for the door and nodding toward Tara, he says quietly, "Tell her I'll be back in a bit."

Tara hangs up, but before I can sit down again, she holds up a hand to stop me. "What I've been trying to say is if you *don't* get a glowing review from Carmen—if you mess this up—tomorrow will be your last day."

Her words hit me like that Buddha paperweight to the gut. It's an impossible task. The world's grumpiest bodyworker has to impress the world's fussiest client? I feel like I'm an anesthetized squirrel being sent into a lion's den.

But what choice do I have, really? I've backed myself into this corner. I've got to fight like hell to keep this job. This Carmen Bronze character doesn't know who she's—

"Joan, are you okay?"

"Yes, why?"

"You just threw a punch into the air. You're not planning to *hurt* Carmen Bronze, are you?"

I laugh like that's absurd. "Of course not."

"You'll be at your best?"

"My very, very best." I don't have a best. Tara and I are both in trouble.

As I close the door, Tara calls after me in a singsong voice, "Tell everyone I'll be a few minutes late to staff meeting."

Staff meeting. I forgot. Now, there's a place where I could really go apeshit.

TWO

Twenty-five minutes later, and without an apology for her tardiness, Tara claps her hands to silence the chatter in the Wellness Room. From a box at her feet, she pulls out a squat tub of body scrub: the Miracle Maple Body Accentuator. She's hoping for excited gasps. We don't deliver.

"You guys! Maple! Vermont is the Maple Syrup Capital of the World, am I right? I'll pass the jar around. Don't touch the salts; we can reuse this."

Not only did Tara just issue me an ultimatum, but now I have to fawn over the overpriced product that she's over-ordered and that we're expected to upsell to our clients, as if someone who comes in with a sore hammy needs a thirty-dollar tub of salt scrub. I'm *terrible* at upselling—out of laziness, but mostly because it feels manipulative.

I'm sitting next to Carlie, an old-timer who's been a body-worker at the Apex for two decades. She's seen half a dozen spa managers take the helm, from the Bikram-practicing power-hungry type to the low-talking, whimsical leader who ate lunch in silence alone on the lawn. She was more dismayed than anyone when a national hotel chain bought the Apex—an iconic and beloved Vermont institution—and installed its own management, which included Tara, an MBA graduate from Florida State who's still charmed by local maple syrup and has no massage therapy experience.

Tara doesn't get our New England ways. If the Apex were a car, it'd be an old Mercedes that's driven into the ground. Why replace a car like that? Or the sidewalk, or the wallpaper, or the paint on all the chipped green shutters on the windows? There's a mustiness at the Apex that no amount of cleaning solution can conceal. If guests expect pure opulence—or just rooms that aren't drafty, doors that close tightly—they don't get it. It's all part of the charm, and judging by the Apex's long history of exclusivity (it was apparently a favorite of President Teddy Roosevelt) and high demand, it works.

Of course, most of us in the room couldn't afford to stay here—let alone splurge on the Miracle Maple Body Accentuator treatment, even with our staff discount.

Carlie leans over and whispers, "At least it's not pumpkin spice." That was last year.

The tub circulates around the room. I tap my foot. When is this meeting going to be over?

I have big plans tonight: binge watch *Battlestar Galactica* and pray my cat, Sweet Bird, doesn't kill anything else, leaving a constellation of bloody entrails to shovel under the hedge.

The evening could include a steamy bath to soothe my aching body, my arms and hands sore from giving three back-to-back deep-tissue massages, but I'd have to clean the tub first, scour the grimy buildup. Plus, I'm avoiding anything that could spark quiet contemplation. I don't need to reconnect with my inner anything to know how terrible I feel. How terrible the last two years have been.

Today marks two achingly long years since Samuel died, just one week before we were scheduled to start work at the

Apex together and then move to Colorado when we'd saved up enough. The dream was simple: start our own massage business and hike the Rockies on the weekends.

We met at massage school. And Tara's right—we were together for only six short months. But we were fully committed, despite our bad jokes and morning breath and meager relationship experience. His laugh, like a seesaw, so annoying it just made me giggle more. My sarcastic streak, so vicious that sometimes he would declare a time-out, using the same gesture as an umpire. "This is a sarcastic-free zone," he'd say, drawing an imaginary box around the two of us.

In that incubation stage, that rare, raw, naive period that can never be repeated, we tethered our happiness to each other, nestled in our world like we were protected inside a snow globe. Untouchable from the outside.

So I had thought. Losing someone at the beginning of what was supposed to be an epic love story has me feeling as left behind as a worm-hole peach.

"When you use the Accentuator, be mindful of conserving product. Use one teaspoonful per leg," Tara says. She inspects herself in the mirrors, smoothing her dress. She does not look like a woman wrestling with guilt over nearly firing me earlier today.

I reach for the tub from Carlie. It takes all of my might to keep my finger from poking into the bed of salts. I pass it on to Jamal, the only male aesthetician on staff, who must have a million trade secrets because his brown skin is flawless and smooth, his eyeliner applied with a practiced hand. An animal lover, he's more at home with the foster pets he cares for than the people whose eyebrows he plucks. He holds the tub away from his body like it'll bubble up and scald him. Maple, I'm guessing, is an affront to his sophisticated sensibilities.

Jamal passes the tub to Tree, a limber Reiki practitioner with shoulder-length hair, who is sitting crisscross on the floor as if he's mid-meditation. He practices alternate-nostril breathing using his thumb and index finger as he sticks his face close to the salts.

Lou, a fiftysomething wire-muscled bodyworker and tiny-house obsessive who wears a feather necklace, is perched against a bolster, an ankle crossed over his knee, twisting a toenail that's hanging on for dear life. With the same hand, he reaches for the tub.

I close my eyes.

Every bodyworker has their way of getting through the day. Tree gazes into the middle distance; Lou drones on about square footage; Carlie installs a new national parks calendar in the break room every January; Jamal glances at footage from his at-home pet camera.

Mine is jotting about clients and the spa. It beats writing about how sad I am. And right now I long to pull my journal out of my bag and scrawl *Miracle Maple Body Accentuator*, but I can't draw attention to myself. It'll have to wait.

Tara claps again. "Guys, remember—you get fifteen percent commission on products. Let's get those numbers up, up, up."

Meeting adjourned, and everyone scrambles to their feet. I overhear Tree asking Jamal and Lou for their smoothie orders. Had he asked me, I would have said, *Fruit plus ice cream, minus the fruit.*

But Tree won't ask me. I boxed myself in a long time ago, made it clear that I wasn't in for anything—no lunch dates, no after-work drinks. For two years, my answer is always a mumbled "can't."

But today I need to talk to Carlie, and I tug her aside. "Hey," I whisper, "have you ever heard of Carmen Bronze?"

Carlie's eyes bulge as if a strong hug might pop them out of their sockets. "Is she coming back?" She presses a palm to her chest.

"Yes. Tomorrow. I have her."

She staggers backward with relief and then lifts her hands heavenward. "Thank god." She points her clasped hands at me and then back up to the ceiling. "Sorry for you, but thank god."

This sounds worse than I imagined. Carlie's usually unflappable. "Any advice? What should I know?"

Carlie cuts the difference between us, takes ahold of both of my shoulders, and says, "Run for the hills."

THREE

In the spa's waiting lounge the next afternoon, I announce the absurd fake name I've been given for Carmen Bronze, who is apparently concerned about privacy: "Gertrude Putyourbottomson?"

If she was going for discreet, this name doesn't cut it. Three people sitting on cream-colored upholstered chairs look up at me, and I give a hell-if-I-know shrug.

A petite woman too short to pass amusement parks' roller-coaster height requirements stands up and tosses a magazine on a table as if it's spurned her. This? *This* is the pint-sized middle-aged lady with the massive bestseller list? The one who has every massage therapist within a fifty-mile radius shaking in their Crocs and overmedicating with homeopathic arsenicum to stay calm?

Carlie's warning now seems a bit silly. I could take Carmen Bronze in a fight, if necessary, and for some reason, this boosts my confidence. After all, it's only a massage. How hard could it be?

I nod, she nods back, and then *she* leads the way down the corridor.

Her tight brown curls bounce as she walks, the corkscrews so perfect it looks like she wound strands of hair around her pinkie finger before setting them free to spiral from her head. I reach up to touch the ends of my own hair: chin-length, brown as a leather suitcase, stringy. In contrast to the rest of her harsh features—hooked nose, dark eyes—Carmen wears delicate pearl earrings. It's been ages since I've worn earrings to work, or since I've worn them, period.

My smile is my best asset, looks-wise, though it's as shy as a shadow-spooked groundhog. When my full smile emerges, it reveals one crooked tooth that appears to be leaning out of a Rockettes chorus line to see what everyone else is doing. I'm five-foot-eight, and after a doctor once remarked that I was "big-boned," I've never shaken the feeling that I take up a lot of space. I felt my physical best when I was hiking daily with Samuel. Now my longest walk is down the corridor to my therapy room.

"It's this one," I say, and Carmen pushes her way inside, hopping up onto the massage table. She's radiating a dizzying amount of energy and begins talking at a frightening speed. "I've got a four o'clock, so let's make this fast," she says, slapping the table. What does that mean? I can't make a sixty-minute massage go any faster.

I'm about to ask my standard questions—Where does it hurt? What kind of pressure?—but Carmen beats me to it.

"Here's the deal—I'm tight, tight, tight." Carmen mock-pinches her own shoulders three quick times. "I'm on a deadline. My agent's jabbing a fork into my ear. Have you ever had a fork jabbed into your ear?"

"Um, no."

"It's not pretty. I mean this figuratively, of course. Most people don't get me."

"I got it."

"Can you dim those things?" Carmen squints at the recessed lights, already subdued.

I'd rather not. It's as dark as a movie theater, but I need a good review, so I'll do whatever she asks. "Sure." I inch the dimmer, and the objects on the side table—a bottle of oil, a singing bowl, and my tote bag containing my journal—grow faint.

"A little more."

I try to keep the annoyance out of my voice when I say "no problem." I'm going to have to grope my way around the room. A lone candle flickers in the corner. I can barely detect the print hanging on the wall, but I know it's an image of the sea swallowing a swollen sunset, just like I know the written command typed below it: "Awaken to this very moment." What if I hate this very moment?

"Can you turn off that horrid New Age music?" Carmen asks.

"I'm sorry, I don't have control over the music." It's piped into my room, and I can't turn it up, turn it down, or, for god's sake, change it.

"Forget the music. Just wring me out to dry. Give me a good once-over. Pulverize my muscles. I want to be mush when I leave here so you have to scrape me off the table with a spatula."

"Figuratively," I offer, to show that I *do* get her.

"No, literally."

Ugh, fail. I had an uncle who used to pile a stack of quarters next to his plate when he dined at restaurants. Anytime he decided the waitress messed up—it was always a woman—he would visibly slide a quarter off the stack and pocket it. Is Carmen taking quarters off my stack? If I started with four stars, am I down to three? This is a nightmare.

Sleeves rolled up, I hover my hands over Carmen's back as if I'm about to thrust them into a large vat of bread dough. Then I begin, spreading oil onto her skin. She weighs as much as an empty laundry basket, though she's far from frail. Her body is lithe and lightly muscular, and her skin is smooth. But her muscles are as tight as promised, with sharp pellets, like little BBs, under her skin. She grunts and groans as I dig into her lats. In an effort to save my thumbs, I move to the head of the massage table, where I use my elbows to slide the skin back down toward Carmen's sacrum, giving my hands a break for a merciful but short sixty seconds.

I press my thumb into her right shoulder blade, gliding across her oiled skin and fanning the muscle just below the surface. Her rhomboid minor is inflamed—likely a by-product of all the writing she does. I imagine her sitting at a vast desk overlooking a bubbling brook, typing her books at a leisurely pace, and I can't help but feel a pang of envy. I wish I could ask her where she gets all of her story ideas, but I've got to pretend she's Gertrude Putyourbottomson, not a famous novelist who doesn't want to be hounded with questions while she's getting a massage.

I dance each fingertip across her rhomboid to the spine. Just right of the spine, I pivot my thumb, working it like a snowplow to push the skin and muscle up toward Carmen's neck and skull. Wisps of her curly hair get trapped underneath my thumb, and I pull them away, slick with oil.

This isn't going too bad. I might be able to pull this off.

As soon as I've formed that thought, the massage turns into a game of Whac-A-Mole.

"There, yes there," Carmen says. I press there.

"Over an inch." I inch over.

"Too far left." Shifting right.

"Too far right." Shifting left.

"Circular motion." I hula-hoop my thumb.

"Scratch for a sec." I scratch.

"Tickle." That's a rare one.

"Karate chop." I thump her with the edge of my hand.
"Hard!" *Wham.*

"Now soft, like a whisper." I barely brush her skin.

"Little raindrops." I lightly tap my fingers.

"Belly flop." Um, whack? I whack.

"Beached whale." My hand flops from the palm to the back of my hand.

"The worm." Is *Candid Camera* still a thing? I inch my fingers up Carmen's spine, caterpillar-like.

"Tic-tac-toe, but a cat's game." I draw an imaginary grid, the X's and O's canceling each other out. None of this makes any sense. I feel like I'm yes-ma'aming a madwoman.

When I resume my usual massage, Carmen shouts, "Harder!" I worry my thumb will puncture her skin. "Are you even pressing?"

This massage is slipping away from me. *I can do better*, I'm tempted to say. But I'm also starting to hate Carmen Bronze, and I loathe the idea of having to cater to someone's crazy whims just because of her celebrity status. Doesn't she have anything better to do than to write nasty reviews that get people fired?

I move to Carmen's left leg and pull the bottom of the sheet up to reveal her foot, calf, and hamstrings, tucking the sheet under her hip to discreetly hide her left butt cheek. Then I press the heel of my hand into the base of her calf, speeding over the hump of her leg toward the back of the knee. My thumbs go to work, side by side as one lever, deeply pressing on the calf to separate the gastrocnemius muscle. It's a slow movement, always with my hands stroking upward toward the heart. When I squeeze the Achilles, it gives me a moment to inspect Carmen's feet. I have to know what I'm in for.

Feet I loathe, with their tiny flecks of lint between toes and sharp, jagged toenails, their possibility of bunions, warts, flaky heel skin, thick calluses I could drive a tack through, athlete's foot, and just plain foot funk.

"No feet," Carmen announces, much to my happy surprise. She lifts her hand behind her back and points as if I'm a cleaning lady who missed a spot. "Spend the rest of the time on this knot right here."

I fumble around in the dark for the bottle of oil on my side table.

"Ha-hem." Carmen clears her throat. "I'm waiting."

"I'm coming." *Talk nicely, talk nicely.* "I just can't see." I knock the bottle of oil to the floor and then crack my head on the massage table standing up. Carmen sighs, dissatisfied, and I work with the slow sullenness of a disaffected teenager in heavy black eyeliner. My uniform is tight and rumpled, with sweat stains under the pits—I'm the one getting wrung out from this massage.

My hands have all but ground to a halt, and I will them to pick up the pace.

"Do you want to turn over?" I ask, my voice too loud for the room. Carmen has become eerily quiet for someone who was just barking orders, as if she's accepted that this is a mediocre massage. What will Carmen say to Tara? Do I care? Right now, I just want this to be over. I'm sure I'll be full of regrets later when I'm jobless, forced to move into my parents' basement.

The timer buzzes and I'm finally done. I stop abruptly. I didn't budget my time well, and I wasn't able to give Carmen my finale, the melting scalp massage, followed by a finger pressing into her third eye between her eyebrows. It's surely over for me at the Apex.

Carmen lies lifeless on the table, a corpse on a gurney. I lightly touch her cold, bony shoulder.

"Take your time," I whisper.

I shut the door quietly, possibly for the last time, and tiptoe to the lounge, where I fill a paper cup with water and walk briskly back down the hall, holding the cup in front of me like I'm racing with an egg on a spoon.

Outside the door, I lean against the wall and tap my foot in the orthotics I feel, at thirty-four, too young to wear.

Lou steps quietly from his therapy room and nods at me before scuttling down the hall to get his client a cup of the same cucumber water. One small upside of being fired and debt-ridden and living in my parents' basement is that I won't have to hear Lou talk about composting toilets ever again.

Carmen opens the door wearing her white robe, which could wrap around her twice. I present her the crinkled cup of water. Instead of taking it, Carmen snatches my wrist with the quickness of a barracuda, yanking me back into the room.

I gasp.

She slams the door and squeezes my wrist tighter. "Your manager, the one with the tresses. Tah-ra."

"*Tare*-uh," I correct.

"She wants a report of your performance."

I'm silent, shaken, trying to wriggle my wrist out of Carmen's strong grasp.

"It was a D, at best. It looks like it's bye-bye baby for you."

"I—you're not exactly a cakewalk," I protest before I can stop myself.

"I'll ignore that." Carmen drops my wrist but steps closer to me, her beaky nose at pecking height of my sternum. She's small, but I'm terrified of her. I'd inch backward if there was anywhere to go. "Listen, I've got a proposition for you. You scratch my back, I'll scratch yours."

"Didn't I just do that?" I joke weakly. Whatever she's proposing, I don't want it. Except if it involves never seeing each other again.

"You help me"—she gestures to herself and then to me—"and I help you."

Wary, parched, and spent, I croak, "How?"

Carmen puts her ear to the door, pausing to listen—for what, I'm not sure.

"Not here," she whispers.

I avert my eyes to, *damn*, the sunset image on the wall, and then she names a rendezvous point—Deb's Diner—for the next morning to discuss her proposition in private-ish, with eggs and coffee involved.

"Nine a.m. On. The. Dot." Carmen pokes me in the chest with each word. "And don't tell a soul." She flings open the door and barrels down the hallway, causing Lou to flatten against the wall, sloshing his client's cucumber water onto the socked toes sticking out of his Birkenstocks.

FOUR

When I finally exit through the heavy employee door, spilling out into the last few hours of daylight, I blink, sigh. I tromp heavily across the gravel parking lot, rooting in my bag for my car keys and a Snickers bar. Once inside my car, I unfold the top half of the wrapper, take a bite, and check my phone.

One text from Cher, my oldest, dearest—and, okay, *only*—friend, inviting me for dinner. I didn't hear from her yesterday on the anniversary, so maybe this is her way of making up for it.

There in 20, I text back with a string of pizza emojis, hoping she'll take a hint.

Cher's cooking is obscenely healthy. Post-Carmen, I'm craving a drive-thru meal, wiping french fry grease on my pants on the way home. Not a kale salad. But I haven't interacted with another person outside of work for a solid week, and even though things are strained and weird with Cher since our blowup this summer, she's still my best friend. Her hugs are spine-popping, in a good way, and I could use one right now. Totally worth pushing some veggies around on my plate.

As I pull out of the parking lot, I survey the Apex. It's strange to feel chafed working at such an indisputably gorgeous place. A central courtyard lined with rosebushes connects the spa with the main building, which has a window so tall it'll perfectly frame a fifteen-foot Christmas tree in a few months. Out front, as guests hand their keys to the valet, eight fluted columns stand watch, each too massive to encircle with both arms.

The Apex is one of the reasons that Newchester, in southern Vermont, has become a tourist town, although I'm no tourist. I was born in Rockford, a tiny neighboring town where housing is cheaper. My mom's parents were patient and industrious dairy farmers who eked out a living on a small parcel of Vermont's rocky soil. My dad, a transplant from Maine, ran away from a lifetime of heaving up lobster traps to work as a car mechanic for the last forty years, running his own shop. Mom just retired as a housecleaner. They're both in their mid-sixties, and they inherited, if nothing in dollars, a sense of resourcefulness from the generations before them.

For a solid half-mile, the road from the Apex is made out of bricks, and my silver 1999 Honda Civic hatchback bumps along like a horse-drawn wagon. I pass dozens of outlet stores that have popped up over the past few decades. There are huge B&Bs with little wooden signs hanging on hooks swinging in the breeze, a second-tier option for the people priced out at the Apex.

It's 5:30 p.m., and the moon is already visible. The maples overhead reach across the road like separated lovers, green leaves in the first stage of turning gold and red, a truly spectacular sight despite the traffic it will bring. Newchester is smack in the middle of the leaf-peeping circuit, with the Apex Inn & Spa a main attraction.

In the next few weeks, traffic will constipate the streets as day tourists from New York drive their cars at the speed of a snow sled ebbing to a stop, studying the GPS on their smartphones for longer than a light cycle.

I take a right on Somerset to dodge a line of cars at a stop-light ahead. On a side street, I push into fourth gear, and just like that I've crossed an invisible economic line, leaving behind the moneyed mansions for the well-loved but worn-down houses dotting the road, refurbished log cabins and long ranches set back in the woods. A white trailer appears on my right, with a barking dog attached to a long leash in the yard next to a muddied ATV four-wheeler, a faded "For Sale" sign fashioned to it. I round another bend, downshift into third, and catch a glimpse of the sparkling river the road has been chasing this entire time.

When I reach Cher's, I park in her designated client park-ing spot next to a sign that says "Shady Grove Massage." She's attained the holy grail: her own profitable, in-home massage business. Shady Grove is flourishing as much as the medicinal shade plants in her garden. Cher has the touch. Plus, there's the herb—her clients can get one of the best ninety-minute massages in town *and* a dime bag.

I find her in the kitchen, with its counter space the size of a fingernail, humming as she breaks apart garlic cloves. Her hair, red as a fire ant, is pulled back with a bag tie. She looks like an adult Strawberry Shortcake, with pale skin and freckles orbiting her nose. Her loose-fitting jeans are smeared with dirt. Hogging every available space on the wooden island that also serves as Cher's cutting board are glass jars filled with brown rice, mung beans, green lentils. A string of white Christmas tree lights tacked above the window gives the room a cozy glow.

"Get over here," she says, coming around the island to give me the hug I came for. I close my eyes and let myself pretend that our friendship is what it's always been. I'm expecting her to apologize for not reaching out on the anniversary of

Samuel's death. Instead, she releases me, picks up a garlic bulb, and says, "You're just in time to help me make pesto."

Did she forget, or is she deliberately withholding because of our fight?

"I'll pass," I say, heaving off my sweater and pulling up a rickety stool.

"Salty dog." Cher slides a bulb over to me anyway and then takes a hit from an already lit joint, her movements as cool as a smoke ring. She offers it to me, but I wave her off, and she stubs it out in a ceramic dish.

From the laundry room, I hear the rhythmic sound of the dryer likely tumbling towels and sheets after her day's work. I'm in awe of what she's achieved with limited outside help.

Cher and I bonded in seventh-grade band class when we both bleated out "Hot Cross Buns" on rented clarinets and were subsequently plunked into the last chairs with no ambitions to improve. While she was a musical dud, Cher's mom was a talented cabaret singer who, looking for work elsewhere, began performing on cruise ships that set sail from Portland, Maine. She'd be gone for weeks at a time, crooning up the coast to Bar Harbor and then to Nova Scotia, finally docking again at Prince Edward Island. During those weeks, Cher stayed with us, sleeping on the trundle bed in my room. Eventually, her mom permanently moved to PEI, and we became Cher's surrogate family. She texts with my mom more than I do.

After high school, I went to the University of Vermont, where I lasted one semester, dropping out when self-doubt and the bursar's bill caught up with me. At the same time, Cher was gallivanting around Southeast Asia, sleeping in hostels for four dollars a night. We knit back together in our mid-twenties, when I was in my third year working at a bowling alley, serving bottles of Bud Light Lime to rowdy bowling leagues every Friday. Cher was home for good by then, and she had a plan: train as a massage therapist, work at the Apex to gain experience, and then start her own business.

And she did it.

I fiddle with the bulb, peeling off the papery wrapper.

"Roughie?" Cher asks.

"Roughie." I'm hesitant to reveal my strikes at work, but I speed my way through Tara's ultimatum and describe Carmen Bronze putting me through my paces. "And if I performed well, Tara said she'd wipe my strikes clean."

"So did you?"

"I think so." I think *not*. I don't mention that I'm meeting Carmen Bronze in the morning to find out my actual fate. I can still see the crazed look in Carmen's eyes when she hissed, "Don't tell a soul."

Or maybe I'm holding back because I'm insecure about all of my shortcomings when I compare myself to Cher. And because, after our fight this summer, I trust her a little less.

Cher's still staring at me, and I grow defensive. "What? It's harder for me than it is for you! You're a natural. My body hurts. People piss me off. The Apex policies are unfair." I was supposed to be there with Samuel. This, I don't say.

She shakes her head and begins to cluck. "I tried to tell you—"

Cher *did* try to warn me that massage therapy might not suit my disposition, but I saw her success, her freedom to call the shots, and I wanted that, too. After the bowling alley, I worked a string of other fairly low-paying jobs, including as an exhibit docent at the Lincoln Family Home—"Don't touch that; please don't touch that either"—and as a "customer experience representative" at Enterprise Rent-A-Car in Bennington, a lame title for someone who pressures people into upgrading to midsized sedans and scares them into purchasing unnecessary auto insurance.

The outlook for my future was bleak. I needed to craft a plan, just like Cher had done. I needed an actual career, not another gig that let me barely coast by.

I actually googled "best paying jobs no college degree." On the list: elevator repair person, nuclear power reactor operator, funeral service director, X-ray technician, pilot. I deleted "best paying" and hit enter. Massage therapist was fourth on the list, and the schooling would take ten months to complete rather than four years. While it didn't feel like a perfect fit, I was genuinely interested in anatomy and the notion that I could ease people's pain by understanding the body.

To pay for the $8,000 tuition for massage school, I took out a credit card loan that I'm still paying off at an exorbitantly high interest rate. I get nauseated thinking about it.

"Not now, Cher, please. I don't need a lecture every time I come over." I plunk the garlic bulb onto the counter and rest my hand on top of it, the stress of the day overtaking me. I would never tell Cher this, but I'm envious that she loves massage therapy and I don't. That people choose her, hand over their own hard-earned dollars because she has an instinctual ability to help them. She's an excellent bodyworker—strong, methodical, empathetic—the kind of woman clients collapse into, trusting she'll give it her all each session.

Whereas my clients likely think they've pulled the short straw.

Moreover, I'm envious of her heart, fully intact and beating, her romantic attention flitting from one person to the next like a honeybee gathering nectar, having a big old blast.

My heart is still broken. Smashed beyond repair.

Cher turns away from me to pull out a worn-out food processor from the bottom rung of the kitchen island. A heavy, dusty cookbook topples without its bookend. She holds up a finger to pause our conversation, and then she pulses the basil, garlic, and olive oil, filling the kitchen with the aroma of fresh herbs. She dips a finger into the thick green sauce to taste it, reaches for the sea salt. Then she leans over the counter, her face close to mine.

"You need to get it together, Joan," she says. "It's not like you live in a war zone or toil in a meat factory or have a dozen kids to feed. You have a pretty good life, even if the Apex is a corporate behemoth and total environmental nightmare and you answer to the 'man.' A lot of other bodyworkers would kill for that gig."

My cheeks flush from a rush of embarrassment. To defend myself I say softly, "The anniversary was yesterday." I tilt my head down so my bangs cover my eyes.

"Shit. I forgot. *Shit.*"

Cher tucks a strand of her red hair behind her ear and reaches across for me, setting a hand on my hand. The simple motion, and the strength of her touch, unleashes my pent-up sorrow. A tear the size of a fat raisin slinks down my face. More follow, a steady drip. I slump, laying my head on the kitchen island, my other forearm a pillow, my hair mingling with garlic wrappers.

"I'm sorry I was so hard on you over the summer," she says, the first time she's fully apologized for what she'd previously defended as "tough love."

More like brutal love: She'd gripped my shoulders and practically shouted, "It's time to move on, for god's sake! You two barely knew each other!" I left her house in tears after accusing her of being a terrible friend, and we didn't speak for all of August. Over the last few weeks, we've been taking timid steps back toward each other.

I murmur a "thank you" into my arm.

"It's just that I see how stuck you are, and I'm worried about you. I want you to find some peace, to start healing. But of course, I know there's no timeline for that. So, I'm sorry again."

The thought crosses my mind that she wants me to heal because it would be less burdensome on *her*. Still, I raise my head a smidge and give her a weak smile. I'm bone-tired from the stress of the day.

"Have you thought about going back to therapy?" Cher ventures.

I grind my molars. "Ugh, no."

"How about journaling, like your therapist suggested? Maybe that would unlock things."

"You try writing about someone's death." I have tried this, more than I care to admit. I never get past writing the line *It was a sunny September day when Samuel went—*

"Your therapist said it could help. Maybe there's some merit to it."

"There's also merit to burying something and trying not to think about it again."

"Look, Joanie, you need an action plan, okay? Otherwise you're going to keep spinning your gears and racking up strikes at work until you do get fired. It doesn't have to be journaling about Samuel, but it has to be something. A grief group. Meditation. A pottery class. A string of one-night stands. Anything. You choose."

I remain silent. I hate all of those ideas.

Her cell phone chimes, and her troubled face brightens as she sees the name of the caller. I nod for her to take it. She goes to the living room, talking in excited, hushed tones. I hear, "I miss you, too."

When she steps back into the glow of the kitchen, I ask, "New lover?"

"She's on her way over." Now Cher blushes. "Do you mind if she joins us for dinner? I think you'll—"

"You know what, it's cool. You do your thing. I'd love to meet her soon." I take the out, irked by Cher's suggestion that I do something to get my life back on track. Like it's so easy.

"I'll tell her not to come."

"Do not do that. Seriously." I stand up from the stool, grab my bag. "I'm tired anyway."

"You haven't eaten. Can I pack you up some"—Cher glances at her offerings—"pesto?"

"No, thanks. I have food at home." Drive-thru party.

Cher glances back down at her phone. "Your mom keeps asking me if I want random things from her garage." She flashes me a picture that's popped up. "I'm not even sure what this is."

I squeeze my eyes shut. "She's doing that to you, too?" My parents are in the process of selling our family home and moving into a smaller, single-story condo. Mom read an article in *AARP* magazine about downsizing. Since then, she's been repeating the phrase "this is just too much house"—like it's an aristocratic country estate instead of a modest split-level they bought in the '80s—and she's begun rifling through boxes in the garage to determine what to sell at a tag sale, what to keep, what might net a surprise windfall on *Antiques Road-show*, and what to bestow upon me and, now, Cher—despite my objections. "Feel free to say no. To any of it."

Cher peers closer, tilting her head to study the image. "Is this an old metal jack-in-the-box? Those were always terrifying."

"Anything is possible."

"Does she have one of those huge gumball machines?" Cher's eyes grow big with excitement. "I've always wanted one of those."

"Ask her. If she doesn't have it, she could get it. You know Mom would love nothing more than a task like that." Mention to Mom that you're out of tissues, and she'll be at Job Lot the next morning. Accidently let on that your toaster is on the fritz, and she'll bop over later with three toasters she scooped up at tag sales.

Cher's fingers are flying over the keyboard, and I know a gumball machine is in her future. Sure enough, Mom texts back immediately and Cher snorts, holding up the phone so I can read: Sharon, a brain tumor coming right up!

"She's got to stop using voice-to-text," I say and laugh.

Cher maneuvers around the island, pulling me near, engulfing me in a garlicky hug, and I hug her back, but I can feel myself withdrawing, or maybe she's retreating, or we're both pulling back. Between our bodies is a growing space where our hearts would usually meet. I wonder if the harm done over the summer is irreparable. If we'll just never be the same.

Anyone observing us from the window would see two old friends, our bond as tight as sisters', basking in the presence of each other, completely at ease. But I know otherwise. I know that underneath the laughter and the banter, something is amiss. I feel a pinprick of anger at Cher that her apology can't erase.

And just like my pain over losing Samuel, I'm not sure that anger will ever go away.

FIVE

I'm shoved so close to Carmen Bronze in the crowded entry-
way of Deb's Diner that I could lick her cheek. Had I been of
sound mind after her massage, I would have suggested anywhere but here. It's packed with locals defying the Starbucks
next door and the Panera down the block—folks I likely know.
We stand out as an odd pair: Carmen, an obvious out-of-
towner in a tight black leather jacket and black jeans, and me,
a townie in an overworn hoodie, slouchy jeans, and knockoff
UGG boots. All the clothes within reach when I rolled out of
bed this morning.

Carmen taps an atlas-sized plastic menu against her hand.
"I'm not the queen of patience."

Is that so? I think. A server zips by and shouts, "Just a sec."
Carmen leans past the coatrack to watch the server amble
down a thin aisle lined with red booths and Formica tables.
Every swivel stool at the counter is taken, nine slouched
backs greeting us, and I fight a pang in my heart.

Samuel and I preferred the counter. We'd marvel at the fast
pace of the line cooks as we lingered over bad coffee until one
of the servers shooed us away.

Another reason I should've suggested a different place.

"Table's ready," the server says, and Carmen hands the woman her menu to carry. The server flashes me a "What's with this lady?" expression that I ignore.

"I'll have a coffee, stat," Carmen says and shimmies into the booth. "Cream and sugar." She looks at me, expectant.

I unzip my hoodie after sitting down, unsheathing my arms from the sleeves. "Yes, same for me. Thank you." Carmen nods to the server, who writes down our order on a small pad and walks to the kitchen.

"Now, why write that down?" Carmen says. "Who can't remember two coffees?"

"That's probably also our bill, so she'll rip that off and give it to us after." Carmen's obviously never worked in a diner.

She unwinds the long white scarf around her neck as if removing a bandage, leaving on her slim black leather coat. She's compact, like a gymnast or a ninja. Her dark brown curls are hopelessly erratic and her mouth has long, deep arcs on either side that look like they're leaning to get away from the things she says. There's no way those are laugh lines. Her brown eyes dart around the diner like she's casing the joint.

I'm just as jumpy. What does Carmen want from me?

Something out the window catches her attention, so I look, too. It's a wedding party congregating on the steps of the all-white church with a towering steeple across the street. Get a blue sky like today, and the pictures will be amazing. A photographer fans out the bride's dress, grabs the groom by the elbow to maneuver him closer to his wife, and scampers down the steps.

"God, I hate weddings."

"What?" I ask. "You're a romance novelist. Aren't you supposed to love weddings? Isn't that the whole point—happily ever after and all that?"

Carmen scoffs. "I write about love, but none of my novels end with a wedding. Never. Nope. Too many horrid dresses, uncomfortable wooden pews, suffocating churches, cloying vows, un-adorable ring bearers, chatty aunts, grabby uncles, sweaty groomsmen, sugary cakes, unoriginal surf-and-turf menus, god-awful speeches that go on forever, that YMCA song—"

The coffee arrives in beige ceramic mugs, putting a stop to Carmen's barrage on weddings.

"I'll have Greek yogurt with fresh fruit," Carmen orders.

"Regular yogurt okay?" the server barks back, making me love her.

"Fine, fine." Carmen waves a dismissive hand in the air.

I order scrambled eggs with bacon, thanking the server again as Carmen checks her phone and stabs her keypad with her pointer finger.

"I don't trust these things." She holds her phone up. "NSA, they're always listening." Then she stuffs the phone into her bag, leans back, and stretches her short arms across the back of the booth as if she's gearing up for a Ferris wheel ride with a sweetheart, her leather jacket creaking with every movement.

"I'm going to be honest with you, Joan. Your massage yesterday, it was dog doo-doo."

I pick at the silver rim of the table. Is this why Carmen asked me here? To humiliate me further?

Carmen continues. "But I kind of like you, Joan. I want to know more about you. You hate your job, right?" Her interest in me is more than a little shocking. Why does she care?

I open my mouth to answer, but Carmen cuts me off. "Table that. Here's the deal. My agent thinks I'm up here for some R&R. But really, I'm sniffing out a new book idea. If my agent gets wind that I have a new idea brewing, she'll be up my ass in no time having a tea party."

I nod as if it's common for someone to have a tea party up one's ass. The server refills our coffee mugs, and Carmen rips into a new packet of sugar.

"I'm not going to tell you much about my next book, but I'll say this: I'm going to set it here."

"Here?" I insinuate the diner. Carmen rolls her eyes, exasperated that I can't keep up. Wrong. *Idiot!*

"At the Apex. My heroine, she's a massage therapist. She's a . . . She's a . . . " An idea seems to be forming in her brain. "She's a down-and-out working mom. Are you a mom?"

"No kids."

"She's a down-and-out working *woman* who despises her work. But she meets someone . . . someone . . . Are you single?"

"Yep." My throat tightens.

"She's a down-and-out working *single* woman who detests her work. She believes love will never find her again, and she's become cold—"

"Okay . . . "

"—and crabby and rude."

"*Okay* . . . "

"Frumpy."

I tilt my head.

"And overweight."

I signal with my hands for her to move on.

"But she meets this man, this brute of a man"—Carmen cups her hands as if they're overflowing with the girth of this brute's balls—"whose muscles have hardened. I'm not sure from what yet; maybe I can find a disease that does that."

Carmen pulls her phone back out and talks into it, presumably recording: "Disease that hardens muscles. But non-life-threatening. Doesn't hurt the libido." She winks at me and returns the phone to her bag.

I'm as baffled by Carmen as are the people sitting behind her, who keep returning the tail end of her scarf over the top of the booth only for Carmen to lob it back a moment later. Breakfast arrives.

"You hate it," Carmen says, stirring her yogurt.

"No, I—"

"It's in development. Early stage. Anyway, here's where you come in."

Finally. I set down my fork.

"I know nothing about your industry. Massage, that is. Except I know a good massage from a bad one." Carmen gestures toward me. *Touché.* "I need someone on the 'inside' to tell me about it." She says "inside" as if she's referring to prison. Her mouth opens like a laundry chute for the next spoonful of yogurt and fruit, and she begins talking again as she chews her way through a large berry. "Not just, what's it like? You know, working with your hands and all that. But who are your clients? Where are they from? What do they ask for? What's it like being employed by a mega-spa?" Carmen points her spoon at me. "I'm thinking you're just the person to be my eyes and ears. Tell me ev-uh-ry-thing. Every juicy detail."

I'm startled by this development. I cross my arms, hands cupping each elbow. "I don't know," I stammer. "I'm not sure it's right, ethically?"

"Sure it is. This is how I do all my research. How do you think I wrote *The Zookeeper's Secret*, which I'm sure you've heard of?"

I haven't.

Carmen grazes the inside of her bowl with her finger, licking off the last of the yogurt. "Well, I had no idea what happens in a zoo, besides animals humping each other day in and day out, plus all the shitting. I had to have someone on the inside give me the play-by-play. I certainly don't have the time to sit around a zoo watching kids tug on their mothers' sleeves and point at the giraffes. 'Look, Mommy, tall.'"

"I'm not the right person for this."

"Sure you are. I peeked at your journal. You're writing all kinds of stuff about your clients like some sort of weirdo."

My face flushes with embarrassment and anger at the thought of Carmen reading my journal without my permission. "What the hell? You can't just rifle through people's bags and read their journals. What's wrong with you? And I'm *not* weird." I pick up my napkin just to fling it onto the table in a show of fury. I have the urge to knock over what's left of her coffee and storm out.

I'm also sickened to think that she may have read the last page of my journal, the place where I'd tucked away my failed attempt to write about Samuel. *It was a sunny September day when Samuel went*—I squeeze my eyes closed.

"Settle down, settle down. I didn't go snooping. Your bag toppled over and the notebook fell out. I read a page or two." Carmen presses her hands down in the air. "It's a strange pastime, but so what? Whatever gets us through the day, am I right?" She doesn't apologize, but her gaze is softer. For the first time since we've met, she seems like a human being. Maybe she's struggled herself and underneath her fast-talking bravado and suit of leather, she can access empathy. I relax my balled fists under the table.

"Consider it a blessing that I peeked, because now I'm offering you a paid gig for amping up what you're already doing."

I lean forward, intrigued. Maybe this wouldn't be so bad.

I keep my job, plus make a few bucks on the side—and all I have to do is tell Carmen what it's like to be me? Even though I'm interested, I want Carmen to chase me a little as payback for thumbing through my journal.

"Well"—I clear my throat—"I'm really booked at the moment. I have a *lot* going on." As in, Netflix, Netflix, Netflix.

"Baloney. You're as free as a spare tire, doing nothin'." Carmen manages to be right and rude at the same time.

"I wouldn't know where to start." As always, self-doubt elbows its way in. I have a journal with some random scribblings. Carmen wants that? Or does she expect something more—an assignment I'm likely to flub, given my track record?

"Look." Carmen scooches her dishes to the edge of the table, a directive for the server. "I'm not asking you to write *Moby-Dick*, for the love of a whale's blowhole. I'm hiring you to be a research assistant. This is standard practice, believe it or not. Lots of writers do this. Just keep a journal, write some notes each night after work. Then I'll take your notes and work my magic." She snaps her fingers in the air as if this is how all good literature appears. *Voilà!*

Before I can respond, she levels her gaze at me, her face grave. "But just to clarify before we move on: You're not an *actual* writer, right? Not harboring some secret authorly aspirations? Because I'm done working with that lot."

My forehead crinkles, as if that's the most preposterous thing I've ever heard. "No. Nope. Not a writer. No aspirations but to get through each day."

Carmen wags a finger at me. "That's what I thought."

"You said 'paid.' What do I get for baring the soul of the Apex?"

She makes a grand show of writing a number on a paper napkin and sliding it across the table, Mob-movie style. It feels ridiculous, but I won't lie, it's also kind of exciting. The only other thing I have planned today is hand-washing my bras, and there's a big question mark about whether I'll actually do it. Now a famous author is making me a secret offer.

I'm expecting five hundred bucks, tops, as I unfold the napkin.

"Five grand!" I give a "whoa, Nelly" whistle. That would almost cover what I still owe in massage school debt.

"Shhh," Carmen says, putting a finger to her lips. "If I wanted to announce it to the diner I would have just said it out loud."

"Oh, right, sorry."

"I'm prepared to pay you half today and half at the end."

I hold my face with both of my hands, chin in my palms, and shake my head in disbelief. Is my luck actually changing? If I get on top of my debt, I might even be able to leave the Apex, maybe go to Colorado like Samuel and I had dreamed about, plopping my bags down like a hopeful orphan in a new land.

"I see you shaking your head no, but is this a yes?"

"Yes," I say and laugh. "Yes!"

"Thatta girl." Carmen whips out a thick contract from her oversized bag—she came prepared—and pushes it dramatically across the table for me to sign. Eager to hit the road, she taps her pen on the edge while I quickly scan the document.

"Shouldn't I take some time to read this? Have my lawyer review it?" Hilarious. I don't know any lawyers.

"The most important things to know: You can't breathe a word about this to anyone. You have to handwrite your research in a notebook—I don't trust computers after that phishing scam targeting authors. And going forward, we'll refer to this simply as 'The Project.'"

I see that the agreement spans nine months and that I'll be required to turn in three installments of research for The Project: one in January, one in March, and one in June. The rest of the legalese makes my head spin, and I give it the same lack of attention I gave Facebook's new privacy notice before I clicked "Agree." I pluck the pen from Carmen's hands and sign on the line.

We exit into the parking lot like old friends, the end of Carmen's white scarf bobbing behind her. Then she presses a thick envelope of cash into my hands. I know it's uncouth to count money in front of people, but I can't help but peer inside, gasping at the crisp $100 bills that appear to have been ironed flat.

I've had a knot in my stomach all week from Samuel's anniversary, Tara's threat, Carmen's demands, and Cher's lecture. Now the knot releases a little.

I, bumbling, grumpy Joan Johnston, have finally done something right. I saved my job, and I'm going to put a dent in my debt. For the first time in a long time, I feel a stirring of hope for my future.

Carmen loops her scarf twice more around her neck. She plucks up a motorcycle helmet hanging from her bike's handlebars and puts it on her head, stuffing her curls inside and buckling the strap under her chin. Her curls are so unruly they threaten to spring the helmet straight off her head like a geyser.

"I'll see you in early January with your first research installment." In a flash Carmen is gone, swerving out of the parking lot, a few regulars watching with their mouths agape.

SIX

I've never purchased a book at a supermarket, yet here I am in front of the paperbacks at the Price Chopper. If I'm going to work for Carmen Bronze, I should probably thumb through one of her novels. Just as I suspect, her latest title, *Love in Midair*, is on the shelves. I stare at the cover, an image of a woman clutching a rose in her teeth, sitting on a flying trapeze, while a muscled lover reaches up to her from the ground.

I place the book cover side down in my basket. I'm turning away when I spot the calendars for next year already for sale, with their funny dog images, Zen rock collections, and "wine o'clock" themes. The one that catches my eye has a bright orange flower on the cover. A California poppy. A megastar in the wildflower kingdom.

Fucking wildflowers. I squeeze my eyes shut, and instantly I'm there on my couch, Samuel spooning me, his lips on my ear describing one of the world's rarest phenomena: super blooms. He knew everything about wildflower explosions in the most barren of lands. I'd asked him to tell me more in his dramatic and bold voice, as if he were auditioning to narrate a nature program.

"Underneath that heat and hostility, that dust and sand, are wildflower seeds lying dormant," he'd said, his mouth

tickling my neck. I'd inched my body back toward his, pressing against the pouch of his belly. "Just when you think
nature has pushed the seeds to the brink, that they've shriv-
eled up, the rains will fall—no one can predict when—and
the seeds, which trusted that this day would come, bloom to
blanket the scorched earth."

I'd imagined a torrent of color, creamy oranges and vibrant
blues, visible even from space.

As he'd said the words "Chile's Atacama Desert," it was all
just too much, and I'd turned my body toward his, interrupting his soliloquy with a deep kiss, entangling my fingers in his
dark curls.

Samuel had kissed me back, bee to pollen. Surly old me,
who couldn't watch a romantic comedy without poking fun
at all the cheese, felt like *I* was blooming in rapid succession,
blues and pinks and oranges flooding my mind.

This was what I'd been waiting for. Samuel, my abundance
of rain.

He'd paused our make-out session to ask, "Will you go with
me some day? To see a super bloom?" Of course I would. I
would have followed him anywhere.

What fools. I keep my eyes closed until the threat of tears
pass. Leave it to a flower to push me over the edge today. I
steady my breath and decide to get dinner before I cause a
scene.

The hairnetted kid behind the deli counter sighs as I eye
the vats of prepared foods—large bowls of gummy coleslaw
and potato salad on a bed of ice, withered pieces of romaine
lettuce beneath the bowls as sad decorations.

On his plastic employee name tag, the actual name is
missing. Instead, it just says DELI. A mistake nobody's bothered to fix.

"Are those new potatoes?" I nearly touch the glass case.

"Uh-huh," Deli replies, already reaching for a large plastic tub.

"Guess you already know what I want."

Deli peeks up from the case. "Lady, you're here, like, every other night." And then he dips his head back into the case.

I'd like Deli to know that there was a time I made a killer red sauce with farm-stand tomatoes and window-box herbs, my kitchen heating up with the heady aroma of thyme and oregano. I'd stir the pot, smack my lips on the red-stained wooden spoon, and nod with a certainty that now escapes me. Samuel stood behind me, ready to taste it, too, preferring my lips to the spoon.

Deli presses the lid onto the tub and crowns it with a large sticker price without making eye contact with me. I have the urge to snap the plastic glove at his wrist.

"Anything else?" he asks. A young woman in tight yoga pants glides by, and Deli whips his head to the left to watch her.

Rolling my eyes, I walk away without answering him. My basket swings like a pendulum ready to bowl over anyone in my way.

I step into an express checkout lane before seeing that Lou is the customer ahead of me. Before I can back out, he spots me.

"Joan of Arc!" he exclaims. I wish he would stop calling me that.

"Lucifer," I say back.

"Very funny." Lou's cradling his own basket in the crook of his elbow, a veritable garden of sprouting vegetables. The contents of my own basket are the picture of loneliness: rotisserie chicken, potato salad, candy bar, cat food, pain reliever, romance novel. I scooch the cover under the tub of potato salad.

"Excuse me," says the cashier, and Lou jumps.

"Oh! Ready for me already. And how is your day, good sir?" Lou, who sometimes speaks like he's at a Renaissance fair, hefts his basket onto the belt without bothering to unload it. The cashier mumbles, "Good," and then Lou turns his attention back to me.

"And milady, how was your shift today?" Lou's lost most of the hair on the top of his head, a perfect crop circle of baldness. The rest of his hair he gathers into a stunted ponytail that doesn't even reach his C1, the vertebra at the very top of his spine. He's got the strong nose of an action hero, someone who could kick your ass, but in truth, he'd hold the door for an ant rather than step on it. I know he's nice, but his constant niceness is just plain annoying. This is who I am now, and I dislike it much more than I dislike Lou.

"Well, I'm not fired, so I consider it a good day," I grumble.

"Is this organic?" the cashier clutches a bunch of carrots. Lou nods yes, and I grab a magazine from the rack and flip to an article about butt exercises. Reshelve.

Lou peers down at me, face tripping into worry. "I hadn't realized you were on the chopping block. Are you okay?"

I sigh. Why did I have to mention that? Lou's the last person I want to be chatting with right now, with my feet aching and my stomach grumbling. "I'm fine. It's more my fault than anything."

"Is this organic?" the cashier interjects, holding up the kale as if his fingers are crab pincers.

"Uh-huh." Lou nods curtly and then fixates on me. "You know, the Apex wasn't always like this. Back when I first started working there, the management was much more humane, more forgiving. Now they"—Lou makes a fist—"squeeze us dry. So maybe it's not as much your fault as you think."

"My friend Cher worked there back then. It seemed different, from the outside."

Lou's expression grows wistful. "How *is* Cher? You know, we had some wild times at the Apex before she went out on her own."

That's odd. Cher never mentioned that to me. "She's good," I say slowly.

"Is this organic?" The cashier palms a head of cauliflower.

"Yes! All organic!" Lou's eyes widen a little. He swings back to me. I feel a shot of pleasure watching Lou get steamed. An awkward silence falls between us, and I don't do anything to keep the conversation going. He pops a knuckle and then, reanimated, says, "Hey, what's your favorite muscle?"

I *definitely* have a favorite muscle. It's the psoas, the long muscle that connects the leg to the torso on each side of the body, running deep below the surface like the Chunnel connecting the United Kingdom to France. The psoas is a fight-or-flight muscle, in charge of big movements, leaps and bounds.

Or, conversely, it allows the body to tuck into the fetal position, a protective stance, a curling inward, the position I wanted to stay in forever when I found out about Samuel. *It was a sunny September day when Samuel went—*

"Is this organic?" the cashier asks again, balancing a cabbage on top of his fingertips, an unpracticed Globetrotter spinning a basketball.

"It's *all* organic." Lou slams his hand down next to the basket. The cashier startles, and the cabbage teeters off his fingertips, falling to the floor with a thud.

Sensing an opening, I gather my basket and back out of the aisle. "I forgot something," I mumble.

Lou calls to me over the mints, "And don't worry, Joan of Arc, I won't tell anyone about the literary porn you're buying." He winks, and I look down, my face scarlet-letter red.

Somehow Carmen's book has jostled its way to the surface of my basket, and I feel as exposed as those nearly bare breasts and the rippling Fabio-esque six-pack on her cover.

―――――――

My house, a rental, is small, snug, perfect for the two of us. Me and Sweet Bird, that is. He's a massive white cat with one black splotch on his side that looks like a genetic whoopsie. When I tilt my head, it resembles the shape of a rooster's wattle.

He's also a massive jerk whom I named before I really got to know him. If I was naming him today, it'd be A-hole. He scratches up my furniture with impunity, plops down in the middle of anything I'm doing, ruining puzzles or ripping magazines, kneads my face ruthlessly in the mornings, pukes for no reason and then proudly licks his paw like it's no big deal while I fetch the paper towels, choking back my own puke— and all the while, he doles out minuscule ounces of love and affection, just enough to keep me jonesing for more.

If Sweet Bird were a person, I'd be in an abusive relationship with an egotistical maniac. But he's a cat, so I forgive him.

Sometimes I even admire Sweet Bird, the way he's smaller than so many things yet entirely undeterred from charging forth into the unknown. I'd take an ounce of that right now.

In my galley kitchen, so narrow it's like preparing food in a hallway, I dodge Sweet Bird's first strike at my leg, tipping cat food into his bowl before he can come at me again. I cart the entire chicken and the potato salad, plastic containers and all, along with a can of Fiddlehead IPA and Carmen's book, into my dining room, sitting at an old and worn farm-house table Mom scored at a tag sale. Most of my things are her tag-sale finds: the checkered tier curtains on the windows; the butter dish with *butter* written in cursive on the side in case I forget; the basket of decorative gourds she dropped off, one so phallic that I lifted it up to her, inched my eyebrows up suggestively, and said, "What should I do with this?" She slapped my arm.

Behind me is a blue couch passed down from my grandparents after my grandmother died from dementia. The color is similar to the strip of blue that bloomed in her adult diapers, alerting my mom, who took diligent care of her in the last two years, that she had peed again and needed changing. I wish I didn't associate the two: my couch and soggy diapers.

The framed collages above my couch are the true representation of me. I made them in my early twenties, cutting up images from Dad's old *National Geographic* magazines, creating something abstract and vibrant. They continue to be the only art that adorns my house, six eight-by-ten white frames hanging two inches apart.

I pop open the plastic lid containing the football-sized chicken and peel off the papery, peppery skin with my fingers. Sweet Bird stretches his paws up toward me, readying to pounce. I feed him a token piece of chicken and he threads through my legs, pressing against my calf appreciatively, being nice because he wants more.

Licking my fingers, I crack open Carmen's book. The female trapeze artist's partner, whom she secretly loved, died after he fell during a performance (*bleak*—jeez, Carmen), and she blames herself. A new partner arrives, handsome, beefy, wise, the magnetism between them undeniable. Will she be ready to love again? To catch again? Be caught? I read the first two chapters. It's hard to believe that this syrupy love story came from Carmen.

"Okay, there it is, a heaving bosom," I say, pushing the book and the chicken away. "New rule, Sweet Bird: Nix any books with the lines 'Her bosom heaved' or 'His member hardened.'"

Yet a few mouthfuls of potato salad later, I can't help but reach for the book again. What *does* happen next? Carmen's plotlines are as weak as watery ketchup, but her prose is fun and titillating, the lust dripping, the inevitable sex scene steamy and romantic. I move to the couch, Sweet Bird curled at my ankles.

It's 2:00 a.m. when I read the final pages. The trapeze partners have retired from the circus, not wanting to risk their lives any longer. They walk away from the only lives they've known, the throngs of people clapping for them with their hands buttery from popcorn, the sticky cotton-candied children grabbing at them as they push through the crowd. The spotlight tails them until they leave the big tent for good, hand in hand, to an unknown happily ever after.

I set down the book, embarrassingly jealous of these fictional characters.

I think again about my grief therapist and my botched attempts to journal about Samuel. I rub my hands over the cover of Carmen's book. As much as I hate to admit it—and I *really* hate to—Cher was right. I am stuck. I haven't processed the loss of Samuel. I do need and want to move forward, but I don't really know how.

That night, as I turn onto my side, curling into a tight ball, I dream of Samuel, of the dawning of our own love story.

SEVEN

From the moment I met Samuel in massage school, I was smitten. I wasn't the only one; the entire class loved him for his easygoing nature and infectious enthusiasm for everything, from fixed-gear bikes to pickling recipes, the way he goofed off to lift our spirits as we all drooped by hour five of instruction.

Samuel was dyslexic, and identifying anatomy terms like "posterior" and "anterior" made his brain swirl. This was where I shined, reciting anatomical positions like I was singing "Head, Shoulders, Knees, and Toes." Samuel needed to get a solid grip on these terms, so he could fully understand what was ticking just below the surface of the skin, not to mention pass our certification exam. For weeks, I'd been tutoring him after class, basking in the extra doses of him, realizing that I'd been as deficient in daily sunniness as a Vermonter in vitamin D.

"This," I said, "is plantar flexion and adduction." I stood barefoot on the hardwood floor. Our massage school was spacious, housed in an old, revitalized mill where workers once made buttons, and then paper, and then plastic crates, and then nothing. I rolled onto the outside ridge of my foot.

He grinned. I grinned.

"You have the loveliest smile," he said.

I swatted at him. "Focus." On the inside, I lit up. Was it possible he was smitten with me, too?

One day, the two of us were paired up to give each other practice massages. This was routine, practicing on a partner.

Having a crush on your partner was not.

It was the first time I'd physically touch him. And he me.

Besides Cher's hugs, my parents' arm squeezes, and now these practice massages, I hadn't really been touched since I broke up with my last boyfriend, Alan, over a year ago. Not that he had been a barrel of affection. He'd rather play a strategy board game than peel my clothes off, and when we did have sex, his penis was pokey, like the bayonet of one of his soldiers guarding Ural on a Risk board.

All of this meant that I was jittery and nervous as Samuel and I negotiated entering our therapy room, who would lay hands on whom first, feeling each other's bodies, albeit through a layer of clothing. Keeping our clothes on didn't make things much less awkward, since sweat had visibly dampened the underarms of my T-shirt. I insisted he lie down first, face in the cradle, as I windmilled my arms around and fanned underneath my armpits.

Then, finally, I began the slow, methodic work of plying muscles apart. I smoothed the fabric of his shirt as if I were preparing a tablecloth, and then I trailed my hands from his shoulders to his lower back, where I pressed with the heels of my hands. He wasn't doughy, but he was a little squishable, with ample love handles and some extra pounds padding his broad shoulders. He was also fit from hiking and cycling, and his butt, I couldn't help noticing, was kind of perfect. I fought the urge to run my hands over the back of his neck and up into his messy crop of dark curled hair.

I leaned my face closer and inhaled, smelling the citronella bug spray he used, plus a hint of licorice: Tom's of Maine toothpaste. The wholesome concoction made me swoon. Samuel was earthy-crunchy lite, a step above making his own baking soda toothpaste, thank god, a man who, as far as I could tell, still believed in wearing deodorant.

Kneading the lower trapezius, I took another gulp of his intoxicating scent, my face so close to his curls that I could have nudged one with my nose.

Then I smelled something else.

I paused my hands over his body and wrinkled my nose, incredulous.

"Did you just fart?" I said—accusing my *actual* crush of farting. But the stench was undeniable.

Samuel mumbled something I couldn't understand.

"Huh?" I turned my ear to him, wanting to pinch my nose.

He lifted his head an inch and turned it to the side. "I think that was you." He set his face back in the hole.

"That was *not* me," I said.

Facedown, he nodded his head yes.

"It was not!"

He picked up his head again, turned to the side, and whispered, "You're excused."

"Oh my god, you know it wasn't me." I jabbed my thumb into his arm.

Samuel tried to stifle his laugh, shaking the entire massage table on its skinny legs. I teetered, repressing a giggle. Samuel roared, and he pushed himself back into child's pose. He softly beat his fist into the massage table as he laughed.

"That position is going to make you fart more," I said. My laugh gave way, a dam bursting.

"It smells," I said through breaths.

Samuel nodded, barely able to speak. "It's lingering," he finally managed.

"Oww." I moved my lips, stretching my jaw. "My mouth hurts from laughing."

"My stomach muscles!" Samuel clutched his belly. We chuckled, winding down, and I became aware of how quiet the room was without the laughter. He lay down again but propped himself up on his elbows. We smiled at each other.

"Let me do you," Samuel said.

"What?"

"Do you," Samuel repeated and then reddened. "Massage you. It's your turn."

"We're probably out of time." I tugged at a corner of the sheet.

"We have ten minutes. Let's do this."

Samuel hopped down from the table, not caring that his hair was matted on one side. I hemmed and hawed, moving slowly, paralyzed by sudden shyness. It was one thing for me to massage him, but for him to massage *me*? True, we were professionals, but the act felt unbearably intimate.

He eyed the clock.

"We now have nine minutes. You're taking away my practice time. I'm beginning to think you're not serious about this training."

I hoisted myself up onto the massage table, placing my face in the cradle. We both forgot to change the face cradle cover, and my mouth grazed where his mouth had been, my face resting against the still-warm paper, as if the two of us were slow dancing cheek to cheek.

"Let me know if this pressure is okay," Samuel said. He softly planted both palms on the sides of my spine in the wide-open prairie of my lower back, his fingers outstretched as if he were tracing his hands to make a kindergarten drawing of a turkey. He took a deep breath, and I softened with his exhale. He glided his right hand up my spine, pressing the heel of his hand as he went, and then pulled his right hand back down as the left hand moved up, a lever and pulley.

Every time my shirt began to bunch and ride up, he tugged it down, covering any inch of exposed skin. Moving from the base of my spine, he pressed his thumbs inch by inch up the vertebrae. I'd never been touched like this—a deep caring, a quiet listening to my body and a response from his hands.

My shyness melted into the table, dispersed into the air like burnt sage, and I was devoted to every movement he made, tracking his hands yet untethered from my thoughts. It felt *so* good. So eyes-roll-back-into-my-head good. So sigh-out-loud good. And not just because he was skillful; he was taking the time to get to know me.

Discovering and understanding me all at once.

Those nine minutes sailed by, and when I pushed up from the table, Samuel stared at me in awe, as if he, too, had been found. Or found me, the person he'd been looking for. As if he wanted to whisper, *It's you*.

EIGHT

Mom is giddy: I have a use for the rickety desk that she plucked from a free pile three years ago, only sturdy enough to bear the weight of a MacBook Air. Or in my case, a notebook.

"Are you sure this thing is safe?" I say, swaying it with the touch of a finger, the structure so flimsy I could knock it over with my exasperated sighs.

"Of course!" Mom reaches out to steady the thing. "Someone wouldn't give away a broken desk."

"Um. I think that's exactly how it works. People give away *broken* things."

Mom tsks at me. She brought Dad along, too, as if she needed his help moving the desk. Now that it's angled in the corner, he stands with his hands in his jeans pockets while Mom busies herself scrutinizing my house, delighting in all the items I'm using that she gave me, taking stock of the missing ones.

Dad rocks on his heels, unsure of what to do with himself. Every time I see him, he appears shorter, more concave in his shoulders. He was tall in his youth, but years spent as a mechanic stooped over the innards of cars have curved his torso like the handle of a candy cane. His Croatian ancestry shines through in his tulip-bulb-sized nose and long ears.

Mom told me that she was drawn to his presence, calm and steady and reassuring.

Mom's physically more agile than Dad, but she looks a good ten years older than him. Her hair, at sixty-three, is stark white, making her a dead ringer for the late Betty White, with the same befuddled eyes as if she's confused by every joke. It's not uncommon for people to stop her in public. At this point she says, "Betty White?" before they suggest it.

Dad nods toward the desk. "Does this mean what I think it means?"

"That you're going to find me and Sweet Bird dead under a pile of desk rubble?"

"That you're getting back to writing." His eyes twinkle, hopeful. I haven't told them about The Project. The desk, I'd said, was a place to "put my bills and stuff."

I roll my eyes. "Dad, no. I haven't done that in years." When Carmen asked if I was a writer, I'd told her the truth. I gave up on that idea years ago.

"Doesn't mean you can't start up again." My dad was a steadfast supporter of my writing life, beginning around the age of eight and fizzling out ten years later. I read my stories to him after school while he was finishing up at his garage, his head under the hood of a car, me sitting on a stool. Still pegged on his office bulletin board are the faded writing awards I won. He doesn't seem to get that plenty of kids burst out of the gate on fire for a hobby—aspiring cellists, baseball players, dinosaur experts—only to become accountants or sanitation workers in adulthood, never pitching another baseball or uttering the words "Triassic period."

And thus, becoming a real writer wasn't for me, or in me. That became painfully clear in college. But it hasn't stopped my dad from nudging me back toward it. Or texting me with story ideas: A story about two women on the lam. That's got some legs to it, no?

Yeah, Dad, it's called Thelma & Louise.

Mom returns from her snooping, deeply disturbed. "You're not using the laundry basket I gave you."

I sigh. "I told you I didn't need it. I have one."

"Well, where is it? I'll drop it at Cher's."

"Mom, Cher doesn't need it, either." It's hard to have patience for this, even though I know that all of Mom's possessions are hard-earned—she scrimped and saved for the expensive ones and scoured tag sales and bargain bins for the rest, a day-old-bread shopper. Bestowing us with these items is her love language.

Because I work in the Apex's spa, a sort of higher ground where Mom would never have dared step during her years as a housekeeper at the inn, she thinks I've arrived. Last year for her birthday, I gave her a gift certificate for a massage at the spa. Instead of using it, she propped it up on her dresser, just short of framing it. I wonder if the gift certificate will be one of the items she re-gifts back to me.

Indifferent to both Dad and me standing there, she begins voice-texting. "Cher," she says, her mouth close to the phone, her voice louder than it needs to be, "do you need an extra laundry basket?" Then she stabs her pointer finger at the screen to press send.

"Mom, you should read over your messages when you voice-text. They always come out weird." This is not the first time I've suggested this, but Mom looks shocked, as if her phone wouldn't possibly let her down.

She brightens her phone again to read the message. "'Sharon, do you want any chicken nuggets?' Huh."

"See, you need to check them."

Mom speaks louder into her phone: "Whoops, I meant laundry basket." Then, without checking, she stuffs her phone into her purse.

Bless them, I've had enough. I clap my hands and usher them toward the front door. "Thank you for the desk. I love you. But I have . . . bills to pay. Mom, if Cher wants your laundry basket, I'll bring it to her."

On the stoop, Dad kicks a white bucket half-filled with sand. "You need to refill this before winter," he says.

"I know, I will. Bye!" I close my door and bolt the lock. Through the door window, I see my dad pressing an expert hand to each of my car tires, checking their air pressure, and I experience the same feeling I always have after I see my parents: a collision of tenderness and regret, loving them deeply and wishing I had been more tolerant.

I know that Mom's using this paring-down exercise as an excuse to check on me. Asking "Are you doing okay?" is too intimate a question for my parents. Instead I get old cookware and not-so-subtle glances around my house for signs that I'm eating and not living like a shut-in. They've been doing this since Samuel died, a man they never got to meet.

"Soon," we kept saying to our parents. "Soon." We weren't ready to let in the outside world, keen to stay in our snow globe, protected, curled around each other, for just a little longer. But that "soon" never happened.

I'm grateful Mom and Dad keep showing up, I really am, but I'm running out of storage space.

Back at my desk, I see that Mom's left me something else. It's a purple hardcover notebook. As I fan through the empty pages, a note falls out, and it is not Mom's handwriting.

It's Dad's. It says, *In case you decide to start again.*

The guy just won't give up. Yet I hug the notebook as if I'm pulling the idea close to my heart. And I'm touched. Dad's never even placed an Amazon order, so there's no way he bought this gift online. He browsed for it in a bookstore, picking through the selection, deciding this was the perfect one for his daughter, the onetime writer, standing in the checkout line among dozens of books by real authors. In his mind, I belong among them. It's so tender that I feel like I could cry, but I don't.

It's also absurd, his belief in me. I was a *child.* I almost wish I'd never won those contests. Somehow I need to disabuse him of this notion that I'm a writer-in-hiding, or these little gifts, his pressing texts, will never end. He thinks they're helping, but they only slam me into my failures.

I shake my head, open the desk's lone drawer, and stuff the notebook inside. The desk shakes as I shut the drawer.

I have work to do, not silly notions to chase. Work for The Project. I borrow an uncomfortable dining room chair from the table, pushing it up to the desk. On the desk, I place three other notebooks—college-ruled composition notebooks with black-and-white covers—and a packet of pens. I readjust the placement of the pens so many times that I begin to worry about my brain.

Now all I have to do is sit down and get started.

Only, two days pass. And then another.

On Thursday, instead of staring at the desk or rearranging the pens, I take the next step, indenting a pen cap with my teeth marks. It's something, but it's still not writing. The sun has set, and my desk lamp lights up my notebook like an interrogation: *Tell me everything you know.*

I write: *Massage Therapy Notes.* I cross this out.

Observations from a tired hag. I strike it.

Carmen Bronze has three nipples. This I heavily mark through.

I throw my pen, stand up, nearly topple the desk, and pace. Carmen Bronze had been clear: "Don't get fancy. Just barf everything up on paper."

Inhaling as if I'm preparing to sprint, I readjust the chair, sit back down again, bob my leg, crack my knuckles, and then think: *Nachos. I should make nachos.* I look longingly at the kitchen.

Nachos it is.

My phone rings, an unknown caller. Raised on watching *Unsolved Mysteries*, I never answer an unknown caller. I send it straight to voice mail, my mind on cheese and salsa.

It rings again, same number. This is one persistent robo-caller—or murderer. Voice mail. Give me those chips.

I'm wrestling open the chip bag in the most indecent of manners when my phone rings for the third time. Doesn't this person know that I'm trying to write? Finally I answer it, my voice hostile. "What is it?"

"Don't you ever answer your phone?"

I frown at the receiver. "Um, who is this?"

"It's me." Me? I don't recognize the voice, so I mentally scan the roster of people who have my phone number, totaling about ten.

"I'm going to need more than that."

The caller lowers her voice to a hushed whisper. "Carmen Bronze."

I drop the chip bag as if she's at the window, witness to my epic procrastination. "Oh, hi!" I say, a little too chummily. "I was just sitting down to work on The Project." Which is true, mostly. I'm also really, really hungry, and I reach down to silently extract a chip from the bag. "Carmen, why are you calling? I thought you didn't 'do' phone calls." I take the tiniest, most inaudible nibble.

"I make the rules, I break the rules."

Something about her ominous tone makes me shudder. I take another mouse bite of chip with just my front teeth.

"Anyhoo, I'm calling to check in on your progress."

My progress. My *lack* of progress. Once again, I feel like she's at the window, peering in. She's not, right? I walk around the house, checking each window. "It's only been a week," I say, looking outside.

"Exactly! How many notebooks have you filled so far?"

"Filled?" Oh, god. Carmen may have grossly overestimated my productivity level. While paying down my credit card debt with that first two-and-a-half grand felt incredible, I've had a nagging suspicion that I would come to regret this arrangement. Suspicion confirmed.

"I'm guessing two," Carmen says.

"I've just been warming up." I roll my shoulders, and then I move a pen from the left side of the notebook to the right, straightening it. "I had to buy supplies."

There's silence on the other end. I picture Carmen's dark eyes boring a hole into something, and I'm grateful we're not face-to-face.

At last she speaks. "So you're telling me you've written . . ."

"Well, nothing." I lift a finger for emphasis when I say, "Yet."

"Nada, nothing, nil, zilch, zero, diddly-squat, a big fat goose egg?"

It sounds worse when she puts it like this. Should I read her the line about her nipples?

"But I'm planning to get started now," I defend myself. "After our call. Right after."

Even though I'm stressed, I'm salivating from tasting the minuscule morsel of salt and hard-pressed corn, and I'm longing to take another, bigger bite. I break the chip in half so that

Carmen doesn't hear it snap, and then I place the chip into the back-left quadrant of my mouth and begin to slowly, silently grind it down with my molars.

"There hasn't been this level of procrastination since da Vinci took fifteen years to paint the *Mona Lisa*," Carmen says. "Every time I see that smiling mug, I think 'What was the holdup?'"

"I'm not procrastinating. I'm *preparing*."

"I thought you were a repository of knowledge."

My brow furrows as I recall our diner meeting when I told Carmen the exact opposite, trying to convince her I wasn't the right person for the job. "I never called myself that." Growing bolder, and hungrier, I pop the other half of the chip into my mouth.

"Well, stop snacking all day and get to work."

I cover my mouth with my hand. "I'm not"—*crunch*— "snacking."

"Listen, Joan, I need you to put everything you have into this. There's a lot at stake for me with this next book. Act with urgency. Like you're rescuing that baby who fell into the well back in the '80s."

"Baby Jessica?" I ask, shocked that she would stoop so low. I know that baby's name because the horrific story scarred me for life. My parents tuned in for days as they watched the fifty-eight-hour rescue of the eighteen-month-old who fell over twenty feet into a well in Texas. It's the reason I never step on sewer grates.

"Yes, that's the one!"

"That's *awful*, Carmen."

"Thank you." She's pleased. But then her tone ices over. "Since you're incapable of moving at anything other than a slug's speed, I'm going to light a fire under your ass. Consider this your Baby Jessica: If you don't write five pages in the next five days, I'm taking my money back."

A hot flash of panic rips through my chest, leaving my heart walloping. I don't have that money to give back. Not now. And not in five days.

I begin to stammer. "Done. Well, not done yet, but it *will* be done. Done-zo. Yep. In five days. No problem."

"And just so we're clear, I'm expecting one filled notebook for our first meeting. I should have spelled that out."

"One"—I'm repeating this as if I'm writing it down even though I'm not—"filled . . . notebook. Okay!" If I sound overly chipper, it's because I'm trying to mask the fear that's coursing through my veins. An entire notebook? *Yes*, she should have spelled that out. Or maybe I should have asked. It's hard to think straight, let alone ask questions, when Carmen's around.

Should I say that *Love in Midair* has been the first book I've been able to concentrate on since Samuel?

Or that sitting down to write floods me with memories from another era, when I traipsed around with words easily, fluidly, before self-consciousness settled around me like a forever fog, so thick I couldn't see the page if I brought it up to my nose?

No. I trust Carmen with my feelings about as much as I trust a sewer grate.

"Wunderbar!" Carmen says. "Now I'm off. I have a dry cleaner I need to go ream out. How hard is it to get a boot print out of a white scarf? Bye for now."

And that's when I create a new embarrassing moment, one for the record books, when I say, accidentally, "Bye. Love you."

Love you? I'm 89 percent sure she'd already hung up.

And 100 percent sure I didn't intend those words for Carmen Bronze.

Back at my desk, I begin again. Or rather, I begin. Without overthinking it, I start with my all-time favorite topic: worst clients.

Notes for Carmen

1. *The clients who start undressing before I leave the room. Or who sit up naked after the massage, dangle their legs over the table, and want me to give a play-by-play of what I discovered about their fascia. "Was the left side as tight as the right?" they ask, scrotum bobbing or tits blasting at me. If I protest or look away, they say, "Don't worry, I'm really comfortable with my body." Okay, but I'm not. The sheet over you is not just for your modesty but also mine. Just because I'm touching your bare skin doesn't mean I want to get flashed. This isn't a sauna, or a locker room, so stop dropping trou or the towel. I'd rather not just avert my eyes. I'd rather avert the whole experience by being out of the room, door firmly closed, before you disrobe.*

2. *The clients who have no body fat. I lose my bearings, thinking muscle is bone and bone is muscle, and it feels like I'm tripping over my fingers. I'm not sure if there's a direct correlation to weight, but in my experience, my skinnier people tend to be my "Evian water" clients—never fully satisfied with what the spa has to offer, no matter how premium, giving resigned sighs as I ask if the pressure is okay for them, like they had known all along I wouldn't live up to their expectations.*

3. *The clients who believe my ability to "press harder" is inexhaustible. In fact, I can only press so hard. More than once I've had to say, "This is my limit. If I press harder, I might hurt myself." It makes me feel inhuman, the way clients bleat out "harder" as if I'm one of those massage chairs*

people sit in when they get pedicures, pressing the dial up, up, up. I do have a breaking point. Besides, sometimes harder pressure is the last thing a client needs, especially for an injury. Sometimes a light touch is better, rotating around a tender spot instead of going directly at it with all of my might. Clients want me to be a trained expert when it suits them, but ultimately, they want me to cow to their wishes, stuff my knowledge into the aromatherapy jar. And if I have three clients in a row who want me to pulverize their muscles, I'm toast.

4. *The clients who take for-ev-er to come out of the room after the massage. When I say "take your time," I never genuinely mean it. The longer a client spends getting up—sighing, stretching arms overhead, meditatively putting on the robe, contemplating the sunset message on the wall—the shorter my break will be. And it's not really a break. I have ten lean minutes between clients to strip the sheets, tidy the room, take a sip of water, go to the bathroom, rest my hands, possibly eat a snack, and scrawl a few thoughts in my journal. Get a bit of sun on my face so that I can reflect on the massage and gear up for the next one, if there is a next one? Not likely.*

I sit back to assess my work. It's more of a rant than anything else, but it's a start. One page down, four to go.

NINE

Notes for Carmen

If I hate the Apex so much, why don't I go out on my own? Sounds so easy. I mean, I can work from anywhere, right? All I need is a massage table, right? If only all that were true.

I can't just wake up on a Monday, declare myself a one-woman shop, and by Friday have clients knocking down my door. No, no, no, my friend. I've got to have some money to invest. Do I already own a table? What about a hydraulic table that moves up and down and is easier on my body? Do I rent a space? Do I own a home with an extra room? Do I want strangers in said home? How do I furnish the space? Do I have the money to buy insurance for my business? Do I actually have any business savvy at all? Should I hire an accountant, and can I pay for that? Do I have savings to carry me through while I build up my clientele?

No, no, I do not. I have the opposite of savings.

There are perks to working at the Apex—or any other busy establishment. We call it "walk in and work," which literally means just that: I can walk in the door at the Apex, set down my bag, start working, and then leave it all behind at the end of the day. I don't have to devote any time, energy, or nonexistent extra cash to marketing, hanging flyers on community boards, building a website, managing reviews, cleaning a studio, booking appointments, or doing laundry.

As a full-time employee of the Apex, I get health insurance and three sick days a year. That said, the Apex takes a hulking 70 percent of every massage fee, and the tiered pay structure takes a doctorate degree to figure out. I'm on the bottom of Tier II. We do earn tips, but not everyone tips.

If a client cancels—or worse, multiple clients bail on the same day—I don't get paid but have to stay at work for the entirety of my shift, where I'm required to do "sidework": folding towels, replenishing the massage oil, ionizing the hot stones. I can't dash out to run an errand or make the most of the afternoon. These are the rules that bruise me, grind me down.

I may never see the same client twice, which has its pluses and minuses. It's fine with me if I never have to lay a hand on certain needy clients ever again, but it would also be nice to help a person progress, to see how my work undoes a stiff shoulder over the course of a few weeks.

There's not much I can control at the Apex—the music, the art in my therapy room, the name of my therapy room, the type of oil we use. The hefty Apex Employee Handbook instructs me on all the things I must never do: dye my hair a bright color, wear facial piercings, grow my nails long, swap clients with another therapist, take tips directly from clients, park in front, use any unsanctioned spa product, offer to work with clients outside of the spa.

While every bodyworker tries to hold on to some semblance of individuality, the massages are supposed to be nearly identical, in spite of the client's presenting problems, so that we're all performing the same routine, simultaneously working on our clients' necks behind our closed doors. Each client smells the same oil, hears the same music, experiences the same circuit they know and trust. We are, essentially, a product and a service.

There's a revolving door at the Apex, and it isn't the one the guests glide through out front. I've seen at least eight therapists leave to launch their own businesses only to slink back six months later, eaten alive out there. Though sometimes it works, and bless those people who give us something to aspire to.

Let's face it: both income streams are unpredictable and our earning potential is limited because, as bodyworkers, our bodies have limits.

Notes for Carmen

Go ahead and ask it, just so we can get this out of the way: Do I give happy endings? Now let's all have a good, long laugh. Finished? Was it as satisfying for you as it was for me? Because, wow, do I love getting asked that in a jokey, nudge-me-in-the-ribs manner when I mention my profession.

The answer, ladies and gentlemen, since you are all so riveted, is no, I do not! But I have certainly been asked to give happy endings, couched in all sorts of references. "Sensual" massages, a favor, "full-body" massages, an "odd request," an "extra mile." Do I want to make a little extra cash? Do I want to meet up later and massage you and also, oh, maybe spank you? Just last week, a man pulled ever-so-slightly on the fabric of my pants and indicated with a nod to his erection under the sheet. I snapped my pants free, mumbling, "I'm sorry, this session is over," and bolted out the door. Yesterday, I was massaging a man's arm down to his wrist, then turned his hand over to rub his palm, when he clasped my hand in an intimate way. "I'm not comfortable with that," I said. It didn't seem like enough to end the session, but I was uneasy for the rest of it.

I didn't get into this profession because I wanted to be solicited sexually. I think some people believe it serves me right because I chose a job where I touch nearly naked people.

When I was practicing on clients during clinic hours in massage school, I was assigned a man who was super-peeved that another therapist wasn't available. He was just livid, and I was extremely nervous. I wanted so desperately to be good at this, and here was this guy who was convinced I couldn't hack it, even before I began. But by the end of the massage, I felt his body shift. I had tapped into something beyond musculature, and he softened. Softened toward me and toward the world. When he got up, he apologized profusely, and I was elated.

I wrongly thought each experience would be like that.

TEN

On my way to work, I nearly back over Sweet Bird, who is cleaning himself in the driveway, giving exactly zero shits that I'm yelling at him out the window and honking my horn. Out of options, I have to get out of the car to go *physically* move him, setting him on the stoop and praying he doesn't instantly return to his driveway spot.

Just as I put the car into reverse, Mom calls. I'm never getting out of here.

"Hi, Mom." My foot is still on the brake.

"Do you want my Longaberger bread basket?" she asks.

"No, thanks."

"But what if you want to deliver bread to someone?"

"Mom, have you ever known me to *bake* bread?"

"How about the seashells that Aunt Nancy brought us from Hawaii?"

"Wasn't that twenty years ago?" I balk. "Why did you hang on to all this stuff?"

"That trip was a big deal for your aunt. And some of these shells are just exquisite. Oh, I can hear the ocean." I picture her holding both of her hands to her ears, a phone in one and a shell in the other.

"I'm going to pass on that, too, Mom, sorry."

Her frown is almost audible.

"Okay . . . but I *am* dropping off a few boxes at your house, and you can't say no, because they're your things," Mom says. "We won't have room to store them when we move into the condo." It's clear she's relishing saying "condo."

I lurch the car into park. "Whatever's in those boxes you can just trash. If I haven't been missing it, then I don't need it."

Mom's horrified. "Oh, honey, no." I hear her lift open the cardboard lid on one of the boxes. She exclaims, "Here's that essay you wrote, the one about the Liberty Bell. Remember when it won that award in middle school? We were so proud of you."

I adjust my rearview mirror and check my teeth for food. "You couldn't *pay* me to read that again."

"And all of your diaries. With their cute little metal keys."

"Toss 'em," I say, as if we're discussing packets of soy sauce. I don't need to rehash unrequited crushes and anxiety about Mom ironing Guess labels onto the back pockets of my Lee jeans.

"And your short stories. There are gobs of them. You would just hole up and write and write. Sometimes it was hard to get you to come down for dinner."

She's right. The honest truth is that I wanted to be a writer with all of my might. While other kids were playing capture the flag in the dwindling summer twilight, words were my playmates. I lived for the simple pleasure of writing, and for the power I wielded in building entire worlds and determining my characters' fates.

By brandishing a pencil and an eraser, I could make my heroine a dog-loving softball player who could pitch faster than any boy in town.

Scratch that. A dolphin-loving pirate girl who would convince her one-eyed pirate father to save an endangered pod.

Scratch that. A nerdy, shy kid who used her science kit to tame a wild snotblob stalking her school.

Scratch that—and so the ideas rushed in, and I grabbed on to each and every one of them.

The ride got bumpier in high school. I no longer wanted to be known as the Short Story Champion. Brainy was boring. Creative was childish. And I didn't want to stand out. *At all.* I wanted to fade into the background so no one would notice my awkward body and my knockoff designer-brand clothes.

I'd always thought of myself as a reader, but I struggled to connect to the books assigned in English class. In the afternoons, I shared fewer stories with my dad because I was writing less—and then barely at all.

"I don't want those. Mom, I have to get to work. Traffic's going to be a nightmare." It's the height of leaf-peeping season, with the trees at their brightest, and tourists are here in droves.

She ignores me. "Here's some of your college papers." From my one semester in college. "Looks like another one of your stories. Says 'Intro to Creative Writing.' Oh, gosh, there's a lot of red marks on it."

I bow my head and press my fingers into the bones behind my eyebrows. "Please incinerate that." I know what story she's talking about. It's *the* story. The one that my professor scribbled all over, writing in huge red scrawl, *Get serious.* Just the thought of it makes my heart feel leaden. There's absolutely nothing worse than falsely believing you have writing talent and being rudely awakened to the fact that you do not—okay, there *are* worse things, like droughts and famine. But at the time, I was mortified, and I imagined my professor shaking his head and thinking, *Poor dear.* I scampered away, tail between my legs.

It's the last thing I wrote since I started journaling about the Apex, and now for Carmen.

"You might not want it now, but you'll want it *someday*, trust me. Dad and I are going to swing by next week."

"Mom, please *do not* bring me those boxes. I will never want them. Not now or someday." The thought of that story being near me—honestly, I'd rather have Mom deliver the bread basket.

"Sorry, honey, Dad's already loaded them into the car." This can't be true, given she was just rifling through one.

I rub my eyes with the heels of my hands, fighting back a headache. "Fine. Just leave them outside my front door." That way, it'll be just a few steps to the trash can.

"Love you," she says.

"Love you," I say, and this time it's directed at the right person.

I shift the car into reverse, giving the rearview mirror a passing glance. There's Sweet Bird again, stationed directly behind me, apparently in the only spot in this huge wide world where he wants to lick a paw. I clench the steering wheel and scream in frustration.

———

Maple trees have the best party trick, and today they came to dazzle. I might bemoan the tourists, but I never tire of the beauty that is October in Vermont. There's always a week in particular when the leaves are at their most spectacular, as if they're throwing their arms out wide, puffing out their chests with pride, and as locals, we can sense it, call it. "It's peaking," we say.

Just like I'm privy to all the shortcuts in town, I also know the trees far off the beaten path, the maples that have never served as a selfie backdrop. My favorite tree happens to be on the edge of what was my grandparents' property in Rockford. It's only a few minutes out of the way, and I need to see it before the leaves fade away on a slow chlorophyll drip.

At the property—an old farmhouse set back from the road—I pull over next to the aging rock wall and step out of my car, walking up to a tree whose leaves are lemon yellow. As a child, I played under its low branches for years, pretending to be Anne of Green Gables.

I brush my hand over the grooved bark and exhale. It's cold enough that I can see my breath, but the morning sunlight filters through the leaves, casting a golden glow that warms me, causing ripples of nostalgia the way autumn tends to do. God, I miss being a kid, when my biggest concern was figuring out how the heroine in my story would sneak an extra ice-cream sandwich. Real life, adult life, is hard.

Because there's no one around, I hug the tree, resting my cheek against it. "Thank you," I murmur to it.

I step back, and like a true tourist, I snap a photo with my phone, which I send to Dad.

Peaking, he replies, and I smile. And then, because he can't help himself, he writes: A story about a group of youngsters who get lost following train tracks. That's got legs, no?

I swear he's just looking at his bookshelf. Or his DVD collection. Yeah, it's called Stand by Me. I start to put my phone away, but then add: Dad, can you please not bring those boxes over? Take them to the dump instead.

To which Dad replies: What boxes?

Before I go, I marvel at the beauty of a fallen leaf, this one buttery yellow freckled with brown spots. You know what? It's time for a change. I'm going to be patient and kind with everyone I meet. I'm going to write a cache of pages for Carmen. I'm going to—

Something tickles my ankle. I pull my pant leg up and see a tick crawling across my skin.

"Ahh!" I yell, swiping it away and making a mad dash for my car.

ELEVEN

Lou catches up to me in the Apex parking lot, despite my best efforts to outpace him.

"Joan of Arc!" He punches me in the soft spread of my upper arm.

"Ow," I say.

"Top of the morning to ya!"

Ugh, he's insufferable. I throw a glance his way, and he looks as chipper as he sounds, totally inappropriate for someone about to start six hours of somewhat hard labor.

I, on the other hand, am the picture of a lady who's given up: hair brushed in five strokes, coat zipper busted, and my bag, not a knockoff of anything, hanging sadly from my shoulder. It is the color, I now notice, of newborn poop. I hitch it higher onto my shoulder, and my coat swings open, inviting the cold air's handsy touch and exposing my rumpled uniform.

Lou's toting a small African drum under an armpit, and by the way he's lightly drumming I know he's dying for me to ask him about it. There's absolutely no way I will, but Lou doesn't wait.

"This is a djembe." He gives it a loud, unskillful slap, as if he's popping someone on the rear.

"Isn't that cultural appropriation?" I say, payback for the "literary porn" comment at the grocery store.

He halts and frowns. "Is it?"

"Little bit." I try to blow past him again, but I make the mistake of turning to look at his downcast face. Jeez, Joan, give him a measly crumb of kindness. Did I already forget my vow under the tree? Pausing, I gesture toward the drum, forcing out a compliment, something that feels at least half-true. "It's a beautiful instrument." And it is.

Lou brightens, relieved, face shining with excitement. "This drum was bestowed upon me by my spiritual adviser. I know this sounds a little kooky, Joan, but I didn't choose the massage profession, this profession chose me. It was a calling." Oh, here we go. I've heard this story. Many versions of it. "This necklace that I wear"—he flutters it at both of us—"was also given to me by my spiritual adviser after I emerged from a three-day sweat lodge. I drank my own sweat to stay alive. And it was during, oh, maybe the fortieth hour when I looked down at my hands and saw them as vessels, and how they're connected to every other human being . . . how they could offer hands-on healing . . ."

Sure, Lou's a blowhard trying to one-up anyone playing the "Who's the most spiritual?" game, but there's only truth behind his intentions. He became a bodyworker to help people. Beats my story: I was broke and lost. Maybe that's why, as I watch his mouth move, I'm wilting on the inside.

Or maybe it's because I've heard this story sixty gazillion times.

I can't help but wonder why Lou even bothers with me. Everyone else at the Apex seemed to have gotten the memo: Joan's not accepting new friend requests. Wouldn't it be great if I could, in moments like this, flip on a neon-pink "No

Vacancy" sign above my head? I'm full up. Not taking visitors. Keep on driving.

I know that makes me sound cold. That it makes me an outlier in a sea of people linking arms. But if I linked arms, I wouldn't be able to keep my own head above water.

". . . and that's how I started playing this drum," he says, patting the tight skin to make a hollow tap. "Hey, you wanna catch a Krishna Das concert tonight?"

"Nope, I already committed to a Krishna *Don't* concert."

Lou's eyes widen, worried he's missing out on a hot new act. "What? Who's that?"

I shake my head. "No one. We're going to be late."

"If you change your mind, chanting starts at eight." Lou begins to chant in Sanskrit under his breath, *"Seetaaraam seetaaraam seetaaraam jaya."* He opens the heavy employee door, taking a jester's bow as he holds it open for me.

Inside, I put several strides between me and Lou. The spa is fully booked today, and it hums with activity. Near the display of crystals, Tree ceremoniously places a stone in a client's palm, closing her fingers around it like he's entrusting her with a secret treasure. Next to them is a giant floor display of the Miracle Maple Body Accentuator salt scrub, dozens of tubs stacked in the shape of a pyramid.

If I were going apeshit today, I'd pick up the forty-dollar kelp-spirulina-volcanic-ash candle and use it as a bowling ball to topple the entire structure.

But I don't entertain those thoughts anymore. I'm on the up-and-up.

Except for the fact that I'm spying on the place.

Carlie zips past with a one-gallon jug of massage oil to top off the bottles in our therapy rooms. Bless her, she always does the sidework the rest of us hate.

I hear Heather on the phone in reception saying, "We no longer offer Chinese spooning, but we do offer Danish knifing." Why is every new service named after silverware?

Clients, mostly in pairs, walk slowly in their white robes, putting on an air of reverence, of a daily meditation practice, as if most of them hadn't just rushed to get here, cutting one another off to take parking spots.

Tara is amid the thrum, standing out in a smart, bright blue pantsuit, especially next to Tony, head of maintenance, who's wearing Carhartt pants, a long-sleeve black T-shirt, and a black Mountain Hardwear vest. Tara toes a worn area of carpet, apparently giving Tony his next assignment. He pulls a small notebook out of his back pocket, removes the short pencil that was resting behind his ear, and with a quiet nod of his head adds to what's undoubtedly an epic to-do list.

I'm so struck by the earnestness of the gesture, of his devotion to this place, that I almost forget I'm in a bad mood. *He's handsome*, I think. All brains light up when they see something pleasurable; it's not personal.

He must feel my gaze, because he glances over and raises his notebook in the air as a hello.

Blood rushes to my face and I return the wave. Jamal, strutting toward me runway-style, mistakes it for a greeting.

Before Jamal joined the Apex, he worked at a spa franchise in Albany that grossly underpaid and overworked him. He came to us like an injured bird, flighty and distressed. It took him weeks to let his guard down, to crack a smile, and it's a relief to see him confident. His experience being mistreated at that spa might be why he's drawn to helping animals most in need—old cats that no one else wants, two-legged dogs in wheelchairs. His dedication to these castaway pets is truly admirable, especially given that most of them cycle through his house, dying from old age or illness.

As he passes me, he leans in like he's handing me a naughty note. "Check out Tara's latest memo," he whispers, and I, despite myself, tingle with the excitement of being included in the workplace gossip.

Tara's memos are infamous for their poor taste and lack of self-awareness. I poke my head into the break room, see that I'll be alone, and find Tara's memo pinned up on the corkboard. Ah, it's about the tipping scandal that broke at Sattva, the massive yoga and spa center in the Berkshires.

Just like the Apex, Sattva collects massage therapists' tips in labeled envelopes that get sent to accounting—both cash and credit card tips. Accounting tallies the tips in order to tax them, and the therapists each receive their tips in their next paycheck. One squirrely accountant at Sattva was skimming from these tips, and netted close to $20,000 over a few years before he was discovered. The news sent shock waves through the massage community, and Apex employees started asking about our tips.

Tara's memo in response is quick and concise: "Thank you for your concern about the tips you receive from clients. Rest assured that we follow strict guidelines and that all accounting is monitored. Please spend your energy thinking about how you can continue to elevate our community here at the Apex."

She signed it "In loving service."

Elevate this, I think, giving Tara a mental middle finger. We have a right to make sure things are aboveboard, and Tara could be a little more sympathetic about our legitimate worries. If it could happen at Sattva, it could happen anywhere.

I'm about to turn away, but I stop. Is this the kind of dirt that Carmen wants? I've been counting down the days—likely two—until I'll hear from her again, demanding to know my progress. True to my word, I wrote an entry yesterday and the day before.

I glance behind me to make sure I'm still alone, and then I pull out my journal to copy down the memo verbatim, making my fourth entry for Carmen. It feels illicit and wrong, so I'm jittery when Tara appears at my locker a few minutes later.

She folds her arms across her chest.

"What's your secret?"

My mouth grows dry. "Excuse me?"

"I just can't believe it." Her hair floats down to her shoulders, perfectly trained.

"I can explain—"

She leans back, cupping an elbow and pressing a crooked finger to her mouth. "I'm all ears. Please explain to me how the infamous Carmen Bronze graded your massage an A-plus. I still can't figure it out."

Ooooohhhh. Now I understand. I nearly snort with relief, even though there's a not-so-veiled insult in Tara's skepticism. An "I thought you really sucked" subtext.

After I signed the contract for The Project, Carmen called Tara, applauding my massage skills—and possibly talking me up *too* much. Nobody's ever given my massage such a high rating, and an A-plus coming from the harshest of critics— Carmen griped that the sliced cucumbers in our water were too thick—doesn't compute. Tara banished my strikes, but I can see she's still wondering how in the hell I saved myself.

I give a sly raise of my shoulder. "What can I say? I've got magic hands." As if to prove it, I lift my hands in the air and rotate my wrists. Traitors that they are, they both crack.

Tara tilts her head, studying me, and for a brief moment I think she's about to call my bluff. But if she has doubts, she lets them go. "Well, maybe I'm going to have to give you all the tough customers from now on."

"They're not *that* magic," I stammer. "Might have been a onetime thing."

Tara steps closer. "I'm still watching you," she says. Then she puts her hands in prayer position, bows, and continues on her way.

Tara's memo, to be handed to Carmen like a decoded message from the enemy, is hidden in my bag. *Oh, I'm watching you, too, Tara.*

TWELVE

After work today, I find three unwanted orphans on my doorstep: the boxes from my parents. The first two contain my old diaries and childhood memorabilia. The last is stuffed with at least twelve different types of bathroom cleaners—Lysol, Clorox, Comet, Soft Scrub—all half-empty, plus four used, withered sponges. *Gee, thanks Mom.*

I'm prepared to dump the boxes of my stuff immediately into the recycling, diaries and all, but when I go to wheel the bin over, I find it stuffed to the gills. My neighbor and I share the bin as part of the rental agreement, and his output vastly outpaces mine. I could stack the boxes to the side, but I don't want my old diaries to be left so exposed. *Dammit.* I kick the wheel with my toe. I'll have to shove these boxes inside my house for a few days.

I haul them one by one into the living room—paper is *heavy*—and stack them temporarily in the corner. "Don't make yourself at home," I say, swiping my hand over the top of the cardboard. Sweet Bird instantly leaps up to perch on top, kneading the cardboard before he settles down to roost. Fine with me. Go to town. Shred 'em up.

I settle into my chair and steady the swaying desk. I've grown affectionate toward the old thing, even though it's like

I'm writing atop a house of cards. I open my journal to the brisk notes I took at work today, pick up my pen, and transcribe them in greater detail to Carmen.

Forty-five minutes later, I close the notebook, satisfied, and pick up my phone. To my relief, Carmen sent me a follow-up text message rather than calling. How's our baby? she asked.

I know what near tragedy she's referring to. Alive and kicking, I text back.

Alive and kicking, indeed. For the first time in a very long time, I'm feeling kind of okay. My job is safe. I haven't done anything weird or rude at work. I'm less consumed by thoughts of Samuel. The Project is proving to be a healthy distraction. And I've paid down half my debt, allowing me to feel calmer in my body, in my bones.

Yes, I congratulate myself. This had been a good idea. A smart venture.

I should heed the warning my mom gave me as a kid when I tried to eat three slices of pizza after being home with a stomach bug: "Don't get ahead of yourself."

Instead, I think: *Filling this entire notebook should be no problem. No problem at all.*

Notes for Carmen
When you're working with the human body, anything can happen. People have acne. People smell. People are ticklish and break into childish laughter when I graze their sides. People have to interrupt the massage to pee, dashing to the bathroom in as little clothing as possible so they can get back to the table in a jiff.

I'm also human. I keep a stick of deodorant in my bag and smear it under my arms if I remember. Sometimes my stomach grumbles so loud it's embarrassing.

People cry on the table, too. They have emotional releases, and I'm not always great in this department. I never know how to respond, or if I should keep going or pull back. Once I actually said "there, there," in an attempt at soothing a client, but I think I sounded like a cold British nanny. Then you've got your over-sharers, who treat the experience as a therapy session, droning on like I'm the shrink who wants to hear about their love lives, doomed marriages, annoying in-laws, financial pickles, job frus-trations, and general existential crises. "What should I do with my life?" someone once implored. I'm only qualified to give Net-flix recommendations, so I said, "You can stream every episode of 30 Rock. That should get you through the weekend."

And people can be downright obstinate, ignoring my requests, blowing off my knowledge, or refusing to comply with the Apex's basic protocols.

No, you cannot bring your child into the room with you and have me semi-babysit him or her while I'm also massaging you.

No, it would not be safe for me to slap you with this birch twig.

No, I cannot allow you to call in to your work meeting and then put yourself on mute while I go at your lower back.

People throw actual tantrums when they are told no. As adults. About a massage.

I guess what I'm saying is, you never know who you're going to get on the table—what kind of body, personality, mood, or trauma. It's a surprise, every time. And we bodyworkers just have to roll with it.

Winter

THIRTEEN

Sybil, heavily pregnant, is insisting on a facedown massage. Normally that's not possible given the baby bump, but the Apex offers something special to expecting women: the donut-shaped pregnancy support cushion. It truly screws us bodyworkers.

We're the ones who have to be the bearers of bad news, politely pointing out that the cushion, with its hollowed-out belly circle and hollowed-out breast sockets, was really made for a Kate Hudson type, who, pregnant, looks like a snake that swallowed a balloon.

Sybil does not look like Kate Hudson. But saying "you're just too big" will go over as well as a plate of unpasteurized cheese.

Instead, I gently say, "I think you might find you're more comfortable lying on your side. We can prop you up with pillows, put one between your knees."

It's not that I want to coast through this massage, the last of the day before the Apex Christmas party tonight, but I was hoping for something easier than what's happening now: Sybil saying, "I want the facedown cushion I saw on the website."

I bristle with annoyance.

Wedging herself into the opening, Sybil shifts and squirms. "This isn't very relaxing," she says accusatorily.

"Again, I think you'll have a great massage even if you're lying on your side. This is likely putting stress on your lower back—"

"I didn't ask your opinion, thanks." Her voice is tight, and I recoil like I've been slapped.

I don't stop to consider what Sybil's gone through during her pregnancy, her craving for the simple pleasure of lying on her belly, or that she might be aching to feel normal, like the woman she used to be, before she enters motherhood.

Instead, all I hear is *You are subservient, subservient, subservient.* And then I'm catapulted back to the session with the client who took a phone call, and to the man who nodded to his erection, and to the older woman who hung her wig on my water bottle, and even to Carmen, who made me dance like a marionette to win her favor, all of them seeming to say: *Only the service you provide to me matters. Your hands. Your physical effort. But not you.*

I push the feeling down and set my hands to Sybil's back. Pressing her body, even with a light touch, only sends her deeper into the caves of the cushion, and she stiffens in alarm.

"Do you think I'm crushing the baby?" Sybil asks, voice muffled.

I should keep my mouth shut, offer reassurance. But if she's so worried about her baby, why not just lie on her damn side? "I thought you didn't want my opinion," I answer, before my better judgment can catch up.

Her voice rises an octave, aghast at me, and she turns her head from the face cradle. "That is not funny. Do you think so or not?"

I give a shrug. "I suggested lying on your side for a reason."

Sybil reaches behind her and flicks my hand away. Then she pries herself up, pushing back to hands and knees, the sheet draped over her back like a saddle.

"You're a monster," she spits. And I'm taken aback. *Am I?*

She folds onto her haunches, gathers up the sheet, and pulls it around her body. The support cushion makes for a precarious perch, and it's impossible for her to gracefully swing her legs over the side. With no other option, she's forced to steady herself with her hand on my shoulder.

Sweat beads form on both of our foreheads.

"I can't believe you call yourself a masseuse," she continues, inching her butt closer to the right side of the table.

My blood boils. "I don't," I hiss. "I call myself a massage therapist." I'm not a stickler about a lot of things, but don't call me a "masseuse." That term is as outdated as smoking on airplanes. We in the biz see this as a derogatory term, a code word for sex work, and it undermines our education and experience.

Sybil has no choice but to put her arm around me so I can help her stand up. At this point, we're both disheveled and panting. My hair is a mess. My uniform is rumpled. Sybil clutches the sheet to her neck. She's missing an earring. We face each other in the dim light of the room, a candle flickering next to the bamboo plant.

"I want a refund," Sybil says, lifting her chin.

"Good luck with that." I give a haughty laugh, also knowing that if she reports me, I'm done for. In another part of my brain, I'm waving my hands furiously to get my own attention. *Abort this self-sabotaging mission.* Sybil will win this fight, it's not even close.

"I'm going to ruin you on Yelp."

I can't stop myself. "I'm going to ruin you on Melp," I fire back. Sybil's eyes widen in question. "You haven't heard of it? It's a site that reviews mothers. I can see the headline now"— my hands underscore every word—"'Mother Crushes Baby for Back Rub, Refuses to Lie on Side.'"

Sybil opens her mouth again, but before she can speak, I open the door. "Take your time getting ready." I step through the door into the bright hallway.

My heart is pumping with adrenaline, and I'm itching for the fight to continue. I mentally dare someone else to come test me. Lou, perhaps. I pause for a moment in the hallway, unsure of what to do next, and then I slip into a single-stall bathroom and lock the door, pressing my back against it.

"Shit."

I pee, and I sit on the toilet for a long time after, lost in anxious thought, my pants around my ankles. Why couldn't I just be more accommodating? More than that, why can't I control my temper? *Am* I a monster? I put my head in my hands and rub my eyes with the heels of each hand, trying to coax a tear.

I stand up, wipe, flush, wash. In the mirror, I examine myself. I try to smooth down my hair. My cheeks are ruddy, my eyes small and far away. A hot shame bubbles up, and I'm filled to the brim with self-loathing.

"You," I say. "You should be ashamed of yourself." And I am. I am. And my next question is *What's wrong with me?*

FOURTEEN

My plan for the Apex Christmas party: Make three loops around the room as part of my spying mission for Carmen and then call it an early night. She's returning in two weeks, and I still have half a notebook to fill.

Second on my list: Find out if Sybil beelined to Tara and whether I'm on the brink of being fired yet again.

Third: Eat a free dinner.

Just as I enter, Carlie thrusts a crystal glass of mulled wine into my hand.

"Did you bring something?" she asks. "You have to contribute a gift if you want in." She's referring to the annual Yankee swap, a cutthroat exchange with players swiping the best gifts out from under one another. Every year, some sorry loser goes home with a dud, like a chintzy, rewrapped teddy bear hugging a heart that was probably won in an arcade claw game.

Or so I've heard. This is the first time I've come to the party, and I hadn't planned to join the swap.

"I . . . uh, didn't bring anything."

"Just get something from your car," Carlie side-mouth whispers as people begin to gather around the tree. Surprising myself, I do, grabbing a brown paper bag of Mom giveaways and shoving it deep under the boughs of the Apex's massive Christmas tree.

Carlie, sitting next to me in a Grand Tetons sweatshirt and a Santa hat, nudges my shoulder as she rubs her hands together. "Don't take it personally if I nab a Starbucks gift card right out from under your nose," she says.

"I won't," I say, growing nervous. A Starbucks card would put my gift to shame.

We're all in a horseshoe shape around the tree, sitting on the Apex's winged chairs and striped love seats. I'm in a black wrap dress that I haven't worn in years, and when I cross one leg over the other, I pull my hemline down over my red tights, feeling utterly ridiculous. It hasn't helped that all of my coworkers, upon seeing my outfit and pendant earrings, reacted with shock, as if I'm usually wearing a trash bag. "You clean up well" doesn't necessarily feel like a compliment.

I look across the U-shape at Tara, who's filing a nail, ostensibly bored. In her red pencil skirt and fuzzy black sweater, she looks like she's dressed for a Republican fundraiser. She glances up, and when our eyes meet, she raises her eyebrows as if to say *How in the hell did we find ourselves here?*

Or is it to say *Sybil marched right into my office—you're toast?*

I can't be sure, and I frown in frustration that I put myself in this position again. I mean, Melp? Accusing an expectant mother of hurting her baby because she refused to give up on some pampering? God, that *is* monstrous. Samuel wouldn't recognize the person I've become. And if Sybil didn't report me, which is shocking, who's to say the next person won't? I've got to get ahold of my anger or I'm going to spiral again, jeopardize my job, and in turn jeopardize The Project. I can't very well spy on the Apex if I'm not working here.

The Project has been a nice distraction, a way to pay off my debt and save my job—but it hasn't touched my grief, which still bubbles up in uncontrollable ways. Like lashing out at Sybil. The Project hasn't fixed my real problem.

I *have* to do something. I can't keep going like this. But what?

A loud pop from the fireplace draws my attention. Two large logs cave in on each other, and Tony springs up, grabs a metal poker, and pushes the charred ruins away from the hearth.

I had wondered if he'd be here. Watching him, I think, *He's actually* very *handsome*.

As he reaches for another log, he winces in pain. I don't want him to catch me staring again, so I move my eyes to the wreath hanging above the fireplace. It's studded with cranberries and fragrant cinnamon bundles, and I nod like I'm appreciating it as a wreath aficionado who has never considered adding sticks of cinnamon.

When I let my eyes venture down, Tony has taken his seat.

Lou stands up and taps his glass with a knife, quieting the crowd and signaling to the pianist in the corner to pause his holiday repertoire. Coils of chest hair have escaped Lou's gold-and-black dashiki. "Before the festivities commence, I want to acknowledge that we are here today on the land of the Mahicans," he says. "Please join me in paying our respects to the spirits of the Mahican people and to the Mahicans who are here with us today."

It's a sentiment I've never heard even though I've lived here all of my life. Out of habit, I want to sneer, because it's Lou, but I don't feel that way. The mood is somber, respectful, heads bowed in unison, and I bow my head, too.

Then Lou booms in a deep voice, "Let the games begin!"

Tree, dressed like a green elf, opens the first gift. It's Bananagrams, and the room goes wild. He clutches the cloth banana to his chest. "Please let me keep it," he whines.

From a silver gift bag with a bright red bow, Carlie pulls out a tub of the Miracle Maple Body Accentuator, and everyone groans.

"That's from me!" Tara says, not realizing (a) we know, and (b) it's not a gift she should claim.

In a ruthless move, Carlie marches across the room to tug Bananagrams out of Tree's pale hands, plunking the salt scrub in his lap. Tree hangs his head.

Tony opens a smudge stick from Tree, which Tree vows is not white sage, since that's being overharvested and should be claimed only by Indigenous people. Tara receives an ocarina hand flute from Lou and frowns at it.

I watch in horror as Lou fishes underneath the tree and hands my paper bag to Jamal, whose teal sweater has an adorable pug wearing a red scarf.

"Who's going to own up to this?" Jamal asks, shooting the bag a dirty look.

I raise a tentative hand. He reaches deep into the bag and pulls out each item one by one.

A Dwight Schrute bobblehead. Mom loves *The Office*. "It's a great show," I say.

Two tea towels laced with an Italian-grape motif. "Can't have enough tea towels," I add nervously. Jamal clears his throat.

One bread basket. "To deliver bread," I say.

Next to me, I hear Carlie say, "Damn, I wish I'd gotten that gift."

Jamal returns each item to the bag and looks directly at me. I'm expecting a rebuke, a deserved takedown, but he smiles and says, "Your Apex family is glad you came this year, Joan. Even if your gift is bunk."

My Apex family. My face grows hot as I notice everyone

nodding in agreement, even Tara, and I tug again at my dress. The sincerity in Jamal's voice, the unconditional acceptance from my colleagues—even after I've rebuffed them for the last two years—is almost more than I can bear. Especially after the incident with Sybil today. What would they all think of me if they knew how I had acted?

"I'm glad, too," is all I can manage to say.

The attention is still on me because it's my turn to open a gift. It's from Carlie.

"This one's real special," she says, winking at me. "Careful, it's a little fragile."

The gift is heavy, and I draw my knees together to cradle it in my lap. I lift the tissue paper, slipping both hands inside to touch the cool, sleek surface of glass. It feels like a crystal ball. But when I pull it from the bag, I see that it's a snow globe. Encased inside are two people on horseback—a woman with a long braid and a man pointing up at a snowy peak.

I barely register Carlie saying, "It's the Rockies. One of my favorite national parks."

All I can think of is Samuel. *Nestled in our world like we were protected inside a snow globe. Untouchable from the outside.* Flipping the snow globe upside down, I send a swirl of snow around the couple.

My eyes flood with tears, and I will myself not to blink. Not to cry in front of everyone when I'm finally joining in like a normal person. All I can do is hold the weight of the gift in my hand.

"Do you want to swap it?" Lou asks.

I lick my lips, trying to gather myself. "No. Nope, I do not." I glance at Carlie. "It's perfect." She reaches over and squeezes my knee.

After the game ends, I bring the snow globe over to my bag stashed in the corner. Before I nestle it next to my journal, I swirl the snow again, my finger to the glass as if I could touch the couple.

It's us, Samuel and me. In our snow globe.

As the snow settles, an unexpected thought takes shape. Maybe the answer isn't journaling my feelings about the love story I lost. *It was a sunny September day when Samuel went—*

Maybe it's writing the love story I wish I'd had, one with the fairy-tale ending. Our story was just beginning, cut too short, but for a moment I imagine filling in the rest. Creating a new story that allows Samuel and me to experience the impossible: a future.

Sure, it wouldn't be real, but it could be . . . cathartic. Fun, even? Fun has been in short supply for the past two years. Samuel and me on a beach vacation. Spending holidays together. Going to Colorado. It sounds a lot better than hashing out what happened, reliving the pain.

I know it's ridiculous, writing a romance novel to fill the gaping hole in my life. Besides, I'm no writer. I gave up on that dream a long time ago.

But it's sparked something inside me. I think about Dad's purple notebook, hidden inside my desk drawer, waiting for me. I can fill it with what could have been. And if writing about Samuel is too hard—it always has been—couldn't I fictionalize us? Imbue fake characters, those two people on horseback, with memories from our time together? Strangely, I think that might feel . . . good.

Crouched over my bag, I hear a jingling sound above my head. It's Tony standing over me in an ugly Christmas sweater with actual bells attached to it.

"Hi," I say, stowing the snow globe and standing up, suddenly nervous. I pull at the cleavage of my dress, wondering if he thinks I look silly in my—

"Nice dress," he says.

My face is aflame. "This old thing?" I say.

"It doesn't look old."

I peer down to examine it, mentally calculating when I made the purchase. "Couple of years. Anyway, thank you." I gesture to him. "Nice ugly sweater."

He frowns. "Is it ugly?"

"Oh, I . . . wow . . . sorry." My hand presses to my cheek.

Tony laughs. "I'm kidding. It's hideous."

"Phew," I say, pretending to wipe and flick sweat from my brow.

"I'm sure you get sick of people asking for your expert opinion, but I have a question about an injury I have."

"Ask away," I say, touched that he thinks I'm the expert in this room of uber-talented bodyworkers. I fight the urge to jingle a bell at nipple height.

"A few days ago, I slipped from a ladder while I was changing a lightbulb, and I tweaked my back. It's been out before, but this feels different. If I . . ." Tony demonstrates reaching up with his right hand, and then stiffens in pain. "See, I can't do that. Doc says I pulled this muscle, something 'serratus'?"

"Serratus posterior inferior."

"That's it!" Tony's eyes light up. "That's the one. Any suggestions?"

"You should book a massage." Embarrassed by what this might be inferring, I rush to say, "It doesn't have to be with me. Carlie's really great, especially with injuries."

"You sound like you know what you're talking about."

I wave him off. "I'm second string. Just don't let anyone Danish-knife you."

He laughs. "I have no idea what that is."

"Nobody does."

For a suspended moment, we smile at each other. His eyes are tawny, like a long-steeped cup of tea. I picture pressing my lips to his lids, and my own eyelids flutter in response. Then they snap open. *Whoa.* This is all coming from left field. I mean, I've worked with the guy since I started at the Apex. I blame the mulled wine for my overactive imagination.

Tara interrupts us, yoo-hooing for Tony from the fireplace. "The fire is dying. Can you take care of it?"

Tony's smile is apologetic. "Thanks for the suggestion. Merry Christmas, Joan." He squeezes my arm as he passes, lighting up my skin with his touch, neurons firing, a mini fireworks display embedded in my body.

Behind me, Jamal taps a microphone, announcing karaoke. Lou's got his lips on the ocarina flute, and Carlie and Tree are embroiled in a fierce game of Bananagrams. I hadn't expected to stay. I hadn't expected to have a good time.

But now, I've got to go. Someone's waiting at home for me. Two people, actually: the fictional stand-ins for me and Samuel. I tiptoe out, quiet as Santa himself.

FIFTEEN

It's safe to say I haven't cracked a single egg since Samuel died. Sprinkled zero fresh sprigs of parsley on an omelet. Diced no peppers. Chopped no onions.

Breakfast is typically a toaster waffle. Lunch a sandwich. Snack a Snickers or a McDonald's Oreo McFlurry. Dinner a deli tub. Toss in a few baby carrots.

This morning, buoyed by my epiphany at last night's Christmas party, plus the fact that Sybil doesn't seem to have lodged any complaint, I'm whisking two eggs with such vigor that Sweet Bird is mesmerized. Or concerned, because I'm also dancing, bopping along to a pop song I found when I turned the dial from my usual NPR. He might not know I can move like this. A slumped shuffle is what he's used to.

"Sweet Bird, I'm making French toast." Cracking the eggs felt powerful, a deliberate destruction. Maybe I'll make my parents a frittata for Christmas morning. That will bowl them over. "Move over, Barefoot Contessa. Holey-socked Joan is in the house." I wiggle the big toe that's sticking out of my sock. Sweet Bird springs for it, and I push him out the cat door. A little cold air won't hurt him.

When I bought the ingredients this morning, I splurged for brioche, and now I float each thick slice in its eggy bath before I place it in the cast-iron skillet Mom gave me, listening to the sizzle. Each time I peer out the window over the sink at Sweet Bird giving me the stink eye from the yard, I see Carlie's snow globe resting on the sill, and I smile. There we are.

Forever safe and happy in our snow globe, Samuel is a cowboy, and I'm a cowgirl—but how exactly did we meet? That's the story I want to tell—the one that leads to this happily ever after. I've been mulling over the possibilities all morning, starting backward. How did we get to that exact moment when we're riding horses side by side, pointing at that mountain? The idea of breathing new life into us is so thrilling that I'm practically yodeling. That would really alarm Sweet Bird.

With the French toast piled onto my plate, I head to the living room to sit at my desk. Can the desk hold the weight of my breakfast? "I'm trusting you," I say to it.

I gingerly open the drawer to retrieve Dad's purple notebook, and I set it next to my plate. Then I take a bite, sit back in my chair, and moan. Damn, that's good. As I chew, I drum my fork against my desk, thinking. Who is my character? Well, people always say "write what you know," so why don't I make her a bodyworker, too? She works at the . . . Summit House Inn & Spa. And I'll call her . . . Evian Jones, a wink to my "Evian water" clients. Like me, Evian is steeped in grief, but unlike me, she didn't lose her boyfriend. No, she's mourning her—I take another bite—mom, who died in a fiery car accident (sorry, Mom). Massage therapy is a calling and she's proud of her talent. I'm drawn to the idea of writing her as someone who loves what she does. I don't want to write about disillusionment. I live that every day.

There's still more to flesh out, but it's a good start. I like myself as her. Or her as me.

And I'm enjoying myself. Much more so than if I were writing about my grief.

On to Samuel. Who should he become? I've harbored a cowboy fantasy ever since I watched Luke Perry play Lane Frost in the movie *8 Seconds* when I was fourteen years old. I confessed this to Samuel, prompting our first and only role play. No hanky-panky. Plenty of cackling as he pretended to walk in chaps.

Yes, I see it: Samuel wearing a dusty, low-slung hat and worn boots, with mysterious eyes and shoulders as broad as a saddle. Scanning the room for name inspiration, I take in my worn corduroys, and then an empty McFlurry cup on my coffee table that I forgot to throw away. Samuel's character's name pierces my mind like an ice-cream headache: Cord McCool.

I press back in my chair, clap my hands, and laugh. Samuel would be getting such a kick out of this.

From the kitchen, my phone chimes. I go get it, brightening the screen to see an Evite notification. I still haven't RSVPed to Cher's New Year's party. The last thing I want to do is hang out with her hippie friends, who, at one past party, insisted on smudging me to cleanse my energy, outlining my body with sage bundles until I was hacking from the smoke. Then they pressed a piece of paper into my hands, urging me to write down the things I wanted to purge from my life—*Smudging*, I'd written, amusing nobody—before hurling the paper into the bonfire in Cher's backyard.

I have nothing to say at these parties. I'm barred from discussing The Project, and I'm not ready to talk about this—whatever it is I'm doing with Evian and Cord. My new hobby. My coping mechanism. The tiny little spark of life that's rekindling inside me.

Then there's the midnight kiss. I'll have no one.

Cher doesn't get it. Her invites imply that holidays should no longer be hard for me, that I should've moved on by now.

"Will not attend." I click my answer almost impulsively, toss my phone onto the couch, and sit back at my desk, swiping a finger over my plate to lick a last dreg of syrup.

Now it's time to introduce Evian to Cord. In the diner, where Samuel and I used to sit.

Before I consider the implications, I flip open my black-and-white composition notebook for The Project and tear out my last entry about the pregnancy support cushion, wanting to use this material for Evian's character, leaving three orphaned perforated edges behind. By the terms of our deal, those three pages are rightfully Carmen's.

For a moment, I pause. Carmen's arriving in less than two weeks.

But it's been so long since anything made me happy, and I'm greedy for this feeling. I don't want to stop now.

And so, pushing her and The Project out of my mind, I crack open the purple notebook and write *Chapter One*.

Snow Globe

Evian Jones perches on a counter stool at Deb's Diner, hoping that the other diners—people she's known all her life—treat her like a stranger. She doesn't want to accept any more condolences or to assure folks that, yes, she's doing all right after her mother's untimely passing.

The truth is, she's not doing all right, and her irritation showed this morning during a session with a pregnant client named Sybil, who insisted on using the prenatal support cushion to lie on her stomach. Just as Evian predicted, Sybil was uncomfortable, shifting and squirming.

"Do you think I'm crushing the baby?" Sybil asked.

"I think you should lie on your side, which is why I suggested it," Evian replied.

As soon as the words left her mouth, she regretted them. Her grief was making her impatient and mean.

All Sybil wanted was a back rub, some relief for her pregnant body—Evian couldn't believe she'd snapped at the poor woman. It wasn't like her.

Evian holds out her cup and the waitress refills her coffee from an arm's reach away. Her dark mood is a repellent.

From the side window, she catches a glimpse of the Summit House Inn & Spa looming over her hometown of Newchester, Vermont. What if Sybil reports her? Evian has the highest rebooking rate, but still, the new management has no tolerance for bad reviews, and even she is expendable. Plus, Evian needs to fly under the radar if she's going to pull off her secret plan: organizing her colleagues to fight for better wages and work policies. The Summit is squeezing the life out of them, and somebody has to stand up for what's only fair. She's nearly done writing her manifesto. But will her coworkers sign on?

She longs to ask her mom for advice. There's nobody else she wants to call. Not Robbie from last night. When he began tenderly stroking her arm and suggesting Sunday brunch, Evian jetted. Not Carlos from last week. He tried to introduce Evian to his son. What's with these men? Evian wants a no-strings-attached, no-Sunday-plans, no-becoming-a-stepmother romp in the sheets. Why is that so hard to find?

Evian senses a presence to her left, some poor soul daring to sit next to her. She turns, only to get knocked on the top of her head by the brim of a cowboy hat.

"Ow," she says, although it doesn't hurt. Everything perturbs her since her mom died.

The hat doesn't budge, meaning the cowboy underneath doesn't, either. His body is angled away from her, studying the outrageously large menu, as tall as an unfolded New York Times. Anyone who has to look at the menu, hell, who dresses like John Wayne, is not from around here, which means he doesn't know whom he's dealing with.

"Stay in your lane, cowpoke," Evian says, louder, rubbing her head.

The hat, and the man, slowly swivel toward Evian, meeting her leveled gaze, and his toffee-colored eyes, delicious as the inside of a Snickers bar, twinkly as gold nuggets, make her feel like she's tripping over herself to get west in a gold rush. To be the first to stake a claim.

"Sorry?" he says with a slight drawl that Evian can't place.

Confident, brassy Evian is for once less sure of herself. "Your hat . . . hit me."

He frowns with a mouth that looks accustomed to it, removing his hat to reveal a head of dark tousled curls. "Pardon me, ma'am."

Ma'am? Oh, no, no, no. Evian's got to remedy this, fast. With her full, Geena Davis mouth and sultry way of moving in the world, Evian can reel most men in with chum, hardly exuding any effort. No one's ever called Evian Jones "ma'am" like she's a 1950s housewife in an apron waiting for a milk delivery.

Before she can toss a poison dart, a quip so clever and cutting it would render him mute, he swivels back away from her. Evian takes a deep breath, smelling leather and dirt and sweat, an intoxicating muskiness that's foreign among the scents of the griddle or the fragrances she's used to at the spa, sandalwood and lavender, infused oils that embody luxury and not a lifetime of *hard work. For the first time in a very long time, Evian is swooning, pinned to her stool lest she fall out of it.*

He's probably as dumb as nails, *she thinks, trying to regain her balance.*

When he orders his coffee, she catches another scent, this time fennel, freshly brushed teeth, Tom's of Maine.

He gingerly readjusts himself on his stool, favoring his right arm.

"Torn rotator cuff?" she can't help but ask.

"That obvious?"

"Let me guess: too much computer time."

He chuckles at this, lighting her up inside. "You've got me pegged. I'm an IT guy."

Evian traces the lip of her mug with her fingertip. "What do you really do, if I might ask?"

"I'm not sure anymore. I used to ride rodeo. But those days are done." The cowboy's gaze is far away: an empty rodeo ring, hung-up reins, Evian can only imagine.

Then Evian's mind shifts, fear settling in like a dust storm.

This guy's trouble; he'll split her heart down the middle, devour one-half of it. The last thing Evian needs is to get hung up on a melancholy cowboy who will drift out of town like a tumbleweed. Besides, she needs to focus on the task ahead: sticking it to the Summit, and sticking up for herself and her coworkers. She's got work to do. No time for distractions.

Before he can say more, she slaps a five on the counter, mock-tips a cowgirl hat in his direction, and says, "Just remembered I'm late for something. See you later, partner." She slips away, willing herself not to peek back to see if he's watching her go.

SIXTEEN

Deli is wrapping my Italian sausages so slowly they might go bad by the time he's pressed the white sticker on top of the butcher paper. It's my fault. When he said he got a *Harry Potter* special-edition box set for Christmas, I made the epic mistake of admitting I've never read or watched it. Deli is now rectifying this dire situation by describing each book's plot in vivid detail. We're on book four, and I'm dying.

If I ever get out of here, I'm making Tuscan white bean soup tonight, with floating coins of sausage and Cher-level quantities of kale roughage. I can't afford the out-of-season tomatoes, so canned tomatoes will have to do.

"That's when Dumbledore . . ." Deli says, and I tune him out, willing his hands to move faster.

But I also smile to myself. It's nice to see him so expressive, so chatty. I notice a difference in his appearance, too. His skin is clearer, and he's tying his white apron around his neck rather than folding it lazily in half at his waist. The spindly stubble on his chin is gone, revealing a pointy, white mountain-cap chin. He still looks about nineteen years old, but more respectable, mature.

Behind me, a woman clears her throat impatiently. I glance over my shoulder to shoot eyes at her, but she whips open a

National Enquirer in front of her face so that only the pom-pom on her ski hat is visible. Then I notice a long white scarf trailing from the bottom of the newspaper to the ground.

"Carmen?"

"Shhh," Carmen Bronze hisses. She tosses the newspaper over her shoulder, not caring who will have to pick it up later. Then she lunges forward, grips my upper arm hard, and pulls me into the cookie aisle. She whips off her dark glasses. Her eyes are mini buttons compared to the oversized frames, and crow's feet branch deeply from the corners, fork tines pressed into dough.

"Are you following me?" I whisper.

"Are *you* following *me?*" Carmen whispers back, leaning close to my face and studying my mouth.

"I live here."

Carmen sighs and releases my arm. Unexpectedly, she snatches a box of cookies from the shelf, puts on the reading glasses that are strung around her neck, and skims the label.

"Poison," she declares. "All poison. They just want to keep us hopped up on sugar."

"Is everything okay here?" It's Deli, who came out from behind the counter to check on me. He's scrutinizing Carmen with concern.

"No, everything is not *okay*. There are twenty grams of sugar per cookie," Carmen says, thrusting the offending box in his face. "Count them. Two. Ze-*ro*."

"I think he's talking to me," I say, intercepting the box. I turn to Deli. "Yes, thank you, everything's fine. This is my . . . aunt. She's . . . very concerned about nutrition."

"As we all should be," she says, crossing her arms.

Deli strokes his chin. "All right. Well, you know where to find me."

"I do. Thank you." I'm surprised and touched that he cares. He backs out of the aisle, studying Carmen the entire time.

"Who is that? Your boyfriend?" She makes a crass finger-into-a-hole gesture.

"God, no. He's, like, twelve."

"Wow, really? Blame it on the milk. Chock-full of hormones these days."

"No, not really. Carmen, what's going on? What's with"—I gesture to her getup—"all this? We're meeting tomorrow morning. Why are you spying on me?"

She inspects me up and down. "I want to make sure you're really going to show. With The Project. My agent has literally crawled up my ass and parked a car there. So where is it?"

"The car?"

"The Project! My god, you're as dense as the traffic across the GW Bridge."

My mind races to The Project sitting on my desk at home, remembering Carmen's words: *Just so we're clear, I'm expecting one filled notebook.*

I'm twenty-five pages shy of a full notebook, give or take, but to me, that's as good as full. Nearly full. Passable, right?

I had *meant* to write exclusively for Carmen this past week, but I couldn't shake Evian and Cord. They're all I can think about, all I want to write about. Finding twenty-five more pages of focus for The Project tonight won't be easy, especially with a soup to make. "Well, I don't have it with me, if that's what you're asking."

"Good, good, best to keep it safe." She pats my knuckles the way an old woman pats the clasped hands of a reverend in the processional after a church service. "So I have nothing to worry about? I had this growing suspicion that you were going to play me." Carmen traces her hand over boxes of cookies, and then she laughs, as though recognizing for the first time how cuckoo it was of her to show up this way. She wags a finger at me. "But you're a good egg, I know that."

"Thank you," I say, my throat constricting as if I'd just downed Harry Potter's goblet of fire.

"I'll see you tomorrow."

"See you tomorrow. Nothing to worry about."

I *am* worried. What sort of game am I playing?

When Carmen's out of sight, I buy the box of cookies that she'd warned me against. I devour half of the fudgy treats sitting in my car in a glazed stupor as I stare out the window, trying to reassure myself that everything will be fine.

Snow Globe

Evian can't stop herself from thinking about the cowboy from the diner. So much so that when she sees him tilted back in an Adirondack chair on the Summit's lawn, hat over his face, arms crossed tightly, she thinks she's lost in a daydream. It can't be him; he was just in her mind.

At that moment, a bumblebee circles his head, and he uses his hat to swat at it, reaching so far over the arm of the chair that he tips himself to the side in the process.

Evian laughs, heading over to him, in spite of her earlier promise to keep her distance, to not get involved. Lying on the ground, legs still hooked around the chair, he looks like an upturned beetle, a very cute and utterly embarrassed upturned beetle. She extends her hand, pulling him to his feet.

"You're determined to make that shoulder worse," she says.

"I'm determined to make an ass of myself, is more like it." He shakes his head in disbelief at his clumsiness but doesn't drop her hand. The skin on his palm is both rough and warm, giving her

the assurance that he can handle a lot. Including her, curves and all. She bats away the thought of his grip on her hips.

"Might as well introduce ourselves," Evian says, nodding to their prolonged handshake. "I'm Evian Jones."

"Cord McCool."

Evian rolls her emerald eyes, lips upturning. "Oh, c'mon. That can't be your real name."

He raises an eyebrow, releases her hand, and reaches for his hat, glancing back up at her as he does. "That can't be yours."

"My mother was a big fan of the water."

"My mother was a big fan of . . ." *He slants his head, burnt-sugar eyes searching the clouds, thinking.*

"The pants?" *Evian offers.*

"The unit of firewood." *Crinkly eyes, a mischievous mouth.*

"Ah, makes perfect sense." *She makes a skeptical face.*

"Would you prefer I was John? Or Dave?"

"No, you're perfect." *Oh my god! Did she just say that out loud? Evian feels heat flooding her cheeks, wishes her blushing wasn't such a tell.* "Well, besides being so afraid of a bee that you'll nearly knock yourself out."

Cord studies her for a beat, making Evian feel self-conscious. "What are you doing here, anyway?" *She gestures to the field, to the Summit's grand buildings.* "How does a cowboy from—"

"Texas."

"—Texas end up at a luxury spa in Vermont?"

"It's kind of a long story," *he says, stuffing his hands into his weathered jeans, the longhorn cow on his brass buckle staring at her. God, he really looks the part. Does he ever just wear normal clothes? Sweats? Pajamas? A T-shirt?*

"Can you shorten it?" *Her eyes are playful, but it's true. Evian has no patience for long stories. Recounted dream sequences are out of the question.*

"*Brevity's actually my middle name.*" Cord shares his tale, making it quick. *He never planned to hang up his hat this early in his career, but after the steer he was trying to rope in Texas punctured his lung and trampled him, nearly killing him, he promptly retired, sending shock waves through the rodeo world. His manager sent him here to lay low and recover, hoping that time away in a place the very opposite of a corral would tempt him back. He's not admitting it, but Evian gets the sense that he's a big deal.*

"*And is it?*" she asks.

"*What?*"

"*Tempting you.*" She's slightly swaying her hips, wishing she was wearing something more provocative than her Summit uniform.

"*I guess I'm still figuring out what Vermont has to offer.*" His gaze is pointed.

Against all the synapses in her brain telling her to walk away again, Evian nods toward the mountain rising up behind them. "*I guess I'll have to show you. Ever hiked during a full moon?*"

"*I'll be damned. I haven't.*"

"*Do you have anything more suitable?*" She gestures toward his cowboy boots.

"*I can drum something up.*"

"*Tonight?*"

"*Tonight.*" He tips his hat.

SEVENTEEN

In Deb's Diner the next day, I'm a yarn tangle of nerves. I'm fifteen pages shy of a full notebook, plus there's the small fact that I've been picking over my notes and using the best bits for *Snow Globe*. It started with the pregnancy massage. Then Evian struggling to sell the Miracle Maple Face Mask. And one of my clients saying "I don't like pressure"—I'm sure Carmen would have loved that line, but I wanted it.

Outside, there's two feet of snow, the roads already cleared by industrious snowplows that beeped their way to sunrise. A family of skiers, their lift tickets dangling from their parkas, tromps past to a corner table, likely steered here by a hot tip that eating at the diner would give them some local flavor. Newchester is a stone's throw from Bartlett Mountain, so when leaf season ends, we get the out-of-towners with their ski passes. A kid about eight years old clomps behind his parents already wearing his ski boots. I'm not a skier, but even I know it's rude to wear your ski boots inside. *New Yorkers.*

Carmen arrives, drizzling her scarf into the corner of the booth, so much fabric it's practically a third breakfast guest. Before she even greets me, she waves down a server with a swift chop of her wrist. The server—not ours—halts next to our table and peers down, steadying a large tray of water glasses, and Carmen dictates an order of coffee with cream. The server scowls, sucks in air, nods, and scurries on as a chorus of ice cubes clinks on her tray.

"You shouldn't order people around," I blurt out. I can't take another meal with Carmen treating waitstaff poorly. As someone who works in the service industry, it's my duty to speak up.

Carmen digs into her deep bag, its mouth as wide as a baby hippo's. She pulls out a tube of cream, slathering both hands and inspecting her cuticles, and only then does she acknowledge me. "I can't, huh?"

"That's right."

She sighs a deep, heavy, bored sigh. "If I must have this conversation, I'll say this: I ask for what I want." Her eyes bore into me, and I glance to the side the way a dog looks away if you stare at it. "I state things plainly and simply. I don't manipulate or conjecture. I'm never passive-aggressive. I cut out excess in conversation, as in 'Coffee, cream. Thank you.' That waitress was balancing a tray of six heavy water glasses. Would you prefer I took more of her time just to say something ostensibly politer, like"—she puts on a high, nasal, whiny voice—"'I'm so sorry to trouble you. I'm dying for a cup of coffee. Is there any way you could send our waitress over or you yourself could bring me a cup of your delicious brew?'"

At that moment, a cup of coffee lands in front of Carmen.

"Now, see," she says. "I'd still be waiting if I hadn't asked for what I wanted."

It's difficult to argue with Carmen, as usual, but her logic doesn't make it any easier to endure her tone, her tendency to see people only for their use in meeting her needs. And I'm a little jealous of that coffee.

"I think the reason you're so bent," Carmen continues, tipping a mini creamer into her mug and then tapping on the empty container with her forefinger for any lingering drops, "is that I know what I want. It makes you jealous."

"That is *so* not true." I can't seem to get comfortable in the slippery booth, plus it's hot in here. Little beads of sweat have surfaced on my lower back.

"You know what you want? You ask for it? You demand what you need?" Carmen takes an oversized gulp of her coffee, smacks her lips, says "ah," almost like she's teasing me. She has two hands wrapped around her mug, all cozy-like, as if she should have her legs bent under her on a couch in Aspen wearing a thick-ribbed sweater, and she peers at me over the lip of it, nearly hiding her smirk. "You're your true self?"

"I'm a . . . I mean . . ." I scoff, my face reddening. "Of course. Who else would I be?"

Evian. I would be Evian. A woman so self-assured she gives off a presidential vibe. Crowds part for her. People listen to her. She has more than one friend, can keep a rosemary plant alive, and earns enough to afford to heat her apartment all winter instead of parking the thermostat at fifty-nine degrees. And most of all, she's falling in love with someone who will never die on her.

"'Kay." Carmen's shrug is halfhearted. "That's not what I see, but I'll take your word for it."

Another server appears, younger than the first, disheveled, her blouse misaligned, strands of hair popping out of her loose ponytail. Her crooked name tag says "Betsy." She's as thin as a balance beam, the fast-metabolism type who forgets to eat, zipping here and there, and then gets away with chowing half a pie.

"Sorry about the wait, this is my first shift, not training," Betsy explains, pushing hair out of her face with her wrist. "They really got me running." She leans the tops of her thighs against the edge of the table to steady herself. A man in a trucker hat at another table waves his check in the air and Betsy gives him an unconfident nod. She notices Carmen's mug. "Oh, good, somebody already got you coffee."

"Indeed." Carmen mock cheers me, unbearably proud of herself.

Betsy pats her apron pocket for a pen and pulls out, instead, a crispy piece of bacon. "Hey, how'd this get in here?" She frowns at the bacon, scans the room for an unhappy customer missing a crucial component of the meal, and then crams the stick of pork back into her pocket, shrugging.

From her deep bag Carmen unveils a pen and passes it to Betsy with a flourish.

"Short stack with strawberries," Carmen says and nods at me to order. Her impatience and the man waving his check in the air like it's a lighter at a U2 concert prompt me to utter, "Same for me."

Carmen's question snickers in my ear: *Are you your true self?*

I'm really in the mood for hash browns, but I bat the craving away.

"Easy peasy!" Betsy says, noting our orders and handing the pen back to Carmen, who takes it and then, reconsidering, presses the pen into Betsy's hands.

"Keep it," Carmen says, as if she's passed her a folded $100 bill.

"Oh!" Betsy grins. "Thank you, that's so kind." She shoves the pen into her apron to meet its neighbor, Mr. Bacon. "Your omelets will be out in no time."

Betsy hurries away, and Carmen rolls her eyes. "Oh my god. Omelets? Who gave her the job? What a loon!"

Still, I can't help but think that my words moved Carmen toward this small gesture of kindness, softened her humanity. Emboldened, I decide to goad Carmen on another topic on my mind. "If you're all about female empowerment," I ask, "what about your books? What about your female characters? Don't romance novels paint a pretty weak picture of women?" I've been mulling this over since I started writing my own personal romance novel.

Besides Carmen's book, the only romance novels I've ever read were ones I filched from my mom's shelf when I was in middle school. Back then, it seemed like brawny men were always saving women from dangerous situations or boring lives.

Carmen sighs again, intertwines her hands, then sets a forearm on the table and leans forward. "Have you ever even read my novels?"

"Uh, yes, one. The trapeze one."

"That's it?"

"Yes."

"*Her Rakish Ways?*"

"No."

"*The Baker's Rolling Pin?*"

"No."

"*Love on a Hot, Tin Roof?*"

I shuffle my feet under the table. "Ahem, no."

"*The Loveless Marriage?*"

"Nope."

"That was a children's book."

I furrow my brow, confused. "A children's book?"

"It was an experiment." Carmen waves her hand in the air to dismiss it, visibly annoyed. "Unbelievable, you critics on your high fucking horses. I shouldn't even have this conversation with you, since it's baseless. But here it is: Every single one of my characters is the ultimate heroine. You know why?"

I press the tongs of my fork into my fingertips.

"My heroine—she doesn't shy away from her wants, her needs, her most base desires. She grabs them, snatches them, as if it's a case of life or death. Sure, sure, there's a formula to romance novels, you could argue that, but that formula isn't played out. It isn't tired. We can't get enough of it because we rarely see it in our own lives. Many women walk around experiencing a slow spiritual death. The women in my books reckon with that. They face those dark thoughts of loneliness, of despair, of a life lived without passion, and they make a different decision. I would contend that the women in my novels do the most revolutionary act: They are their true selves, as we were just talking about before you ordered something you didn't really want."

Oh, lordy. I didn't expect this answer. If I was standing up, I'd be on my heels.

"You writers." She gestures to me, and corrects herself. "Well, not you, per se, but writers in general, they're so holier-than-thou. I've got a little news for you: Every book hinges on a formula, from *Great Expectations* to *Tantalizing Passion*, which was my first bestseller. Some are just more visible than others. Tension, scandal, love, loss—we're all regurgitating the same stories. Some of us happen to have it nailed down and some of us happen to package it so you can read it in one afternoon, on a beach, sipping a daiquiri."

I finally have a glass of water, and I take a drink, the ice falling toward my face, splashing droplets. I wipe my mouth with my napkin, not looking at Carmen.

"Do you know how hard it is to write a book? Do you?"

Actually, I'm getting the idea, but I shake my head no.

Carmen points a finger straight at me. "Well, then, don't tell me how to write my books or that I'm not feminist enough for you. I suggest you get your own life straightened out."

I'm half-impressed, half-terrified, and I have no response.

Betsy arrives, bless her, just in time to curb me bursting into tears. She simultaneously sets down two plates, declaring, "Short stacks, syrup, and a side of bacon on the house—not from my pocket." She winks at Carmen and beelines to the next table.

"Well surprise, surprise—I was half expecting cheeseburgers." Carmen chomps a piece of bacon. "No hard feelings. Let's move on. What do you got for me?"

Bloody hell. I want to sink under the table. I feel chastised and embarrassed and small. And this is all *before* I hand in my progress on The Project. I slide the black-and-white notebook over to her.

"I wasn't sure if you wanted the whole thing or . . ." I inch down in the booth.

Carmen fans through the pages. She glances up at me. "It's not finished. I specified finished."

"Yes, but it's only short a dozen pages or so." I bounce my left knee.

"Or so?"

"I got sick last week," I fib, giving a little cough. "A head cold."

"Hmmm."

"And I ran out of time."

"Uh-huh."

"Let's focus on the positive. There's a lot of great stuff in there. I mean, the notebook is practically full."

Carmen raises her head and peers at me over her eyeglasses. "No, *practically*," she says through clenched teeth, "it is not."

I can't say I'm really surprised that Carmen's a stickler for details.

A few solid minutes pass as Carmen reads and flips, reads and flips, and I again nervously slip my hands between my thighs as if I'm holding in my pee. Abruptly, she closes the notebook, removes her glasses, and pinches the bridge of her nose. She closes her eyes and sucks in a steadying breath, and then her eyes flash open and she levels her gaze at me. "I'm tempted to go back on our deal."

"What?" I hadn't considered this possibility. I mean, seriously, I did put a lot of work into that notebook—at first. It's only very recently that I've shirked my assignment.

"You were right. You're not good at this. Not only would I like my money back"—she outstretches her hand as if I have the cash to give her right then and there—"but I think I'll give Tara a quick buzz on the way home, tell her the truth about your massage."

"I can do better!" My heart is thumping in my chest as I think about how easily Tara had vanquished my strikes—and how she could fire me tomorrow.

Carmen angles her face and side-eyes me. "Can you, though?"

"I'll work overtime!" I blurt. "I'll fill up another entire notebook. I'll write until my fingers blister. You'll have so much dirt on the spa you could write a sequel."

"I have a lot riding on this book." Carmen looks to her left and then her right like she's about to cross a street before leaning forward and lowering her voice. "Between you and me, *The Zookeeper's Secret* didn't sell so well. Turns out my readers aren't big fans of primates. But spas they do love. Juicy gossip and demanding clients they will *lap* up. Scintillating behind-the-scenes details about the wellness industry and the grind of massage therapy—yes, please."

She plunks back against her seat, as defeated as I've ever seen her. "New romance writers are popping up like zits, all of them thinking it's easy to write a book you can read in a day."

I'm not a zit. I don't think writing a book is easy; I'm not full of confidence that I can do it myself. I'm more like a pre-zit, before it pushes to the surface. Underneath the table, my legs are bobbing as if I'm freezing.

"They all want to dethrone me." She sighs heavily. "And maybe I should just let them. It's never been easy, and after thirty-four books, it's not getting any easier. Maybe I should just call it . . ." Carmen stares past me, lost in thought. She almost seems depressed for an author who's at the top of her game. Who has everything all the zit writers dream of.

"Are you okay?" I ask.

"What?" she asks, as if she's coming to after a minor concussion. Then she shakes her head. "Yes. I'm fine. Now, I need a *major* brain dump from you. I need you to take this more seriously than a lump in your breast."

"*Jeez*, again with the little much."

She cocks her head and says breezily, "Your livelihood is tied to mine."

My stomach curdles like the cottage cheese I would never order from the breakfast menu.

I peek up at Carmen, whose look is menacing, taunting, an almost satisfied smirk across her lips now that our fates are intertwined. It's hard to believe that she's the same person who wrote the tender love story that kept me reading when I should have been sleeping. Where, in the depths of her, does she conjure up that? Has she known a deep love? Lost a great love? She's never shown her cards.

Should I show mine? Tell Carmen what I've really been doing—and, more important, why? That I've been trying to release a pressure valve of sorrow that was threatening to burst inside of me?

Before I can pipe up, Carmen shoves the notebook into her bag. "Are we clear now? You come back to me again with an unfinished notebook, even by one page, and I'm speed-dialing Tara."

"We're clear," I say, my voice small, my eyes downcast. "I won't disappoint you again."

She takes another enormous bite of pancakes followed by a slug of coffee and says, "I've got to jet. I've got a dermatologist I have to ream out. If you're going to remove a mole, remove it all." She stands up, coils the scarf around her neck, and seeing that I'm not joining her, slams a twenty-dollar bill on the table, not enough to cover a tip.

"I'll be back in March. You better pony up next time. Or *else*."

I feign confidence. "I'm on it."

Carmen tilts her head, studying me. And then she's off, the fringed end of her scarf waving at me over her shoulder, the goodbye that she didn't give.

EIGHTEEN

"Who'd you spend New Year's with?" Cher appraises me. I'm sitting on a stool in her kitchen, banging my foot repeatedly against the rung. I stop.

I rang in the New Year with two people Cher doesn't know: Evian and Cord. Which also felt like spending time with Samuel.

In Chapter Three, Evian and Cord hike up Mount Summit—an homage to Samuel and me hiking Mount Apex together for the first time. I'm giving this memory to Evian and Cord. It's the first time I've been able to think about it without despairing. The first time I've been able to look at it with curiosity and wonder, as I would a prism paperweight on a desk, turning it this way and that to catch the light.

I left Evian and Cord on the mountain, peering down at the village below. I have to focus on The Project or risk losing my job all over again.

"I just had a quiet night in," I say.

"Well, you missed a great party," she says, and I hear the annoyance in her voice.

"I'm sorry. I've been so worn out from helping Mom sort through eons of belongings. I had no idea they were such pack rats. Which reminds me"—I pull out three items from my tote bag and plunk them on her counter as if I'm a traveling sales-woman displaying my wares—"any interest in a desk organizer, a pair of driving gloves, or these banana hair clips?"

Cher examines a tortoise-colored banana clip. "These are coming back into fashion."

"Are they?"

"Are they not?" She seamlessly eases it into her long red hair, clamping it up into a high ponytail. She looks great. "Too horsey?" she asks, swishing her hair back and forth.

"You should take them all." I push the other two across the counter.

"Just the one." She glides them back, then gives me a look. "So that's it? You've been MIA because you've been lost in your parents' garage?"

"I've also been taking extra shifts so I can get on top of my credit cards." The lie comes so easily, I'm startled by it.

Cher frowns, knowing it's unlike me to work more than I have to.

"Don't worry," I reassure her. "I'm not living some secret life and not telling you about it." I *am*. Why did I have to say that?

But Cher just chortles at the absurdity of me pulling off a double life. It rankles me. I feel less guilty about lying.

She turns her attention to a quart of home-brewed kombu-cha, scooping rounded mounds of sugar into the jar, watching it dissolve into the liquid.

"It's like feeding a goldfish," she says, tapping the spoon on the brim of the jar.

"It looks like snot." I'm grateful for the distraction. No more questions, no more evasions about The Project.

"That," says Cher, pressing her finger to the glass the way children do at an aquarium, "is called 'the mother.'" I roll my

eyes at her reverence for a glob. "And speaking of sugar"—
Cher indicates her mason jar of sweetener—"guess which one
of my clients offered to become my sugar daddy a few
days ago?"

"No!" My hand flies to my mouth. I'm also wondering why
she didn't call or text me right after it happened. Didn't reach
out for support.

About six months ago, Cher had a real scare. A male client
with good credentials—vouched for by another client—
blocked the door of Cher's therapy room after a massage and
suggested that she "deserved her own happy ending."

Because Cher is alone in her house doing this work, she
always brings her cell phone into the room, and she threat-
ened to call the cops when he wouldn't move. He called her
an uptight bitch, hurling insults all the way to his car. Nobody
makes Cher cry, but thirty minutes later she was still shaking
like gloveless hands in an ice storm.

She had called me then. But something in the last few
months has shifted.

Cher nods vigorously. "You know the older couple that has
standing appointments with me every week—Gary and Fran?"

"No!" I repeat, aghast.

"*Yep*. Gary threw it out there so casually, like it was no big
deal. He said, 'If I don't ask, I'll never know the answer.'"

"What did you say?"

"I kept it professional." She shrugs one shoulder. "Told him
I wanted to strictly remain his massage therapist."

"And do you—after that?"

Cher mulls it over. "I'd hate to lose that steady income.
He's harmless, I think."

"God, this job is the worst," I say, trying to be commisera-
tive. "The things we have to put up with. I'm so sick of it."

Cher doesn't respond. Silently, she wipes down her island, and I feel a flash of regret. I've botched my response, though I'm not sure how.

I clear my throat, looking around the kitchen for safe territory, a topic that can steer us back to chumminess. There's a brochure tucked into one of her cookbooks, and I tug it free, thinking it'll be a cheesy advertisement for historical walking tours of Newchester or something else we as locals can poke fun at.

But no, it's for an online business program at the University of Vermont.

"What's this?" I say, holding up the brochure.

Cher snatches it from me. "Can you stop snooping, please?"

Snooping? Since when does my best friend of over twenty years accuse me of snooping? I scoff. "Sor-*ry.*"

She opens the cookbook and jams the brochure back in, slamming the cover.

"Are you going back to school?" I ask, not able to let it be. This is normally the type of life decision she'd hash out with me, and an icy fear flashes through me. Is she deliberately excluding me? Or, worse, is it just not occurring to her to involve me?

"If I wanted to talk about it, I would." She's rewiping the already clean island, and when she looks up at me, my face must show my hurt and confusion, because she sighs, softening her tone. "I don't know. Maybe. I'm just considering my options."

"A business degree? That doesn't seem like you."

"Aren't I a business owner?"

"Yes."

"Well, maybe I want to grow my business. Open a larger place. Hire people."

I open and close my mouth, shocked. She's never said a word about this.

"It's early days yet. I'm just toying with ideas."

"I'm good with ideas."

Cher smiles like she's indulging a child who wants to help make dinner but can't be trusted with the knife. "Joan . . ."

"What?"

"Nothing. Thanks for the offer. I'll let you know." It's the way she says it—as if I'm the last person she'd turn to—that makes me yank up my own drawbridge.

I gather Mom's giveaway items and scoop up my coat. "Well, I've got to get going."

"Already? You just got here."

"Mom needs me." The words come out before I realize there's a jab in them. Someone needs me. Mom needs me, her real daughter, and not Cher, whose mom does not need her.

"Want some help?" she asks.

The truth is I'm not even heading to Mom's. "All good," I say. Now it feels like Cher's the crestfallen one, the person on the outside.

Pulling out of the driveway, I regret the exchange with a ferocious pang, wishing for simpler times when we were giggling on my trundle bed, me closer to the ceiling, Cher closer to the floor, both of us closer to each other than we are now.

NINETEEN

For a solid week after I meet with Carmen, I journal with the fervor of a Brontë sister as I try to make good on my promise to give The Project my full attention. I don't return any of Cher's texts, barely linger to talk to Deli at the supermarket, and turn down Lou's invite to go in on Chinese takeout for lunch, instead eating in my car as I write and write and write.

I've also fallen behind on my Goodwill runs, my parents' pile of castoffs growing as large as a trash can, which is where most of the items belong. The boxes of memorabilia they dropped off a few months ago remain unopened in the corner of my living room.

For Carmen, I write about "practicals," the massage industry's version of tryouts. You can't just *vouch* for being a good massage therapist; you have to physically prove it, sometimes giving a massage to the person who will be your boss. Yes, it's hella weird, and I botched mine with Tara—had I already massaged her left leg?—who for some reason hired me anyway.

I write about office politics and the power the front desk staff wield because they make all of the massage bookings, determining who might have an easy slate (all Swedish) and who might go home with their hands throbbing (deep tissue).

Some therapists are brownnosers, bestowing little gifts and compliments on the front desk staff, while others take a fear-my-wrath approach.

Carmen begins sending me more postcards with menacing phrases or questions. *Working overtime?* says one postcard sent outside of Buffalo. *It's your livelihood,* says another, with a "Wish You Were Here" palm tree image on the other side. She signs these only as C.B.

I tuck these postcards away out of sight to focus on the task at hand.

And I'm successfully keeping Evian and Cord at bay, their story paused. They'll be there when I emerge from The Project. That's what I tell myself. But I can't help missing them—missing the light their story brings to my life.

───

Last client of the day: Nancy. Deep tissue. Sixty minutes.

I lightly place my hands on top of the thin sheet that separates me from Nancy, resting them on the outskirts of the spine, where, underneath the rib cage, the kidneys pump and pump, the body's Brita filter. This first step warms up the client's body and readies the two of us for the mutual exchange of touch, a rare intimacy between strangers.

I peel back the sheet to reveal her back, tucking the sheet into the elastic layer of her underwear. I warm my hands by rubbing them together—no massage oil just yet—before planting my palms on either side of her undressed spine, spreading my fingers wide to take up space, like I'm imprinting a Hollywood Star. *I was here.*

When I set my hands on Nancy—a woman in her fifties with short, silvered hair who wore a Talbots duster cardigan before she disrobed—her sharp intake of breath seizes my attention.

Again, Nancy gasps, sucks in a stab of air. I can feel the pace of her heart through her back, a quickening of her pulse.

My next deep breath is an invitation to align us, to calm her. After another shallow intake, Nancy exhales with me, long and slow, and we're in sync, rowing a boat together, oars in and out, in and out. Nancy's back visibly sinks an inch as her body begins to relax, resign itself.

Unwinding is a process. Some people can let go immediately, unclasping the handles of all of their baggage, while others hold on for dear life, avoiding the surrender.

I pump massage oil into my hands and spread a light coat across the expanse of Nancy's freckled back, her skin likely looser than it was when she was younger. On top of the oil, my hands skate up and down, moving the sheets of muscle underneath. The next five minutes are dedicated to each shoulder blade, tucking and pressing and unpinning at the typical places of soreness around this great, sliding glass door of a bone.

As I knead my way up the spine, I notice a terrific knot beckoning, a rigid and angry stone, larger than a pebble. It's a trigger-point moment, and I press hard and long on the knot to signal to the body to let go of the myofascial gridlock.

The knot slips in one gulp, reabsorbed by the body, a release of toxins into the bloodstream and into the brain, and a release of who knows what else. Fear? Disappointment? Rejection? Whatever it is, it travels up Nancy's thoracic spine and her throat, slipping out as an unabashed yell, as brief as a single foghorn signal, ricocheting off of the walls of the massage room.

Have I hurt her? I step back, holding my hands up in midair.

Nancy shakes with sudden, raucous sobs, a private distress unleashed, muzzled slightly by the face cradle.

No, she's not hurt. This is an emotional release. I've seen it before but never like this.

Teardrops pelt the carpet. Rather than stiffen as she cries, Nancy melts further into the table, her body heaving.

What should I do? No amount of training can prepare you for these moments, and I'm not sure if I have it in me to give her what she needs. This woman should be on Cher's table at her house. Or Carlie's. Lou's, even. Poor thing got the worst of the bunch.

Nancy's cries continue, and I hover my hands over her body, unsure. I cock my head to the side, recognizing something in the desperation of her sobs, a sorrowfulness that's almost unbearable. I recognize myself.

I hear Cher's words: *Move on.* Tara's insinuation: *You should be bouncing back by now.* It's clear as day, as if that sunset image on the wall is flooding me with sunrays of knowledge. Nancy's right where she needs to be. I understand her. I am her.

Slowly, ever so slowly, I plant my palms on her back again as an offer of solace, of steadiness. This touch I can do. I can hold her pain, even if it makes me uncomfortable. Then I move my hands to where the knot had been, stacking one on top of the other as the muscle trembles and pulsates before the body relinquishes its heartache.

As her crying subsides, her breathing steadies, tears slide down *my* cheek. Samuel. It's been more than two years—why does it still hurt like this? I tuck my face to my shoulder to brush them off, careful to not let them hit Nancy's back.

When our time ends, Nancy opens her eyes and puts a hand on my arm. Neither of us say a word.

The pain inside me wells up as though she's stuck a sharp finger in my knot. I manage to slip out the door before the dam breaks. Passing Lou in the hallway, I race for the relative privacy of the staff bathroom to lose my shit over old news.

TWENTY

Lou rushes in just as I'm swinging the stall door closed behind me. "Joan of Arc, what's wrong?" He crouches down; I can see his bent legs.

I try to speak but can only gulp, a goldfish who took too much of a leap. I shake my head, scared that I'm having a heart attack, or am dying, or will never breathe again. I clutch at my chest.

"Okay, okay," Lou soothes. "Let's take some deep breaths together." He inhales in and out of his nose. "Just like this. Come on, Joan, you can do it."

On the other side of the metal door, I attempt a ragged breath, and then another and another.

"Yes, good," Lou coaches. "Can you open the door?"

For some reason, I do. But then the gentle look in Lou's eyes almost sets me off again.

"I'm sorry," I say when I can finally speak. "I'm fine, seriously." I leave the stall to splash water on my face.

"You don't need to apologize, Joan, and you don't need to be fine."

I pat my face dry with a paper towel, and then I slide to the floor. Lou immediately takes a seat next to me. When I begin to talk again, my voice monotone, the story tumbles out of me, as if I've yanked open a closet door stuffed full of plastic balls for a kid's ball pit, yellows and reds and greens bouncing over and under my protesting arms, impossible to stop or block or shove back in again.

"It was a sunny September day when Samuel went—cycling for the last time," I say. I'm staring at the wall, but I'm far away, recalling the sky that day, a crisp blue that made me want to take a bite out of it, store all that beauty in my belly for the coming winter. "It was still biking weather, and Samuel had been excited to cycle on a back road, taking in all of the fall colors. It was his favorite time of year." I smile faintly, remembering his enthusiasm, but it melts away. "He was following the river outlining the base of the mountain, and the shoulder on the side of the road was the size of a wisp of hair. You know the road I'm talking about?" I turn my head ever so slightly to see Lou nod. Of course he knows it. There's been a wreath marking the spot on the side of the road ever since, decaying in the elements.

To Samuel's right, the river sparkled. To his left, the mountain rose quickly, the oncoming lane shimmying up against it. He approached a series of tight curves, as the sign warned with a squiggly black arrow.

I share the next part with Lou as if I'm reading from an accident report, robotically. The police determined that a car trailing Samuel tried to pass him, ignoring the yellow do-not-pass line, giving him a wide berth by swinging into the other lane just as an oncoming van barreled around the curve. The van swerved left to avoid the collision and the mountain, getting nicked on its right bumper, but in the process the driver swung into Samuel. Both drivers survived, but the impact of Samuel's bike into the side of the van killed him. My lips curl inward, tasting salty tears. "And that was it. A couple of seconds and he was gone." I shake my head, disbelieving, even after all this time, how a person can be there, and then not. Touchable, and then disappeared.

Lou shakes his head with me. "I'm sorry, Joan. I knew what happened, but I didn't know the details."

I barely register Lou's comment, still lost inside the memory. "I was buying new socks at the time. At Walmart. I couldn't decide: low-cut or mid-calf. Low-cut or mid-calf." I roll my eyes to show the shallowness of my indecision. "I didn't want to make the wrong choice." My laugh touches on the maniacal. Lou doesn't join me, but makes a *mmm* sound. "The moment his body hit the van"—my palms slap together violently—"I was handing cash to the clerk. Or taking the plastic bag and turning to leave. In that flash of time, everything changed."

I'd walked out of the store, blinking in the sunshine, unaware that my happiness—my future—had burst.

"Do you know what made it worse?" My arms are crossed over my chest, cupping my shoulders as I slightly rock in place, back and forth, like I'm sitting in a porch rocking chair and not plunked down on the cool linoleum floor of a shared bathroom.

Lou shakes his head. "I can't imagine how this gets worse."

"No one called to tell me he died. We'd been planning to meet each other's families, but we hadn't done it yet. And I guess in the midst of everything, they forgot about me."

They forgot about me. It still pinches my heart, twists my stomach.

"Oh, Joan. That's awful."

"I hadn't heard from Samuel all day, so I drove over to his apartment. I was annoyed with him. We had plans, but he wasn't answering his phone. When I pulled up, I saw a crowd of people, some of them crying. There was a police car."

I told Lou everything. How somone perched on the edge of the crowd broke the news to me, saying it so matter-of-factly, side-mouthed. As if I were just another gawking passerby. I swung my hand to my mouth with immense force, stifling any sound.

Backing away from the group, I squeezed my mouth viciously with my hand, shaking my head, whispering, "No, no, no, no, no, no." I sprinted past the family and the cop talking in hushed tones, and entered Samuel's apartment through the back patio, where I knew his sliding glass door was always unlocked. I needed to speak with him urgently. My first and only thought was "I *have* to talk to Samuel about his death." Only he could comfort me. I pulled out a chair at his kitchen table and waited for him.

"Come home," I demanded. He never did. No one stepped inside. The family remained outside, huddled. I stayed inside the house until the driveway emptied and the sun had set. Then I called Cher, who shuttled me home and took care of me for the next week.

At the funeral, a few of Samuel's friends recognized me, and they touched my arm softly with extended fingers as I leaned in to Cher. But his parents couldn't pick me out of a crowd, nor could his childhood friends with their arms around one another, nor could his aunts and uncles who brought plates of food to share afterward at a home where I wasn't invited.

I was status-less. Not fiancée. Not wife. Not even ex-wife. I was the new girlfriend who'd barely shared a blip of Samuel's life.

After the casket was lowered—Samuel would have balked at this, preferring, I imagined, to be scattered among his Vermont forests, not decaying in a box wearing a pair of pressed khakis I had never seen—I approached Samuel's mother, a round woman in black slacks with eyes like his.

"I'm Joan. Your son and I were dating," I offered. "I'm so sorry for your loss." His mother nodded, looking off somewhere in the distance, searching the horizon for someone who would never return. Was she remembering him as a boy, so young and innocent? She nodded while I spoke, but she didn't truly hear me. Then someone put an arm over her shoulders and ushered her away as if she were a dementia patient who had wandered out to the lawn.

I swivel my face fully to Lou now, beseeching him. "You know what I wish I had said? 'Your son and I were madly in love. We held on tightly to each other inside a comet until it burned out too quickly. I'll never recover. Not in a million years.'"

"God, Joan, I'm just . . ." He raises then drops his hands, helpless. There's no right thing to say.

I spent months replaying that moment, wishing I had said more, held her attention, hugged her, wept in her arms. I wanted to be close to Samuel again, so of course I wanted his mother to wrap me up in an embrace that never came, to hear her say, "I'm sorry for *your* loss, too."

I spent an equal amount of time being furious with Samuel. Why wasn't he more careful? Why did he ride on that toothpick of a shoulder, given everywhere else he could have ridden? I wanted to throttle him for being too enthralled with the world, too sure of his own skills. Eventually, the anger dissolved like a sugar cube in coffee, and a darkness descended.

After the funeral, I went back to his apartment, but the sliding glass door was bolted. Who boxed up his things? Did they think of me when they found a second toothbrush, my sandals, my pajama bottoms, distinctly not Samuel's? And where did they go, our possessions, our world? I cupped my hands to the glass door to see inside, but the room was stripped bare, no indication that we had existed.

"It's as if it wasn't real. That we'd been erased. But it was real, right, Lou?"

He clears his throat, his voice breaking a little. "Yes. It was real."

For two years, I've lugged this heavy pain around, but I've never cried like this before—not even at Samuel's funeral. And I've never voiced these feelings, not even with my parents or Cher. I feel like Nancy back on the massage table, her breathing growing steadier after the release of so much. I look at my shaky hands, feel the throb in my temples. "Thank you," I say to Lou. *For being here for me in this moment, despite how I've treated you since we met.*

"Of course, Joan of Arc," Lou says, patting my hand. "Of course."

TWENTY-ONE

Ostriches bury their heads. Turtles recoil their limbs. I hole up in my house, refusing to leave for three days. I call in sick to work, I don't answer my phone, I let The Project languish, and I revert to my packaged-meal days.

On the fourth day, Mom sends Dad, who knocks on the door before letting himself in. He brings with him a plume of frigid air, and he stamps his boots on the mat before stepping out of them and walking into the living room, where I'm stationed on the couch.

"Hey, kiddo, I brought you a new ice scraper." Dad holds the scraper by its long, retractable handle. It beats the $2.99 stubby little scraper I'd be struggling with if I left the house. Temperatures dropped to below zero last week and have stayed there, making all of us in this frozen tundra wonder why the hell we live here.

"Thanks, Dad," I mutter. I watch him survey the scene, knowing Mom will ply him for details. Me in grubby sweats, eating from a Ziploc bag of uncooked ramen noodles sprinkled with their MSG flavoring. There's nothing strewn on the floor because I haven't been doing anything except abandoning half-filled water glasses on various surfaces mid-drink, as if I couldn't be bothered to quench my thirst.

"Where's the beast?" Dad asks, meaning Sweet Bird.

"Out cavorting." Last week, Sweet Bird was mystified by my upswing. Now he's radiating concern about my downslide. Or about as much concern as an asshole cat can show. When he's been kneading my face in the mornings, he's retracting his claws first.

"Hit a rough patch?" Dad begins busing water glasses back to the kitchen, three in each hand. He's talking about Samuel without talking about Samuel.

I'm tempted to lie, but there's no hiding what's going on. When he returns to the living room, I say, "I thought I was better. I thought I was beyond this."

Dad put his hands in his pockets, rocking from toe to heel. We both know this is Mom territory. He clears his throat and forges ahead. "There's no finish line. No point where you say *finito*. Take all the time you need. All the time in the world."

How do I not know this already? Missing Samuel never just ends. That's a wrap, folks. Let's call it a day.

I sit up and sniff. "I needed to hear that. Thank you."

He walks over to the boxes in the corner, and he rubs his fingers over the pockmarked cardboard from Sweet Bird's claws. Without looking at me, he says, "There are some gems in here. Reading through your old stuff might be just what you need to get out of your funk."

I roll my eyes. "That's the last thing that's going to help."

"A woman who rediscovers writing. That's got legs to it, no?"

Now I just feel annoyed. "Dad, please drop it." I don't tell him that I've been writing, just for myself, and that it was helping a little. And it doesn't matter anyway, because I left Evian and Cord on that mountain, and that's where they're going to stay until The Project is done.

He rubs his hands over the box again and then taps it for good measure. "Just saying. I mean, what else are you going to do? Get another glass of water?"

I can't help but laugh. Dad crosses the room, leans down, and kisses the top of my head. "And no matter what you do, answer your phone. You know how your mom worries."

It feels like I'm in a serious moment in a sitcom. "Okay. Promise."

For ten minutes after Dad leaves, I stare the boxes down. And then, as if they've talked me into something, I stand up and say, "Oh, fine."

I rummage through the first box, stacking up several children's diaries with their wobbly metal keys. There's a crumpled certificate from third grade, giving me an E for "Excellence" in English. My heart-stopping essay answering "What does freedom mean to you?" where I waxed poetic about the Liberty Bell.

Not ready to tumble down a tunnel of teenage angst, I set aside two high school diaries, their black covers a mature choice, I remember thinking. Then I make a pile for photographs, averting my eyes from one of me in a T-ball uniform. I was as athletic as stale bread, and I whacked that T-ball stand as if the whole purpose was to hit *below* the ball.

Underneath the T-ball trophy given to every player, I spot something that makes my stomach drop, even all these years later: my college story that I had, pitifully, thought was pretty good. I ease it out of the box.

It's been sixteen years, but I still remember writing this thing at my parents' kitchen table. They were both at work, and the house was quiet. As the words flew out of me, I experienced an oncoming rush, as if I were on a roller coaster inching to its highest peak, the noise of the wheels grinding against steel, wind whipping my hair, until I crested, and from there, for a split second, I could see for miles, a perspective where everything made sense, the entire story coming together before I plummeted back toward Earth, my stomach in my chest, my chest in my throat, my thrilled yell not audible from below.

I'd planned to chase that sensation for the rest of my life.

Until my professor returned my story covered in red marks. Once I saw his admonishment on page three to *Get serious*, I stopped reading the rest of his edits, never returning to them until now.

I flip to page three, and there they are again—those crushing words in lobster-red scrawl. I squint. Caught up in my emotion that day, I hadn't noticed two other words, tucked neatly underneath the glaring *Get serious* billboard in smaller, neater letters, the same red-pincer color: *See over.*

Over?

I swiftly turn the page and see only more notes about serial commas.

Over?

On the back page of the entire manuscript is a note from my teacher that I had never seen or read. I gasp, my hand to my mouth.

Joan, take yourself more seriously. It's clear you have talent, but you're not allowing your characters to fully materialize. Sometimes your characters are caricatures of themselves and you hide behind the humor. I'd like to see you balance the slapstick with intimacy. I want to hear more from your characters, which means I want to hear more from you—both in your writing and in class. Consider joining the student writing group on Wednesdays so you can keep developing your craft.

Crouching, I tip back on my haunches, as if swayed by a powerful gust, and I reread the passage over and over again. All this time, my teacher had actually been suggesting I *get serious about my craft.* That's what he had meant. To be brave and go after it. Buckle down.

I let my butt plop to the floor and stretch my legs out in front of me.

Why had I quit so easily? How had I let two words—two misunderstood words—push me down so hard that I couldn't get up? What a waste.

Right now, I feel like a rag doll, and for a moment, I consider just being a rag doll, staying on the ground forever, droopy arms and legs, button eyes, no brain. Sweet Bird, who's returned from his outdoor adventure, pads over, sensing I might be a permanent cushion, and curls up on my lap.

I thread my fingers through his fur, lost in thought.

"Get serious, Joan," I say, trying out the words with their new meaning. I mean, if not now, when?

"If not *now*, when?" I repeat. It sounds like another Apex inspirational poster, but it's true. Am I going to let another sixteen years pass me by?

Writing a fictionalized version of Samuel hasn't been just some odd way of processing the loss of him. I'm resuscitating us. I'm unlocking that sliding glass door. But I'm also allowing myself to write again. Cord and Evian have been my on-ramp to something that gives me the roller-coaster highs—that makes me feel alive again.

I'm fighting for my livelihood by working on The Project— paying off my debt, keeping my day job. But when I write for myself, I'm fighting for my *life*, because remaining debilitated, angry, or bowled over without a moment's notice by sadness is no way to exist.

Maybe, just maybe, I can still be a writer. Maybe it's not too late for me. Don't we all have dormant potential coiled up inside of us? Greatness lying within, waiting to be tapped?

Just like Samuel's super blooms. Seeds holding out for perfect conditions: soil, sun, rain.

What I need is a hefty dose of willpower. A readiness to try my hardest and possibly fail. That's the only way to bloom.

I make my way back to my writing desk. I make my way back to Evian and Cord.

Snow Globe

When Evian enters her apartment, she smells oregano, thyme, and homemade tomato sauce bubbling up in its pot, speckling the counter with red dots. In the kitchen, Cord is unsleeving a package of spaghetti, and her heart whacks itself against her rib cage as if someone stopped short in front of it.

She could get used to this.

Evian and Cord have begun shopping together, eating every meal together, and she is learning about him the way she ravenously devoured her anatomy books, absorbing every detail. While Cord had come across as reserved at the diner, he is chatty with strangers, engaging fellow hikers or a couple ordering coffee. He'd twisted around at the movie theater to ask a woman wearing a Cape Cod sweatshirt, "Where on the Cape?" As the previews started, Evian had elbowed him. "Have you ever been to the Cape?"

He'd smirked. "Nope."

He had odd grooming habits, casual about showering but obsessed with flossing. He pressed Evian to floss, too, which only made her reject it more. Every night, he came to bed with a quarter-sized wet patch on his boxers just to the left of his penis.

"Can't you just spend a few extra seconds shaking it off?" Evian implored. He said he'd try, but there it was, as inevitable as the moon.

Evian was a few degrees more selfish than he was. Cord would take the scratchy blanket, the burnt piece of toast, the gross booth seat at the diner, and Evian sometimes woke in the night with a sinking fear that she would never be as giving a partner as he was.

"What do you even like about me?" Evian asked once, propped up on her elbow in bed, steering clear of the pee spot. It was a question she'd never thought to ask anyone before.

"I'm a fan of your entire catalog." He gestured to the whole of her.

Last night, Evian had finally convinced Cord to show her some YouTube videos of him competing in rodeos. Turns out he was a big deal, had huge corporate sponsors, throngs of fans waiting for him after each competition, waving their cowboy hats for autographs. Watching the videos cracked Cord open, and he'd shared how learning to ride horses and competing in rodeos had saved his life. He'd grown up in foster care, rotating through more foster families than he did blue jeans.

"A lot of foster kids end up in jail. Or on drugs." That was almost him.

His dream, he said, had been to open a rodeo training school for other foster kids, but getting badly injured was causing him to waver. "It can be a dangerous business," Cord told her. "What if I'm just putting those kids in harm's way?"

Evian listened, but she didn't answer. Encouraging him to follow this dream would be encouraging him to leave. And she wasn't ready for that yet.

She crosses the kitchen now, whistling at him. "Hey, cowboy."

His eyes flick up at her, a wooden spoon in his hand. "You're going to love me," he says, bringing the spoon to her lips. Yes, she was, in spite of herself.

Evian takes a taste and then moans, pretending to stagger backward. "How did you get so good at this?"

"It was either a lifetime of peanut butter and jelly or learn to fend for myself."

She moseys toward him, removing the spoon from his hand to set it on the counter, and encircles her arms around his neck. "I have good news."

"You did it." A wide grin breaks across his face.

Evian nods. "I did it." Today, she'd gotten the last of her coworkers, even the old-timers and the risk-averse, to sign their names to her manifesto. Everyone wants things to change at the Summit. Better pay, compensation for the times when they are working but don't have clients, a higher employee discount so they can actually afford to get bodywork themselves, more transparency when it comes to their tips. At another spa in the Berkshires, an accountant stole thousands of dollars in tips over five years, and the news had shocked them. Could this happen at the Summit? Evian wants assurance that it won't, not just lip service. "Tomorrow, I bring our list of demands to management."

There is no "or else." Not yet, anyway. Evian's hoping management will listen to reason, impressed by the strength in their numbers. After all, their demands are reasonable. They should want their employees to be happy, to foster longevity in an industry that has a lot of burnout. Right?

Evian wishes there were national leaders she could turn to for advice, or a bodyworkers' union they could vote to join. But rules and policies change state to state, and even venue to venue, so Evian is mostly making this up at she goes along.

If management laughs in her face—then what? She has no idea. "Cross that bridge," her mom would have said. For now, tonight, Evian's celebrating her first victory and trying not to think too far ahead. Arms still draped around Cord's neck, she *threads her fingers through his hair.*

"You're really impressive, you know that?" Cord says, nipping at her jawline.

"Oh, yeah?" Evian tilts her neck back.

"Mmm-hmm." Little kisses up toward her ear, and Evian's entire body responds. She presses against him, and then she returns the favor, nudging his face to the side to tease his neck with her mouth.

"Is this impressive?" she whispers between kisses.

Cord's sigh is hungry, heated. "I love your lips. Yes."

"How about this?" She reaches a hand up the back of his shirt, trailing her fingers over his skin. He shivers.

"Yes."

Her other hand travels down past the brass belt buckle to the fly of his jeans. "Now this," she says, cupping him, "is impressive."

They forget about dinner, satiated by each other.

TWENTY-TWO

Tony booked a massage. With *me*. Not with anybody else.

"It's this one," I say, when we reach my therapy room. I want to cover the placard that announces the name of my room: Knotweed. Of course *I* got the invasive species.

We dance at the door—who should open it, who should enter first—and after a few awkward steps this way and that, I do the honors and stand aside, insisting that he go in. Once in the room, he remains on his feet near the table, arms at his sides, uncertain.

"Please, have a seat." I motion to the table, and Tony hoists himself up as if he's about to have a medical exam. He swings his legs, childlike. I can't help noticing that the sleeves on his T-shirt strain around his arm muscles, but not like he's a gym rat showing off his biceps.

I blush and hope he doesn't notice, tugging at my shirt to let a tuft of air down my chest.

"This is my first massage," he says.

"Ever?"

"Yup." He kicks his legs.

"Well, you're in for a treat." My eyes crinkle, but my insides cringe. *In for a treat?* Gah. I've never said that to anybody. I clear my throat. "How's the injury?" I unfold a white towel only to fold it again and place it back on the stack.

"Still bothering me." Tony sighs.

"Well, if it's okay with you, I won't go directly at your injury since it's still so fresh. I want to give your muscles a chance to heal while also instructing them to relax, so I'll work with some of your complementary muscles." I'm impressing myself. *Not bad, Joanie, not bad.* Tony, too, nods in agreement.

This is the first time I've cared about impressing a man since . . . well, Samuel. I'm surprised with my eagerness to show off my skills.

"You're the expert." He smiles assuredly and I grin back, the moment suspended in the darkened room, the candle flickering. On the wall next to us, the sun makes its unending dive into the sea. Suddenly I don't entirely hate the message on the poster: "Awaken to this very moment."

"So, uh." I motion to the table. "Let's start facedown. I'll be right back."

I step out, and after a few minutes I knock gently on the door. "All set?"

"Yeah, yeah, good to go." Tony's voice is muffled by the face cradle.

Before I enter, I sniff my armpits. Passable.

Tony's opted for no shirt and no shoes, but he's kept on his jeans and socks.

I start my work. *This is your job, Joan,* I remind myself as I take in his body. He's meaty and undefined yet strong. His skin would be called "olive," though I've never fully understood that description. Kalamata? Green? Black? I suspect that he tans naturally. The dark swirling hair on his arms looks like dozens of miniature whirlpools.

Tony is chatty in a pleasant way. It helps that I'm rattling off questions, avoiding the intimacy of silence. Maybe we both are.

He reveals that the Apex poached him from another

mega–wellness center just outside of New York City, where he had worked for eleven years. The promise of a more rural lifestyle had beckoned. His twelve-year-old daughter loves horses and *Star Wars*, and he's torn about whether she's too young for a smartphone. My ears perk up when he says, "My ex-wife lives in Rutland." Duly noted.

I touch him gingerly and then with more emphasis, coaxing the muscles around his injury to spur on the healing process. It works like peer pressure: *C'mon, serratus, all of us other muscles are relaxing. Why don't you?*

When I stay quiet, thinking he'd prefer it, he picks up the conversation like the end of a jump rope, ready to keep playing.

"Why massage therapy?" he asks.

I wish I had a more profound or inspired answer. "I needed a career. And I thought I would like it more than I do."

I instantly regret the answer, fretting that he might think I'm not enjoying myself or that I don't like working on him. I backpedal. "Some days are better than others. This is a good day."

"No offense taken."

When he flips over, I hold up the sheet for modesty even though he still has his pants on. His hands are next on the circuit, but I can't bring myself to interlace my fingers with his like I normally do, spreading out the palm.

It oddly feels too . . . personal to hold his hand.

Instead, I gently pinch the sides of each finger and then seek out the acupressure point on the webbing of his hand, stretched between the thumb and forefinger.

I want to bless him when he says, "Please skip my feet. I've been working in my boots all day."

When I'm finished, I say, "I hope that helps." I wish I could give him extra time, but I have another client waiting.

"I feel better already," Tony says, and I cross my fingers that it's true.

"I'll be right outside. Come on out when you're ready."

Standing in the hallway waiting for Tony to reappear, I lean my head against the wall and close my eyes. It's been so long since I've experienced a sense of longing for someone who isn't Samuel, and I'm shocked to feel it now, especially just days after the grief attack in the bathroom. What is my heart doing, swinging all around like this?

I sense a presence, and I open one eye. Jamal is standing before me, hand on his hip, arm like a protractor, sharp as a right angle. Our dour uniform looks glamorous on him with an added scarf knotted at his throat and his black boots.

"Hey, girl," Jamal says. "Sorry to disturb."

"Oh, no worries. I was just"—lusting?—"resting."

"We all get through, we all get through," he says.

"How's Crumpet?" I ask, trying to recall the name of the dachshund Jamal's been fostering for the last week.

"Moppet. She's good, but she'll only eat her dinner if it comes with a side salad."

"Huh," I say. "I'm just the opposite."

Jamal's holding a clipboard. "I'm going to make this quick." He inspects the hallway. "I'm petitioning management to make our bathrooms gender-neutral. Tara already said no, so I'm taking it higher. Will you sign on?" He flicks me the clipboard, his wrist hula-hooping in a tangle of bangles. "Everyone's signing it."

"Yes, yes, of course I'll sign." I snatch the clipboard.

The door to my therapy room clicks open, and Tony appears, rumpled. Seeing me busy with Jamal, he raises his hand to give a short wave. I glance back down in a panic at the paper; I want to say goodbye to Tony, or something else clever.

I look up and back down. But . . .

Tony mouths "Thank you." He hesitates for a moment, and then he pulls the door handle shut and walks away down the long corridor.

My shoulders fall. Jamal retrieves the clipboard triumphantly and blows me an air kiss. I sink back against the wall as he struts off.

Tony, huh? I'm not ready for another relationship. Aloneness, that's what I've been picturing. Not a mellow man with a pre-teen daughter and a penchant for Jason Bourne films, which he said were his favorite, if he had to choose, which he also said he didn't like to do. How sweet.

I'm jolted back to reality as Tara whisks by. "Is there a problem, Joan? You have another client waiting, and I'd hate to give you a strike for tardiness." She points to her watch, and I'm back in action.

It's dark and cold outside, and tall, dirt-laced snowbanks surround the employee parking lot like the walls of a corral—although maybe I'm just thinking that because of Cord. In the glow of the streetlights, big snowflakes flutter to the ground in fits and spurts. The sky is only spitting for now, but the forecast calls for feet. It'll be snowman snow.

Already the snow is sticking to the ground and to car windshields, but this afternoon when I'd arrived at work, I'd left my wipers saluting straight up into the air, prepared. A few quick swipes with my new scraper from Dad and my windshield is clear.

Sitting in my car, the heat on low, my hand hovers over the keypad of my phone. I want to tell Cher about Tony, but I hesitate. She's leaving in a few days for her usual six weeks in Siesta Key, Florida, where she rents massage space from a friend and makes some mad money from snowbirds also escaping a New England winter.

Usually she wishes herself bon voyage, gathering a group of her friends for boozy margaritas, heavy on the salt, and homemade chips and salsa, but if this is happening, I haven't heard about it. Maybe I'm not invited this year because I ditched her New Year's shindig. I can't bring myself to ask, *Did you forget me?*

It's fine anyway, I tell myself. Tonight, I need to spend some time on The Project. Even if I'd rather spend the evening with Cord and Evian.

Instead of texting Cher, I respond to Mom, who sent me an image of a garment bag.

Want this? she wrote.

Yes, please, I type, wanting to make her day.

I glance up and notice a white van idling at the far end of the parking lot, low beams illuminating the diagonally falling snow. I've never seen the van before, don't know who on staff drives it. I squint and turn on my wipers to remove a fresh layer of snow. The figure in the driver's seat appears shadowy, just an outline of a person.

I gasp. A chill runs up my spine. My first thought, because, again, a steady diet of *Unsolved Mysteries*: it's a serial killer and I'm the next victim.

Without warning, the van's floodlights pour onto me, blinding me, my forearm flying up to block the light from my eyes, and then the driver peels out of the parking lot, the van's back tires spinning hard to gain traction in the slippery snow.

I peek through my fingers, and as the van passes under a streetlight, I swear I catch a glimpse of a white scarf. My hand flies to my chest. Carmen.

Spring

TWENTY-THREE

I enter the library waving my old-school paper library card as if it's an entry ticket to the movies. A young librarian with a nose ring and spectacles greets me, appraising my ancient relic. "You don't need to show that to get in," she says.

"Right." I stuff the card into my pocket and make my way to the section I'd never spent time in before: Romance Fiction.

The town library is beautiful, with a Victorian tin ceiling and wide, dark walnut trim around large windows framing picturesque snow swirls outside. Vermont didn't get the memo that it's officially spring. Temperatures have nudged up from hostile to just merely cold, but the library is warm and snug, slowing me down, steadying my heartbeat. I love it here. I've missed it here.

It's occurred to me as I get deeper into the story about Evian and Cord that I should read other romance novels. If I'm going to "get serious," I should study up.

I spin a rotating metal rack filled with paperbacks 360 degrees when the front desk librarian pops up and asks, "Need some help?"

"Um, well, I'm looking for a romance novel. Or two. But less helpless maidens and vulnerable virgins and more worldly, badass heroines and feminist-loving men."

"Gotcha." The librarian nods as if she gets the question all the time. "Contemporary romance?" she asks.

"That sounds good," I say.

"Historical romance?"

"Sure."

"Paranormal?"

"Nah."

"Erotic?"

My face reddens. "Maybe?"

"Follow me," she instructs, heading back to the front desk in her Converse sneakers, brown stockings, and high-waisted paisley skirt. I follow, watching as she pulls out a bookmark-sized card from a rack and makes precise tick marks next to book titles. "These," she says, "are books from the *New York Times* bestseller list." She turns the card over and scrawls quickly. "And, as an Asian American, here are a few of my personal faves that feature women who look like me—a rarity in publishing." She scoots the bookmark to me and smiles warmly.

"Wow, thanks so much," I say, feeling the glow that happens when a stranger goes out of her way to help me, even if it is her job.

"And finally, not to toot my own horn or anything, but here's a book from the indie press where I also work." She hands me a slim novel.

"Really?" I tilt the spine and read Swooning Heart Press.

"I'm the assistant editor. We specialize in romance. This author is from Maine—a super-sweet lady with a very mean pen. Her prose is"—she mimics a chef's kiss.

"I didn't realize there were indie romance presses."

"Oh, yeah, for sure. It's a very big market. We have a great following."

"Hmm," I say, tapping the book against my palm. "Interesting."

I can't help it: A daydream I don't even dare to name flickers inside me.

Starting my search anew, I clutch the bookmark and collect a pile of books the height of an orange juice container. For good measure, I top my pile with a book of sage writing advice from the world's most revered writers.

I lumber back to the front desk with my stack, setting them down with a thud. They nearly topple but mercifully don't.

"All set?" the librarian asks from behind a book cart. I'm usually intimidated by people who have multiple piercings, since the boldest thing I've ever done is squeeze lemon juice on my hair for temporary highlights, but I'm finding the librarian very approachable.

I'm wrestling the books into my bag when another book catches my eye on the New Fiction rack by the front desk.

Carmen Bronze.

Her name, in red block print, is larger than the book title. Even though she's not here, I feel her eyes on me, hear her voice demanding, *What are you doing?*

Noticing where I'm looking, the librarian says, "How could I forget? Carmen Bronze. You've got to read her!"

I don't want another reminder of Carmen in my house. I can't handle another tap on the shoulder that I'm overstepping my bounds big-time and am wildly procrastinating on The Project. That I'm jeopardizing my livelihood if I don't get on track soon. "I'm not really a fan," I say.

"No?" She looks surprised. "Her books are candy for me. I can tear through one in a day and not regret it. The gossip around town is that she stays at the Apex from time to time. I would freak out if I ever met her!"

"I've met her," I admit before I can clamp my trap.

"Seriously?" She raises her eyebrows, waiting for more.

I try to downplay it. "Oh, it was a fluke thing. I work at the Apex . . . and ran into her once."

"What was she like?"

"She's . . ." Batty. Suspicious. Zealous. "Fascinating," I finally land on. "She's a really fascinating person." Which is true.

"Cool," the librarian says appreciatively. "I'm Quinn, by the way." She extends her hand.

"Joan." I shake hers.

"Hey, you should come to our romance book club. We meet next Tuesday. You just checked out this month's book, so you already have it." She taps a flyer on the desk.

Carmen's returning next Friday for the second installment of The Project, and I need to spend every free moment making up for lost ground. Which is to say I don't have time to speed-read. I should decline Quinn's invitation.

"I'm . . ." Busy. In over my head. Screwed. "There," I say.

———

Carmen Bronze calls me the moment I settle into the car, my book haul in the passenger seat. The timing is uncanny. I scan the parking lot for a white van.

"Hi," Carmen says breezily, as if we're girlfriends who chat daily about nothing in particular.

"Hi?" I answer, more of a question.

"Just checking in. Whatcha up to?" She's so nonchalant that I can picture her unpacking groceries as we talk, ear pressed to her shoulder while she stashes the milk in the fridge and nudges a dog away from the meat bag with her foot. But I know better. Everything about Carmen is calculated.

"Umm . . ." I check the rearview mirror, trying to figure out if she's watching me right now. "Laundry."

"Gotta separate those whites."

"You're taking a break from sending me vaguely threatening postcards?" I don't mention the lurking van, as I know Carmen will deny it.

"Oh, good, you've been getting them."

"I have, yes."

"So I trust you've upheld your end of the bargain. Working those fingers to the bih-zone. Filling up an entire notebook with gih-zold." Why is she talking like that?

I swallow hard. "You're going to be very pleased."

"This novel has to be bigger than big. It has to be epic. It's gotta launch me into another realm."

"Does it, though? I mean, another realm sounds kinda scary. But the status quo, that's always a safe bet. Or even, oh, I don't know, taking your time."

Carmen's voice sharpens. "You have doubts about this book?"

"No, no doubts. None at all." I'm riddled with doubts. Doubts about how I'm going to pull off a full notebook in the next five days. Doubts about whether I'll survive Carmen finding out that I've been busy writing a story of my own instead of filling a notebook for her.

"Good. Me, neither. I trust you completely." Is she taunting me?

"All right, well, my dryer alarm just went off."

"That's funny, I didn't hear anything."

"It was . . . faint."

"Back to it, then. See you Friday."

"Yep, Friday."

"And, Joan."

I feel like I'm choking on a garlic bulb. "Yes?"

"Love you, too." And then the line goes dead. I'm 89 percent sure she's ribbing me.

I hang up and rub my eyes with the heels of my hands. I'll go straight home right now. I can do this if I completely devote myself to The Project from here on out.

Only, I don't.

Snow Globe

The Summit's pool room is dark and deserted, the dim security lights casting a warm blue hue on the steam emanating from the hot tub. Outside, it's snowing huge snowflakes that will cover the stone pathways in a matter of minutes, flakes so large and heavy they seem coated in tempura batter.

Evian reaches for Cord's hand, leading him to tiptoe over the cool tiled floor. Then she peels off her clothes, dropping them at her feet in a messy pile, her body voluptuous and supple.

She misses nothing as Cord removes his shirt and releases that old belt buckle, revealing his taut stomach muscles and ropy thighs, his strong legs. And those dips at his hips where she longs to kiss. With a red-painted toe, she presses the button to start the bubbles, breaking the silence of the room as they roil up.

Submerged in the water, their mouths crush against each other, bodies mashing. The tip of Cord's tongue travels from Evian's collarbone to the place behind her ear, eliciting a shiver. She lightly bites at his shoulder, her fingertips pawing at his back, her nails leaving half-moon indentations on his skin.

When she finally straddles him, she takes him inside in one big rush, gulping him greedily, hungrily. It's been a long time since Evian's had sex with someone whom she lusts for and respects, where both her body and her heart are involved, and the combination unravels her.

When it's over, Evian collapses on Cord, their breathing in unison, their skin red and hot to the touch from the warm water and the merging of their bodies. Before long, they're overheated, and they push themselves up to perch opposite each other, naked on the edge of the hot tub, cooling their torsos as they dangle their feet in the water.

Cord points to the snow, still plummeting, the flakes as large as dimes. "It's majestic."

"Don't have that where you come from?" Evian teases.

"Most certainly not."

Evian twirls her hand in the water and tries to catch a hand- ful of steam.

"It's a snow globe," he says.

"What?" Evian's head snaps up.

"Being in here like this, with you. It's like being inside a snow globe. Untouchable to the outside world. Cozy. Warm."

"Protected," Evian finishes.

"Our own little bubble. Encasing this moment forever."

She stares at him, this man who seemingly came out of nowhere, dangling his bare legs in the frothy water, the air thick and muggy, windows steamed up, and any last remnants of wall around her heart crumble, leaving it bare and beating and wanting.

Evian dips into the water and swims to him, pulling Cord back into the tub, wrapping her legs around his waist, encircling his neck, body to body, not a thread's space between them. Out- side, the snowstorm picks up, rages on, the flakes hardening to pelt the glass. Inside, nothing touches them.

TWENTY-FOUR

I volunteered to bring snacks to the book group, and I went overboard. On the way out of the supermarket, I'm carrying a tire-wheel-sized plastic tray of cured meats and cheeses so massive that Deli has to prop the door open for me with his foot. That's right: Deli asked to be my plus-one for book club after I mentioned the reason for the pound of prosciutto at the counter that morning.

"I get off at six. Can I come?" he'd asked, and it was clear his evening plans were pinned to my answer.

"Don't take this the wrong way, but do you even *read* romance novels?"

"Do you have it on you?"

"The book we're discussing?"

"Yeah."

I'd rifled through my tote bag. "Um . . . actually, I do."

"Sweet. I'll read it on my break."

I pick up Deli outside the automatic doors of the supermarket, a backpack slung over one of his shoulders, a blood-iron hamburger smell trailing him, and we drive to the library. I'd found out his real name, Clay, when he fixed his name tag at work, another attempt to elevate his professionalism. On the way, I confess to calling him Deli in my mind, and he's surprisingly stoked.

"I've always wanted, like, a legit nickname," he says, pounding his fist into his other hand.

"So you want me to keep calling you that in real life?" I drive with the caution of an adult escorting a younger person somewhere. I put my right blinker on a good one hundred feet from the turn. He doesn't notice or care.

"Deli? For sure. That's sweet, man. That's, like, so apropos."

It seems a little too on the nose to me. But then again, I had come up with it. I'm not sure if he knows my name. It feels like we're past the point when I could say, "Oh, by the way, I'm Joan." Now it would be awkward.

Deli chats as if he's been alone all day and with an ease that suggests we hang out all the time. I sit stiffly. He reaches up to feel the scruff on his cheeks, pulling his fingers down to the point of his chin. His day clothes are the same as his work clothes, without the apron. His worn-thin Nirvana shirt had seen more teen spirit a few years ago.

"I'm thinking about getting into voice-overs," he says.

"Voice-overs? For commercials and stuff?" We drive past a young woman standing outside a T-Mobile store holding a giant arrow directing cars into the parking lot. I lock eyes with her and I swear she mouths to me aggressively, "Come and get it." I don't come and get it but keep going toward the library.

"Yeah, voice-overs for all kinds of stuff. I can do a lot of voices." Deli impersonates a weather forecaster—"Bad news, folks, it's a rainy one"—and then morphs into a southern female flight attendant for Southwest Airlines cracking a joke about seat belts. Both are believable.

"That's pretty good! Had my eyes been closed, I would have thought I was on an airplane," I say. "But eyes on the road," I feel I should add, pointing peace fingers from my eyes to the lane ahead.

"I can do a British accent, too. 'For *Masterpiece Theatre*, I'm Laura Linney.'"

"I see where you're going with that, but Laura Linney is American."

"So?"

"Well, her voice wouldn't be British, even though *Masterpiece Theatre* is."

"Whatever," he grumbles, not appreciating the feedback.

"Can you do Laura Linney?" I ask, trying to fix things.

"No." We drive in silence while he ruminates. Now I know what my mom felt like driving me around.

He eventually pulls out of it. "Did you catch that T-Mobile girl back there? That was my ex. Pretty sure she was swearing at me when we drove by."

I stop myself from saying, *I think you dodged a bullet with that one.*

Once in the library, Deli and I wind our way to a back corner where light talking is tolerated. When I introduce him to Quinn, I say, "I hope you don't mind that I brought a friend. This is Deli."

"Like the sandwich," he offers.

Quinn extends a hand. In her burgundy corduroy overall dress, the silhouette a trapezoid, and a buttoned-to-her-neck blouse, her wardrobe again screams hip librarian.

I set up the snacks on a small table, taking care not to make a lot of noise as I pry off the plastic lid to the platter.

"Gosh, Joan, I just meant some pretzel sticks," Quinn says, peering at my offering.

"I'll take it back," I joke, pretending to repack the food.

"Joan," Deli repeats, almost to himself. Aha. So he *didn't* know my name.

Before the club officially begins, I check my phone. There's a text from Cher. Actually, there are no words, but it's an image of her bare feet in the sand, the blue ocean just beyond. I immediately resent the image. Why do people on beach vacations always take photos of their feet in the sand and then send those images to people who are *very* far away from beaches, who are in fact in the last gasps of winter in spite of the calender announcing spring, an extremely unpleasant time, with everything goopy and muddy and soggy?

I type back #blessed, which I know will peeve her.

Four other people dribble in—fewer than Quinn's aspirations, apparently, as she removes several chairs to make our circle tighter. Now I'm glad I brought Deli, who holds his own during the discussion while I stay mostly quiet and neutral, playing the part of the deep thinker who's not quite ready to share. The group laughs at a few of my wisecracks, instantly endearing them to me. Martha, a book club regular who has underlined most of the passages in her book, speaks confidently about the cultural relevance and timeliness of the novel, while Bob, a military retiree, thoroughly enjoys his second dinner, cracker crumbs making a constellation on his sweater until it looks like an entire galaxy.

After we adjourn, I'm dismayed at the mound of cheese cubes left over, so when Bob asks if he can take a plate to go, I offer the entire platter. "All yours," I say, and he gleefully accepts. Deli takes a potty break—his words—and I help Quinn put the chairs back.

"Joan, how's your book coming along?" Quinn asks as we finish our task.

I jerk my head toward her, caught off guard. "How'd you know I was writing a book?"

"You checked out that book about writing advice. I just took a leap."

"Oh, god, *that* book. I read the first few pages of it and got intimidated." True story.

"How long have you been working on yours?"

"A few months."

"I've been working on mine in fits and spurts for six years."

"Six years?!"

"In between working here and the press, yeah. I think I'm on my twelfth draft now." Quinn drops a paper plate into the trash can and then ties the top of the plastic bag into a knot, lifting it out and over the can. "I just keep plugging away."

I hold up a handful of leaflets that Martha left behind about a women's martial arts class. "What should I do with these?" Quinn snatches them, recycling all but one. The other she pins to the community board.

"What's the genre?"

"Oh, um." I clear my throat. "Romance, actually." It feels crazy to say it out loud. A book? A genre? Me? I feel like an interloper at a literary soiree. A country bumpkin at a gala. A non-degree writer at an MFA barbecue, everyone reciting Walt Whitman while I wonder when the burgers will be done.

"Really? I'd love to read it sometime." My face must be blasting alarm, because she laughs and says, "No pressure, of course."

"Sorry. I'm just not used to the idea of anyone else reading it."

Quinn hands me a business card. "Here. This has my email address at Swooning Heart Press. Send me some chapters whenever you're ready."

I stare at the card. "Oh, I'm not going to submit this to you or anything. I'm not good enough."

"I'll just read them as a friend. It's always helpful to have feedback. And I'm super-nice, I swear."

"Thanks." I slide the card into the back pocket of my jeans, unable to imagine a time that I'd feel brave enough to use it.

TWENTY-FIVE

Carmen's here tomorrow. My calendar announces the date with a fat red circle, following me around the kitchen like an angry eye. All of my promises, all my vows, have been empty, or half-empty: The notebook for The Project remains half-filled. As the sun jackknifes out of view, panic sets in.

In the shower, lathering my hair, I decide I'll pull an all-nighter and fill the entire notebook for Carmen as if I'd been diligently adding research all along.

Clean and dry, I dust off a cheap box of wine that I've been storing in my pantry. I find my one and only wineglass squatting behind taller tumbler cups. It's short and stubby, the kind of glass a mom-and-pop Italian restaurant uses to serve its house red. The wine makes quick work, and before I know it, I'm warm, loopy, and determined.

I confront the mirror in the bathroom. In every romance novel I've read—two more now, thanks to Quinn's recommendations—the heroine always talks to herself in the mirror before she's about to do something major. I give it a go, flicking on the light.

My brown hair is there, being its flat dead-leaf self, and my oversized sweatshirt with the cutout neck does me no favors.

I peer closer. My skin is dry around my nose. A patch of adult acne creeps up the side of my neck like a perennial vine, faithfully returning with every menstrual cycle. My eyebrows, though I don't pluck them, appear scant, grass in a drought. But I note all of this without my usual dismay because there's something else.

My eyes. They're clear as day, as if a grimy plastic film has been lifted. Eyes don't dance. And yet, is that a waltz I see?

Is this happiness? Or am I just tipsy?

I smile, baring my red-wine teeth.

"Sweet Bird," I yell, not breaking my gaze with myself. "Get off my chair. It's time to get to work."

And I do it. I write for hours, making up for weeks of inactivity. I tell Carmen about the time the massage oil was rancid, and how Tara once inspected my nails to see if they were short enough after a client complained that I scratched her. I cop to stealthy workarounds to make my job easier—if I have back-to-back husband-and-wife clients, I don't change the sheets, for example. When I start to wane, I dig out my old massage school curriculum guide, using it to think of other topics: local and state laws that govern the industry, the continuing education courses we have to pay to take in order to stay licensed, how to maintain professional boundaries, nutrition (I'm one to talk).

At 4:00 a.m., I slither into bed, but I'm too revved up to sleep. Instead, I repeatedly flip the pillow to the cool side, fretting that Carmen will see me for what I am: a sneak who's been playing at being a writer on her dime.

From the diner booth, I see Carmen marching across the parking lot, her giant Mary Poppins bag in tow, her gleaming white scarf tossing in the wind over her shoulder. Poor scarf, trailing behind as always.

Outside, it's positively balmy at forty-seven degrees. Two teenagers in front of her are wearing shorts, and the rest of us have heaved off our winter gear in the hopes that we won't see it again for months. Even the short-lived maple-tapping season is over, and the webs of plastic tubing linking tree to tree, umbilical cords of sweet sap, have been shut off with the warming forecast.

Carmen buzzes past the hostess, ignoring a "Ma'am?"

I gulp, steady myself, and begin to stand, but Carmen tosses her bag to the back of the booth, unspooling herself from the scarf. She sits, cracks her knuckles, and then outstretches both her hands, twinkling her fingers.

"Gimme, gimme, gimme," she instructs. "My agent is shoving a Greyhound bus up my ass, and she knows I never ride public transport."

Hiding my nerves, I pass the notebook to Carmen across the table. Carmen reads, halts, scans, flips again. She stops on a page, her finger on a heading.

"Office politics? I didn't think there would be much of this drama, since aren't massage therapists a little more"—Carmen reaches for the word—"evolved?"

"Ha!"

"Ha!"

Are we sharing a joke? It feels collegial.

Carmen grins, elated with this revelation, and I notice a green piece of spinach taken prisoner by one of her incisors. I imagine the bit of greenery yelling out to the rest of the spinach as it travels down Carmen's throat, *Just go on without me!* and then looking around, feeling all alone in that porcelain tundra. *Focus, Joan.*

Carmen scans the restaurant with binocular precision and locks eyes with a server ringing up a customer. "We are ready to order," she mouths, before directing her attention back to me. "My heroine, her name is"—she snaps her fingers—"what rhymes with 'Joan'?"

"Huh?"

"Nothing."

I frown.

"Let's call her Felicity, though I might have used that name in a book in the late nineties. I can't keep them all straight."

A server pops up like a prairie dog. Her face is familiar. Crooked name tag, flyaway hair, distressed breathing, though the diner is relatively calm this morning.

The server flips her notepad to a fresh page, not bothering to look at us. "Morning, ladies, I'm Betsy, I'm new here."

Carmen and I exchange perplexed looks.

"Well, that's quite the racket," Carmen says. Betsy looks up, startled. "You told us you were new back in January."

"Oh, shoot." Betsy covers her mouth. She leans in and whispers, "Okay, I *was* new, but I'm still saying that to my nonregulars because people generally go easy on me."

"We'll go easy on you," I offer. Carmen glares at me as if to say, *Like hell we will.*

Betsy exhales, relieved. "I'm just not that good at this job, you know? But I need it." She laughs and then stops. Repeats, "I *need* it."

"Never would have guessed," Carmen mutters. Betsy's eyes widen; she could cry, it seems.

"Well, I think you're terrific," I announce.

"You do?"

"Uh-huh." I nod and then search for something else to say that isn't bullshit. "You're very friendly and you always deliver."

"That makes my day!" Betsy beams.

I rattle off my order, a simple request of eggs and toast.

Carmen, sulking and fuming, decides that this is the moment she needs a very particular type of omelet with a very particular type of fluffy egg, mushrooms just so, and on and on. I watch Carmen speak, the green spinach bobbing up and down, Carmen asking for "the red peppers diced, not in strips," and my distaste for her rises again like heartburn. Being with Carmen is a bipolar swing. One minute I suspect I might be starting to like her, but the next I want to throttle her much more tightly than that white scarf.

Betsy taps the table twice with the overly large menus and disappears behind the swinging doors leading into the kitchen.

Carmen's back at the notebook, reviewing, halting, nodding. She doesn't look up at me when she says, "And you're not withholding anything?"

How does she know?

"No." I take a swig of ice water.

"Uh-huh."

"Nope." I blot my mouth with a paper napkin.

"Uh-huh." Carmen eyes me, and I smile—a big and toothy wolf-masked-as-grandmother smile.

"Not hiding a thing." I flash my empty palms.

"Wunderbar!" Carmen declares, clasping her folded hands on top of the cover. "We're *finally* getting somewhere."

"So you can call off the white van," I say.

Carmen's a good actor; she looks genuinely mystified. "What white van?"

I give her a knowing look. "Carmen, you don't have to keep tailing me."

"I really don't know what you're talking about. Besides, I would *never* drive a *van*. Gross." She visibly shudders. "Just think who drove that last. A family."

"You're not spying on me?"

"That's ludicrous." *Is it?*

"Okay . . ." I say, relenting but not totally buying it. Maybe I'm being overly suspicious about this. A random van showing up at random times.

That's not the only surprising thing. The notebook has passed muster, and yet I'm not as relieved as I thought I would be.

When I started writing for my own sad self, the idea of Evian being a massage therapist felt borrowed from my life. But now I'm daydreaming about it being a real, actual book someday. In that light, it sure as hell looks like I stole the idea from Carmen. She'd have every right to be livid. My book wouldn't exist if it weren't for her.

"What are you thinking about?" Carmen's eyes are predatory, owlish, sensing a shift.

"Nothing."

"My third-most-hated answer."

"Oh?"

"You (a) weren't devoid of thought, and (b) weren't contemplating the theory of nothingness. What's in that fortress of a brain?"

Desperate for a subject change, I grasp at straws—not literally, there are none on the table—and ask her something that's been on my mind. "I was wondering," I stammer, "when did you label yourself a 'writer'?"

Our food arrives, and we switch plates. Betsy *is* bad at her job.

Carmen seems excited to talk about herself, and, mission accomplished, the spotlight has shifted. "I was born in the Bronx, and I came up in this industry punching my way up. When I graduated from college, do you know what they told me I could be? A secretary, a teacher, or a nurse. Three choices, that's it. I said, 'Fuck you and fuck that.' No one ever told me, 'Carmen, honey, you have a real way with words.' I just decided that I did. I'm successful because I never stopped needling, needling, needling my way in." Every time she says "needling," she presses the table, hard, with her pointer finger, and I cringe a little. She'd be the world's worst massage therapist. "No one else was going to call me a writer. I started doing it myself." She deflates her fluffy omelet with a jab of her fork.

"Hmm." I listen, salting my meal.

"I've never asked permission to be who I am," Carmen continues, "and I've never backed off because I'm afraid to be vulnerable or to fail." When she looks at me pointedly, I could crumble.

It hits me. The difference between me and Carmen—or any real writer out there—isn't talent. It's courage.

"And it's the reason why I now self-publish all of my books. No editor. No publisher. I don't need anyone else's permission. Plus, I keep all the profits."

I press my fingers onto a few freed salt granules, fidgeting. Carmen shoots her arm across the table and puts her hand on top of mine, at first, I think, to stop me. "That's annoying," I expect her to say.

Instead, she pats my hand. "Don't ask for permission, Joan. Nobody is going to hand you the life you want with a bow around it. You have to take it for yourself. If massage isn't your thing, it's okay to pivot, you know? You have dozens of years left. Don't spend them miserable."

I nod, the knots in my stomach releasing. Words of encouragement have even more impact coming from Carmen.

Then Carmen laughs. "Here I am slinging advice when I should be following it."

I'm surprised. "Are you miserable?"

She lets out a sigh. "If I am, it's my own doing."

Is Carmen opening up to me? I lean forward, hoping to get her to share what's going on—but Carmen is already waving away her comment, her eyes looking past my shoulder.

"Is that Betty White?"

I don't have to look behind me to know it's not Betty White.

"Joan!" Mom exclaims, coming up to our table. "You're out!"

I know Carmen wants to keep her anonymity *and* keep The Project a secret. So how am I going to explain her to my parents? "Yes, Mom," I say. "I do venture out from time to time."

Dad appears by Mom's side. "Hi, kiddo," he says.

"Who's your friend?" Mom asks, nodding toward Carmen, who is gawking at Mom.

"Your mom is Betty White?" Carmen says, unable to take her eyes off her.

I wave my hands in the air to clear up the misunderstanding. "She just looks like Betty White. But she is my mom. And this is my"—she can't be my aunt this time—"new coworker at the spa. Her name is . . . Gertrude . . . Putyourbottomson. I'm just taking her out to celebrate her first day."

"Oh, isn't that nice!" Mom's embarrassingly excited that I seem to have another friend. Meanwhile, I can see Dad mouthing the words to Gertrude's last name, trying to make sense of it. "How are you liking the Apex, Gertrude?" Mom asks.

"Call me Trudy, please." I kick Carmen under the table, but she ignores me. "It's wonderful. I just love pressing that flesh. All day long." She makes an exaggerated hand motion that she must think looks like massage. It's coming across more like she's waxing a car. Then Carmen slaps the table hard with her palm.

"Your clients must really enjoy that," Mom says, looking scared.

A server stops next to Mom and Dad, holding two menus. "Your table's ready."

Mom and Dad say their goodbyes, but just as they turn to leave, Carmen says, "You should be really proud of your daughter. She's a good person."

Mom peers down at me proudly, and Dad pats my knuckles.

But am I? When Carmen told me to grab the life I want, she didn't know I had Quinn's business card on my desk at home and Cord and Evian in my purple notebook. She didn't know that I've been thinking, more and more, that I don't want to be just someone's research assistant. I don't want to be just a secret writer. I want to be an author.

I want to publish *Snow Globe*.

TWENTY-SIX

I'm checking my email in bed—a bad morning habit—when Tara's message comes in, short and unsweet: I've used up my three sick days. Any more time off, and I'm paying for it.

I toss my phone to the side and pull off the covers, swinging my feet to the cool wooden floor. I need to dress quickly. I have to stop at Mom's on the way to work to pick up a small fish tank. It's not for me; it's for Lou. Thanks to my Yankee swap gift, her giveaway items are now famous. All my colleagues want to know what Mom's got this week. It's the thrill of her lifetime.

Maybe the free stuff wouldn't be so popular if any of us had money to burn. We're headed into what we at the Apex call the Spring Slump. The holidays have passed, ski season is mostly over, the maple sugar shacks are closing, and it'll be a while before tourists return. The best Vermont can offer is mud. Mud, and a piercing, windy chill that's almost worse than the cold of winter. Until about mid-May, each bodyworker is lucky to get three clients a day. None of us will be fully booked.

Jamal's working a second job at the Armani outlet and Carlie's delivering packages. Lou's taken on some carpentry work. Last year, I had to borrow money from my parents to stay afloat. At least I have The Project this year; I'm counting on the final payment to pay off another chunk of my credit card debt. I'm just praying that I don't drop and break my phone or need new tires. If only we had the base pay Evian's crusading for at the Summit.

In the kitchen, I pour cat food into Sweet Bird's bowl, noticing that he didn't touch much of his dinner. It's a cheaper brand, and he doesn't like it.

Then I stand upright, the thought registering: We should push for Evian's base pay.

If she can do it in *Snow Globe*, maybe I can do it IRL.

I grab a toaster waffle—I'll have to warm it up via car heater vent—and my keys. I know just whom to talk to about changing the Apex's ways.

"Hey, Jamal," I say to him in the Apex hallway. He's wearing a fanny pack, unironically, twisted to the side of his waist. If I did that, Tara would give me a strike for violating Apex uniform code.

"Hi?" he says, not used to me stopping for a casual chat.

"Congrats again about the bathrooms." His petition to upper management worked.

"Thanks," he says. He unzips his fanny pack to get his travel lint roller. The bearded collie in his care has overwhelmed him with dog hair.

"Any chance you want to team up?" I ask.

He eyes me skeptically. "If you're organizing a softball league, I don't want any part of it."

This clues me in to how he sees me. I'm a person with an adult-softball-league vibe who barely trudges around the bases and daydreams in the outfield about the orange-clown-hair-colored buffalo wings she'll eat at the bar after the game. Oh, no.

Then he reaches over and zooms the lint roller over *my* shoulder.

"This has nothing to do with sports," I assure him, peering down at Sweet Bird's fur clinging to my uniform. Wordlessly, I stick out my other arm as Jamal runs the roller over the fabric. I tilt closer to him and say in a hushed voice, "I think we can push for an hourly rate on top of our per-service rate. I've been doing some research, and there are other spas offering that now, paying their employees to do their sidework. Can you imagine?"

"Tara will never go for that," he says, indicating for me to turn around.

"We won't know until we try, right?" I swing my arm in a chummy "one for all, all for one" motion, talking to him from over my shoulder as he swipes the roller across my back.

I turn back to see Jamal suck in his cheeks, his cheekbones letter-opener sharp, and in his hesitation I see an old fear emerge, a woundedness he tries to hide. "I have it so much better here than I've ever had it anywhere," he finally says. "When I worked at the franchise, if someone came in with a coupon—and everyone was always coming in with coupons— we were docked the pay. Sometimes I earned seven dollars a treatment. *Seven dollars.*"

"Oh my god," I say, horrified. I've heard rumors of how bad it could be at some of the mega-franchises, but I had no idea it was *that* bad.

"Trying to get a gender-neutral bathroom was one thing, but asking for more money—I'm just not sure I want to rock the boat. I can't risk my job."

I chide myself for believing that all my colleagues would jump on board, lining up to put their names on something as if I'd asked them to sign a birthday card.

"I understand. I don't want to put you in a tough position."

Jamal rips a sheet from the roller, depositing it into the trash can. He stows the brush in his fanny pack. "What would you want me to do?"

"I was thinking I would write a letter to management if you'll help me get signatures like you did last time for the bathrooms."

He's silent, considering, so I push further. "I don't think we should settle just because it's better than it could be. There are days—weeks, even—when we don't earn much, and a base pay would give us predictability, help us stand on solid ground. I don't know about you, but in those weeks, especially right now, I can't always pay my bills."

Jamal presses his palms together and draws them to his face, tapping them against his lips. "I have to think about it. I'm just not sure."

"Thank you for not ruling it out entirely! Take your time. And now, about the softball league—"

Jamal's face registers more alarm than when I'd pitched him the petition. "What?"

"Just kidding!" I crack up.

"Ugh. I've got a pedicure in five." He turns away, but then he swings back and blows me an air kiss.

I imagine us as comrades for workplace justice, two friends changing the world, but then I ruin the moment by pretending to catch his air kiss and pocket it. Jamal's face falls, and I'm back to being the softball dudette in cargo shorts, buffalo sauce fingertip stains vining up the pockets.

But I don't really care. I've never really fought for anything. I'm a top-rated grumbler. I bemoan things. I stew. I bathe in regret. I blame others, blame circumstances, blame my lot in life. But put up a good fight—no, you could say I've never really fought for anything. Not for my writing early on, not for Samuel's family to recognize the importance I held to him, and not for more sustainable work practices at the Apex. Nothing has motivated me to take unflinching and valiant action.

With or without Jamal, I'm finally doing something about something.

———

Heather from reception summons me with a crooked finger. "Someone's been stopping by for you," she whispers, her blue eyes full of mischief.

"*Me?*"

Heather nods vigorously, and then looks side to side to make sure the two of us are clear of eavesdroppers. The spa is a gossip mill. "It's Tony," she whispers. "From maintenance."

Tony. He *has* been thinking about me. My face gives me away, flashing mottled red, and suddenly I'm as overheated as Evian and Cord lying languid in the hot tub. I touch my neck.

"I told him I couldn't give out home phone numbers. But he said you could have his. Want it?" Heather looks expectant, waiting to hear what this is all about.

I fiddle with a display of jade face rollers, trying to play it cool. It could be that Tony just wants to ask a few questions about his injury, and that's it. In fact, it would be silly to think anything else.

"Yeah, sure, I guess I'll take it." I shrug indifferently, like I'm answering mayo or no mayo on a burger. I avoid Heather's eyes. "I mean, just to see what he needs."

Heather's painted red lips spread into a slow smile. "You got it," she says, and then adds teasingly: "Who would have thought—Tony from maintenance?" She passes me a slip of paper.

I glower at her tone, snatching the paper. I start to walk away, but then I tap the desk, nodding at Heather. "Thank you."

Heather winks, which I hate. Don't wink. There's nothing to wink at.

Still, I can't help myself from bouncing down the hallway like a Super Mario Brother springing from mushroom to mushroom. I can feel Heather watching me, but I can't un-pep my step.

Snow Globe

Evian hangs up the phone and stares down at her notebook. Louisa, a bodyworker in Portland, Oregon, had been gracious with her time, giving Evian the lay of the land up there—how body-workers in the city were banding together to demand change in the industry. Evian had tracked Louisa down through a Facebook search, finding a picture of her standing in front of a banner for the Protect Our Bodyworkers Project at a local farmers' market, where she had been handing out literature about the group's efforts.

Cord appears in the doorway with a steaming cup of tea. "How'd it go?"

She reaches for the mug, blowing the steam away. "It's a long game—collecting petition signatures from the public to support a vague notion of change in the industry—but they're not pushing for anything specific yet." Evian glances up at Cord, who is lean-ing against the doorframe, listening with interest. "But we want specific changes, and we want them now."

The Summit's response to Evian's petition was an overly cheery "Thanks for your input" email, as if Evian has suggested a new brand of massage oil. They were unswayed by the number of practitioners who had signed their names, and business contin-ued as usual.

Undeterred, Evian's been on the phone all morning, seeking input and advice from other bodyworkers around the country.

"Maybe it's time to go public," *Cord says.* "Put a little heat on the Summit, increase the pressure."

Evian points a finger at him. "I might just keep you around."

Cord lingers, hands jammed into his jeans pockets. He clears his throat. "Speaking of keeping me around, I need to check out of the Summit."

"Oh!" *A look of surprise surges across Evian's face, replaced with a sudden understanding.* "Right. It must be costing you a fortune."

"I wasn't paying for it. My sponsors were. But they're done footing the bill."

"Where will you go?" *This is the question that's been pulsating between them.*

"I'm not sure." *He toes a divot in the floorboards.* "But I do know one thing—I want to be with you."

"I want to be with you, too." *Before she can second-guess herself, she rushes to say,* "Move in with me."

Touched, Cord moves closer, taking Evian's hand and drawing it to his lips. "I could do that," *he says. Then he looks at her, his expression pained.* "But . . ."

"But? Oh, god." *Evian withdraws her hand.*

"But I have to be honest about something. Something that's been eating away at me."

Eating away at him?

"What is it?" *Evian says. She's the picture of calm, but her pulse is beating so fast it's going to set some sort of record.*

"I don't think Vermont is my place."

"Oh?"

Cord studies the palm of his hand, picking at a callus. "It's beautiful. There's a lot to love. But I miss the wide-open spaces.

*The mountains here, the green hills everywhere—it makes me feel
a little claustrophobic. Hemmed in, even."*

"You want to move back to Texas." *Evian's heart free-falls, a
hot-air balloon basket snipped from its cables. That's what she
gets for flying so high.*

*But she had predicted that he wouldn't stick around for long,
and she'd gone and fallen in love with him anyway, knowing that
when he left, she would never recover. Not in a million years.*

"No. Not Texas."

Her brow furrows with confusion. "Where, then?"

"I was thinking Colorado—with you."

"With *me*?"

"It's crazy, I know, but hear me out." *He bends his knees a
little so that he's face-to-face with her, and he takes her hand
again, running his fingers over her knuckles with reverence.* "We
could buy land," *he says, sounding like a pie-eyed dreamer.* "I
could start my rodeo school. You could open your own massage
business. It won't be easy to start over, but we'd be together."

"Okaaaay," *she says, slowly processing.* "But why Colorado?"

*He stretches his arms out wide and then flies his fingertips to
touch.* "We meet in the middle. We'll have my wide-open spaces
and your mountains." *Now she can see that he's the nervous one,
his breath held in his upper chest as he awaits her answer. Her
mind rifles through all the reasons this idea is ludicrous, moving
with a man she just met to a state she's never visited, but each
reason is as flimsy as a sapling.*

*What's keeping her here? Not family. Not anymore. Roots,
perhaps, and that's nothing to scoff at. Vermont's all she's ever
known. The Summit?*

*Maybe moving will help her broaden her network, allowing
her to have more impact on the industry. Making a difference has
become her priority, she realizes. That and Cord.*

Evian notices Cord's hands, his thumb caressing her fingers with care, each swell of a knuckle its own journey, and she understands with clarity that the winds in her life are shifting.

"I'm moving to Colorado with a cowboy," she marvels, and Cord lets out an audible whoop. "But first," she says, interrupting the start of their celebration, "I want to finish what I've started."

TWENTY-SEVEN

Should I call Tony? If I'm not careful, I'm going to wear away his number on the slip of paper before I work up the nerve. It'll have as much use to me as a pinpricked condom.

Normally I'd call Cher to talk it through, but now I'm giving *her* the cold shoulder since she took a solid week to respond to my last text and then told me curtly that she'd extended her stay in Florida until May. I picture her with an entirely new group of friends—women who wear flowy swimsuit cover-ups and dip their fingers into large glasses of sangria to fish out red-stained slices of oranges, laughing over inside jokes that I don't know.

So instead, I think about what Evian would do. Evian's got more chutzpah in her left pinkie finger than I'll ever have, and from her I hear, "Hell, yes. Call him pronto."

I dial Tony's number, and impulsively, I also take a bite of the homemade coffee cake Mom left for me on my doorstep along with a chipped dustpan, a flashlight, and a chalkboard in the shape of a rooster that Carlie will love. I figure I have at least three, maybe four, rings to chew and swallow before he answers. Who picks up on the first ring?

Tony, that's who. "Hello?" he says.

Mouth full of food, I try to say his name, and it comes out as "Pony?"

"Who?" Tony is thoroughly puzzled.

Unable to pry the cake from the roof of my mouth, my second attempt is also "Pony?"

"Excuse me?" He's so polite! I would have hung up by now.

"Hah owng." Translation: Hold on. I use my finger to pry what feels like a retainer mold off the roof of my mouth. Free to speak clearly, I explain myself, "I'm so sorry. I took a bite of food just as you answered and then I sounded like a polar bear eating a trout. I was trying to say 'Tony,' not 'Pony.' This *is* Tony, right?"

"Yes, this is Tony, not Pony."

"Oh, phew. I was planning on calling Pony another day."

Tony chuckles, but follows it up with, "And who is this?"

Oh my god! I still haven't introduced myself. It's as if I've never in my life made a single phone call.

"This is Joan Johnston—from the Apex."

"Joan!" Tony sounds truly delighted that it's me, and my heart swells. He's making it easy to forget how badly I've bungled this.

"Heather from the spa reception gave me your number." Baby steps, one word in front of another. I just formed a single coherent sentence.

Tony's voice is soft, shy, and I can picture him nervously picking at a sliver of peeling paint on a door frame as he talks. "I hope it's okay that I stopped by looking for you."

This is where I wait for him to ask me for some sort of massage advice. Something entirely unrelated to me. This is where I prepare my heart to deflate, a tiny hole in the blow-up mattress shrinking the whole thing down so that my spine greets the floor by morning. We're both silent for a beat, and then we both rush to talk at the same time.

"How's your serratus—"

"How are you—"

"You go."

"No, you go ahead."

"Oh, I was just asking how your body is feeling. Your injury."

"It's good, it's good. A little sore still, but you really helped it," he says.

I cringe. Does he think I'm fishing for a compliment?

"It was probably just time that did it. Time heals all." *Time heals all?* Now I sound like a tear-away 365-day inspirational quote calendar.

"Well, listen, I . . . gosh, I'm out of practice." Tony takes a deep breath, and then rattles off his intentions. "I'd like to get to know you better. You seem interesting. Is that a flattering word these days?" *Oh!* He thinks he's bungling it! "I was hoping maybe we could talk."

"Talk?"

"Does that sound weird?"

"Depends on what you want to talk about," I say coyly. I'm flirting!

He's caught off guard. "Oh, ho, anything." He chuckles the chuckle that first got my attention in Tara's office. It's such a willing laugh. "We can talk about anything and nothing. Have a few phone dates, I guess I would call them. I have to take things slow, because of my daughter. I don't . . ." He pauses before continuing. "It's not that I don't want to, but I can't really meet for a date just yet."

I'm flooded with relief. *I* can't really meet for a date just yet. I'm still not sure what I'm up for. I'm in the throes of writing a novel about a fake romance to mend my broken heart, so talking on the phone sounds like just my speed.

Lost in thought, I had forgotten to answer him.

"Are you there?" he says. "Does that sound okay to you?"

"Pony, that sounds perfect."

Snow Globe

A box of oatmeal-raisin Clif Bars. A bright red Le Creuset tea kettle, browned on the bottom like toasted bread. An iron skillet, gleaming with a fresh coat of oil. And a pair of worn cowboy boots that Evian sometimes tromps around in, making Cord laugh as she pretends she's wearing chaps. These are Cord's prized possessions, the items he shipped from Texas. The items that are now on Evian's counter, on the stovetop, in the hall closet.

It's so easy, she thinks, to make room for him.

They've devised a six-month plan to move to Colorado. Evian's decided that she and her coworkers should focus on winning one demand from the Summit management, at least for now. At a meeting last night, they had collectively agreed to push for an hourly wage along with their massage commissions and tips.

Now Evian's organizing a Week of Action and putting together a press release. The Summit bodyworkers aren't walking off the job or threatening a boycott. But they are making their demand public, and Evian's scheduled to give a talk at the local co-op. She feels fired up and renewed and happy.

All around her the forests and bushes and grasses are slowly retreating toward hibernation, and the true fall grandeur is bursting forth in another few weeks, maroons and golds that pluck at her heart and reverberate through her body like a harp string of beauty. She relishes fall, and right now she's placing two yellow potted mums outside her—their—front door and standing back to admire them.

Her mom had loved fall, too, and the season reawakens a quiet ache in Evian. She wishes her mom could have met Cord.

Just then, Cord walks around the side of the garage pushing Evian's bike.

"Can I take this for a spin?" He's yearning for movement, for the rush of wind in his hair, for his body to propel him forward,

and while the bike isn't a horse and the helmet isn't his cowboy hat, it will do.

Evian tests the tires. "Of course. I think you'll just have to pump up these babies first."

Cord holds up the pump. "Got it." Noticing the mums, he says appreciatively, "Those look sweet." Crouching down, he unscrews the top to the tire valve, latching the pump, and then stands up to inflate the tire.

She watches him strap on his helmet. "Be careful, my love." She squeezes his arm goodbye. "Those roads are winding and the leaf-peepers are here." Leaf-peeping season has become a dangerous sport, all of the tourists driving distractedly as they behold the splendor.

"I'll be so careful. I've got a lot to live for." He leans from the bike seat to brush his lips over her cheek.

Forty-five minutes later, she gets a phone call. There's been an accident.

TWENTY-EIGHT

Just before bed, I open my front door to usher Sweet Bird inside, and I spy a white van parked down the street. My breath catches in my throat.

It's *got* to be Carmen. Following me to my workplace is one thing, but sitting outside my home is loony territory, verging on threatening. Although what would she be threatening to do?

I squint, trying to get a good look at the driver's seat, but it's too dark. I slip my feet into my rain boots and pull on a sweater over my pajamas—April nights are still chilly. Crouching down, I steady myself on the pavement with my fingertips before keeping low and sprinting across the driveway to hide behind the trash and recycling bins. Carmen floors it, hauling ass down the middle of the road and out of sight.

I walk back to the house feeling a little pissed, a bit violated, and fairly spooked.

If Carmen's appearance is designed to spur me into action, it works. Since I met with her three weeks ago, I've written less than a tweet's worth of characters for the third and final installment of The Project—and two more chapters of my own book. It was comforting to recall specific details about Samuel—his fondness for his Le Creuset kettle, his addiction to Clif Bars, his summers on Cape Cod—and bestow those details to Cord, breathing life into my character through my memory of Samuel. So many of these little details had been lost amid the fog of grief, and it was a joy to rediscover them again—and to let them live on.

I'd better make a dent in The Project. The only problem is, I've got nothin'. No new notes, no new research. But I do get a harebrained idea. By 10:00 p.m., I'm reading old blog posts from my massage school. I copy verbatim the posts about the benefits of foam rolling and trigger points for insomnia. Then I personalize a case study about a client who had a heart attack mid-massage, pretending the client was mine.

An hour later, I've entered ten fresh pages of content for Carmen into The Project's notebook, none of it my own material. I'm crossing a line, I know I am. I do feel guilty. I want Carmen's book to be a success. I want to honor our contract.

But what does it matter if the heart-attack client happened to me or somebody else? If Carmen wants someone to nearly croak on a massage table, now she knows how it could go down.

Carmen, I assure myself, will be none the wiser.

Here are the things I've learned about Tony on the phone: He can still do a few magic tricks from childhood, like pull a quarter out of an ear. He's a Yankees fan, but he's not a raving psycho about it and promises not to relive games with me (not interested) unless a player gets into and out of a pickle (love those!). Tony and his ex-wife met in high school, and their divorce is the kind you'd hope to have if you ever had to get divorced: amicable. Were they still truly in love, they began to wonder, or were they still together because being a couple was all they'd ever known? Just like you can't rebottle ketchup after you've squirted it onto a hot dog, there was no way they could walk back that conversation. They share custody of Chelsea, and they still spend some holidays as a threesome.

It's surprisingly easy to tell Tony that I've been dabbling in creative writing, picking up an old hobby. I don't, however, tell him what I'm writing. Or about whom.

On the phone today, I admit something. "I *finally* realized who you remind me of, by the way! It's been driving me nuts."

He's quick with the answer. "Tony Danza."

"That's it!" I'm lying with my head at the end of my bed and my feet up the wall above my headboard, L-shaped, just like I did in the '90s when call-waiting and see-through phones were all the rage.

"I hear that all the time. It doesn't help that we share the same first name."

"I won't sing the theme song."

"Please don't," he pleads, but I think he's grinning.

"I really want to, though," I tease. "I might not be able to stop myself." I start to hum the first line of the chorus.

"Don't do it!" I know Tony's at his kitchen table, where he always sits when we talk. He eats a nightly bowl of cereal, and I love that he has rituals that involve bedtime snacks. I hear cereal flakes falling into a bowl, a wave of milk. A crunch as he takes a bite.

I tell Tony about my mom's uncanny resemblance to Betty White. "All the most important people in my life look like actors from eighties sitcoms," I say and then blush. Without thinking, I just identified Tony as an MIP.

Gah! Is it too soon? Do I mean it?

He clears his throat, and I sense his tone changing. *Ruh-roh.*

"Joan, you keep saying you'll tell me about Samuel, but then you don't. I'd love to hear about him."

I swing my legs down and sit up on my bed, holding my phone to my ear. This is the last thing I feel like broaching. "Argh" slips out.

"I'm sorry to be a downer," Tony says. "I've heard rumors at the Apex about him, that he died just before he was about to start working there, but I don't know what really happened. Or how you're doing with it now."

I've dodged Tony's questions about Samuel in the past. But I know that tied up in the question of "how I'm doing with it now" is whether I'm ready to be in a relationship with someone else.

"No, it's okay." I soften my tone. "I'm sort of worried it might alarm you, because learning about Samuel is learning about how I lost the love of my life. That may be hard to hear. I'm not saying there won't be another . . . love." *Maybe you, Tony.* "But the story is heartbreaking, and I think I'm only just coming out of it."

"That's honest. I appreciate that." Tony takes a steadying breath. "I'm not afraid of what you have to say. I thought my ex-wife was the love of my life, too."

I'm relieved to hear him say that. "Okay."

"Okay."

"Here goes."

"Here goes."

I dive into the deep end, and I tell Tony everything. How Samuel and I met, about our instant connection, our hikes, our future plans, his quirks, our happiness. And then, for the second time, I recount the story of his death and about the phone call that I didn't get.

"About a year after Samuel's death, I looked up his mother's address and drove to her house, planning to knock on the door and reintroduce myself," I say, sharing a part of the story that I hadn't told Lou. "I really needed her to know me. It felt like our love story would only be validated if she and I finally met. And I wanted to assure her that her son's last six months on earth had been joyful. But also, part of me"—I pause, hesitant to reveal another side of my nature—"was angry. Didn't she have any curiosity about me? How could she have *not* reached out to see if I was okay? She *knew* I existed. Samuel had talked to her about me. I wasn't sure what would come out of my mouth when she opened the door."

"What did you say?"

I flop back onto my bed. "I chickened out. I stared at her house and then left." Samuel's mom had a meticulous garden with dozens of animal sculptures peeking through the flowers, as if they were playing hide-and-seek. In one corner next to a rhododendron was a miniature arched bridge, and perched on one of the rails was a sculpture of a boy in britches pulled up to his knees, hat askew, fishing. I'm guessing it reminded her of Samuel.

Tony sucks in air, and I can picture him slumped, as tired as I am after recounting the story.

"That all sounds incredibly brutal, Joan. I wish I could hold you right now. Is that okay to say?"

"Yes," I say softly. "And I wish that, too." These phone calls have been wonderful, but I'm ready to experience Tony in person. I'm starting to long for his touch.

We're quiet for a moment. I'm parched, and I take a sip of water. In the silence I consider telling Tony more about my book, the last piece of this story. It's the way I'm getting my life back. It's how I've gotten here, readier than I've ever been to love again. But I feel like I've already dumped a lot on him. Next phone call, next installment of Joan's epic grieving process. Maybe by then I'll have figured out what I'm going to do about Swooning Heart Press and Carmen going nuclear when she learns I've penned my own novel behind her back.

Tony breaks the silence by clearing his throat. "This is sort of an odd pivot, but I want to ask you something because, well, I'm developing feelings for you." He sounds like a Victorian suitor when he says this, and his sweetness makes me blush.

"What do you want to know?"

He blurts, "How do you feel about kids? Or that fact that I have one. Chelsea."

I've taken another drink of my water and I almost sputter. "Wow, you *are* pivoting."

He cringes. "I hope that doesn't sound too job interview-y."

"That's illegal to ask during a job interview."

"Maybe it was too soon."

"No, it's good that you asked." I pace the floor of my room, fiddling with a bottle of ibuprofen on my dresser, trying to decide how to answer. "I'm not someone who's had my kids' names picked out forever. And given my mental state these last few years, my maternal drive has been stalled. I'm not writing off the prospect of becoming a mother someday, but I'm not gunning for it, either." I'm quiet, thinking, before I say more. "That said, I could envision myself having a strong friendship with someone else's child. Which is to say, I would be open to a two-for-one special."

"Really?" He breathes an audible sigh of relief.

"Yeah, I would love to meet Chelsea. That is, if you ever let the two of *us* meet again in person, besides me catching glimpses of you at the Apex as you run around putting out fires. Or trying to respond to Tara's fickle demands."

"I'm ready," he says with conviction. "You're one of my most important people, too." He *did* register my compliment. "I'm out of town next week chaperoning Chelsea's class trip to D.C. Let's set a date when I get back."

"Finally!" I punch the air. And in my excitement, I say, "And about kids—I certainly love the act it takes to make them." I redden. For all of our talking and flirting, we haven't waded into sexual territory. Tony is silent for an agonizing few beats, and then he purrs back to life, as if I've flipped a different switch in him.

"You do, do you?" His voice is lower, sensual.

"Mmm-hmm." *Thank god* he volleyed back.

"Gives me something to dream about tonight." Maybe he's *not* so virtuous.

TWENTY-NINE

I potentially have a boyfriend, but I'm barely talking to the one person in the world I most want to gab with about it. I miss Cher. The reasons for our standoff have gone fuzzy, replaced by an ache for my best friend, who's returning from Florida next week. I can't wait to see her, can't wait to restore our friendship to how it used to be, but I think I might have some explaining to do.

A lighthearted email could break the ice. I type a quick message.

Cher Bear,

I'm sure you're feeling wary about swapping sunny Florida for cooler climes, but I assure you Vermont's in full bloom and you can (mostly) leave the house without a coat.

Can't wait to catch up and learn about all the snow-birds who fell under your spell over the last few months.

X, Joanie

There. That oughta spark things back to life. I dust my hands off as if I've just settled something, and then I click back to my news home page, as I always do, skimming the B-list celebrity news, disaster warnings, and unlikely animal friendship stories, like a buffalo and a beaver pulling ticks off each other near a stream.

I'm poised to take a bite of the pasta puttanesca I made for dinner—a surprisingly cheap option if you forgo the anchovy paste and cut up the olives instead of using them whole—when I pause the fork in midair. My mentor and foe, my rose and my thorn, Carmen Bronze, has made the headlines: "The Queen of Romance Recovers in Hospital."

Say what? I dive-bomb the article but it's sparse with details. What I glean is that Carmen was in some sort of accident two days ago and is recovering in a hospital in Santa Barbara.

Poor Carmen, I think, picturing her alone in a sterile room, causing her nurses to question their decision to care for the sick.

I pick up my fork but halt again, alarmed. Hang on. Carmen wasn't in California two days ago. She was in Vermont, in a white van, parked on my street, spying on *moi*.

How can these two things both be true?

I decide to go straight to the best source. Carmen answers on the first half-ring.

"Is something wrong?" she asks.

"Everything's fine with me. I just saw in the news that you got in an accident. Are you okay?"

"Oh, that." Carmen lets out an exasperated sigh. "My scarf tripped me." Not, I notice, *I tripped over my scarf.* "I've got a lovely row of stitches on my forehead."

"That's awful," I say, but my mind is racing. How could Carmen have tripped in California while she was doing espionage on the East Coast?

"I'm a concussion risk, apparently." Carmen raises her voice, and I picture a nurse rushing in to check her chart as fast as humanly possible. "Which is why they've trapped me here, like in some sort of *prison*!"

"What are you doing in California?" I'm still trying to make sense of this.

"Scouting locations. I think the spa in my book should have a West Coast vibe, don't you?"

Wait, what? "I thought you loved Vermont."

"Oh, god, no. The ticks. The trail mix. The Subaru. The fleeces. The covered bridges and itty-bitty cemeteries. The co-ops. The beards. The microbreweries. The historic downtowns. The shape of the state on a map—it's a leg puffed up with gout." She's not winding down, so I interrupt.

"You weren't in Vermont two days ago? I could have sworn I saw you."

"Must have been some other beauty queen," she says and then cackles. "Ow, that hurts my stitches. Who is this again?"

"Uh, it's Joan."

"Right, right. Anyway, I've got to go. There's a doctor I've got to ream out. If you're going to take out my spleen, take all of it."

"Carmen, you know you didn't have surgery, right? Maybe you do have a concussion."

"Potato, potahto."

"Take it easy, okay?"

Carmen pauses. "Hey, Joan, thanks for checking in. Means a lot."

I feel crushed with guilt knowing I'd called only for my own selfish reasons. After we hang up, I'm left hoping she's getting good medical attention.

I'm also left scratching my head. If Carmen isn't driving the white van, who is?

Snow Globe

Evian is desperate to lay her eyes on Cord, frantic for answers. On the phone, the police officer—a guy named Bobby who had been Evian's junior-year prom date—had assured her that Cord was in stable condition after being hit by a car as he cycled on a winding road following the river, but Evian will believe it when she sees it. She's terrified of internal bleeding, of some yet-undetected injury that will end his life.

She rushes into his hospital room, spinning out of control—but there he is with that goofy smile, lying in a bed, left leg in traction.

"You're alive," she says, kneeling beside him, clinging to his arm.

"By the skin a' my teeth," he says, then winces.

Evian realizes that she's tightened her grip around Cord's black-and-blue wrist. She takes him in, as bruised as a dropped peach, as scratched up as an old tire rim. "Oh my god, look at you."

"I've got road rash pretty good underneath this sexy gown."

"And your leg?"

"Busted. But fixable."

"He's a lucky fellow," interjects a doctor from the doorway, stepping inside and joining them. "Hi, I'm Dr. Reed." She extends her hand to Evian and turns her attention to Cord. "All of his wounds are superficial, except for the break in the femur. And if you have to break your femur, he did it the right way."

"I'm a perfectionist," he jokes, then grimaces.

"And the driver?" Evian asks.

"Not a scratch," says Dr. Reed. "It really is a miracle. Change the circumstances even an inch and, well . . . we might not be having this conversation."

The reality of what happened, of what could have happened, knocks Evian over as if she'd belly flopped from a high dive, and she gasps for breath, clutching her chest. The doctor fetches a chair, easing her into it.

"Hey, hey, Ev, it's okay," Cord soothes. "I'm here. I'm not going anywhere."

She wipes her tears. "You're determined to stay injured."

"I'm determined to make an ass out of myself, is more like it," he says, and she laughs at the reminder of that day, not so long ago, when he'd fallen sideways in his chair outside the Summit and she'd been speared by Cupid's arrow.

"I was so terrified that you'd been taken from me just as our love story was beginning."

"Not a chance, love," he says. "I'm here for the next chapter. And the next."

THIRTY

There's a memo pinned up in the break room today. It reads:

> Under no circumstances should any spa employee use a smartphone, iPad, laptop, or any other hand-held personal devices to watch Netflix, Hulu, HBO Go, or YouTube clips of funny cats while administering Reiki, craniosacral, hot stone massage, or any spa treatment at the Apex Inn & Spa. We're known for our stellar reputation, and we will all have to work hard to restore our clients' trust in us.
>
> In loving service,
> Tara

I scan the room, utterly baffled. Carlie sips a Coke at the table.

"This must be a joke," I say of the memo. I yank open the tea drawer and rifle through the options. Detox lemon verbena. Decaf chai. Who do I have to screw around here for a simple bag of Lipton? I find a lone packet of Earl Grey from the wrong side of the tracks and pluck it up.

"It must be a joke," Carlie says, shaking her head in

disappointment, falling into her habit of repeating what people say to her.

"I mean, who would watch something on their phone during a session?"

"Who would watch something?" Carlie swallows and then sets her Coke down with a tired hand.

"No, really—who did it?" I click on the electric kettle and tear open the tea packet.

"Oh, it was Tree. He was watching *Game of Thrones* on his phone during a Reiki session." Somehow Carlie is always strangely in the know.

"*What?* This is a thing people are doing?" It hasn't occurred to me to keep up with my binge-watching at work. Sure, I check my texts every now and then, but watching a show is a whole new level.

Carlie stifles a burp with her fist. "Yeah, I heard he thought the client was asleep, and he put on headphones and set the phone on the corner of the massage table. But you know Tree—he's sensitive to all that blood and gore, and he yelped and yanked his phone to the ground. Caught."

"That's crazy." I try to imagine juggling an iPad and a hot stone without anyone noticing.

Carlie takes a long sip of her Coke and then under her breath mutters, "Maybe if they'd pay us more, we'd have time to watch shows during our time off instead of working second jobs."

I turn slowly from dunking my tea bag. "What'd you say?"

Carlie looks weary, worn out. "Aw, nothing."

"You said something about paying us more."

"Eh, just griping."

I pull out a chair and sit, moving closer to her. "Did Jamal talk to you?"

"Why would Jamal talk to me?"

It's just the two of us in the break room, but I glance around, feeling jumpy. "I'm working on something that might interest you. About our pay here. Jamal knows about it."

Carlie's eyes grow as wide as the bowl of the spoon I'm clutching. "Oh, yeah?"

"I want—I think we can push management to pay us a base rate."

"Good one." She slaps the edge of the table.

"I'm dead serious."

"Oh."

"You've been here for how many years?"

"Going on twenty. But who's counting?"

"And I bet you're certified to do every treatment on the menu."

She lifts a finger to object. "Everything but Tibetan singing bowls." Lou's cornered the market on that one.

"I'm guessing that even as the most senior staff, the most experienced LMT here, you can't always pay your bills."

Carlie nods. "I have to dip into my rainy-day fund when things get slow, sure do."

"We should have something to fall back on when times are tough at the spa."

She fiddles with the tab on her Coke can. "I don't know. Seems like a long shot. I mean, what's in it for them?"

"Retention. Do you know seventy percent of bodyworkers quit two years out of massage school because of the pay? The Apex and other spas waste so much money hiring and training new people. There was a great study in *Massage and Bodywork*. I'll bring it in for you."

"I'd be interested to read that."

"If I put a petition together, would you sign it?" I'm jumping the gun a little, but I'm so thrilled to be having this conversation.

"Jamal signing it?"

I waver. "He's still on the fence."

"He's on the fence," she repeats.

"But I think having someone like you on board would go a long way. For the others."

"For the others."

I want to throttle her. *Stop repeating me!* Instead, I say, "I think it's time we shake things up around here, don't you?"

"I love your enthusiasm."

"But?"

"But I don't know." *Damn.* "I have to give this some thought." Carlie stands up and tosses her can into the recycling bin. With her hand on the door, she turns back and says, "Joan?"

I look up. "Yeah?"

"Thanks for being so courageous. We need someone breathing new life into things."

It's the first time anyone's ever said that to me.

"By the way," she says, stepping back toward me for a moment. "If you're compiling a list of demands, can you suggest they add a camera in the employee lot? A driver in a white van was lurking out there yesterday. Gave me the creeps, sure did."

I nearly tumble out of my chair.

THIRTY-ONE

Mom wants to know if she should drown a dove. It's a voice text, so I take it she's asking if I want new garden gloves. Sure, I type, hoping I'm right. Then I take a deep breath, square my shoulders, and stroll into Cher's kitchen just like in the old days.

I'm breathing new life into things, like Carlie said. Or trying to.

She's in the kitchen, her red hair held back in what little kids these days call an "Elsa braid." Her bare arms are dotted with freckles that emerged from her time in the hot Floridian sun and are sticking around now that our days here are warmer and longer. Her white maxi dress makes her look like a Grecian goddess. I'm in cutoffs and an old T-shirt.

"Hiya," I say.

"Well, well," she says. She's folding her massage sheets, and she pulls one corner of the sheet to the other with vim. Her withering look makes me feel like I should bow to the floor and beg for forgiveness.

But I'm not entirely sure what I did. Didn't she kick this all off by telling me to hurry up my grief? And I'm the one who sent her an olive-branch email that she didn't reply to even after she'd been home for a few weeks.

Because she's my oldest and dearest, I extend a second

branch. "I'm sorry things have felt shitty between us."

The branch goes up in immediate flames.

"*Shitty?* That's an understatement. You can't even be bothered to answer a text."

My anger instantly rises to meet hers. "Oh, please, you text my mom more than you text me."

"At least she responds! When I text you 'How are you?' and you respond, 'Good, you?' that's not an answer."

"Neither is a picture of a fucking sunset. 'Look how amazing it is here.'"

We glare at each other. I'm the first to look away. Then I sigh and pull out a stool to sit down.

"I think this is bigger than who's texting whom, or how many times," I say.

"I agree." Cher slams a folded square of sheet on top of an oversized stack.

"You go first." There's a mound of dandelion blossoms on the kitchen island—Cher makes her own dandelion oil—and I pick up a flower and twirl it.

"Okay. Let's see." Cher puts a hand on her hip. "I can't remember the last time you came in here asking about me. You're either in need of a pep talk for another existential crisis or you don't need me at all. You ditched my New Year's party with a lame excuse. And you didn't even say goodbye before I left for Florida."

I've destroyed the flower. I pick up another one. "Can I go?" Cher shrugs her shoulder, turning back to her sheets as if she might not listen to my side of things.

"You told me to move on from Samuel—"

She throws up her hands. "I apologized for that!"

I repeat, "You told me to move on from Samuel, and even though you apologized, it still hurts, and it wasn't just a onetime thing. I felt like there were multiple veiled suggestions that I should be better, less sad. Like the New Year's Eve party. Didn't it occur to you that it might be hard to watch everyone else kissing at midnight? And by the way, I haven't been having an 'existential crisis.' My boyfriend *died*. It's called grief."

Cher tugs at a sheet, smoothing it.

"And maybe there was a time when I was oversharing with you, but you've been undersharing. You never tell me about your problems. You're making all sorts of huge life decisions without talking to me. It's like you don't need me anymore. I didn't think you wanted to see me before you left for Florida. You didn't invite me to your going-away thingy."

"So I shouldn't invite you to New Year's, but I should invite you to my going-away party. How am I supposed to keep track?"

I tie the stem of a dandelion into a knot, pulling it tight.

"I didn't have one, by the way. A going-away party."

"What? Why not?"

"Maybe I was tired of throwing my own goodbye party. Maybe I was hoping a certain *someone* would have the where-withal to do it for me. I mean, it's a little embarrassing, throwing your own party year after year."

"Oh." I wince, mortified. "I had no idea."

"And of course I'm not talking to you about my plans for my massage business—you hate this job, and I'm sick of hearing all the negativity around something that I love."

I yank the knotted stem so hard that it breaks. "I don't hate it," I say. "I respect it. I wish I was better at it. I wish it felt like the right path."

We're silent. Cher wrestles with another sheet, flapping it out in front of her so that it momentarily catches the wind like a sail.

"Do you want help with that?"

She shrugs indifferently. I take it as a yes and grab the other end near the floor. We hit a rhythm with the sheets, stepping apart and together as we fold, a line dance. Step out, step together, and fold.

"I'm sorry I don't ask about you more," I finally say, looking straight at Cher. "You just always seem so capable and put together and . . . what's the phrase?" I snap my fingers. "Ah, yes, mentally stable."

She chuckles a rueful laugh, as if that couldn't be further from the truth.

"I guess I don't picture you needing *me*," I continue. "I'm always bumbling and flailing, and you're soaring. I almost got fired at work, and you have a thriving business. I'm still grieving Samuel, and you find love around every corner. I just sold Mom's bread maker on Facebook Marketplace for gas money, and you own your house." In all of our years of friendship, we've never talked so openly about our relationship. Cher is looking down, but I can tell she's really listening. "Sometimes it can be painful to hear about all of the great things happening in your life because it shines a light on all of my struggles. I don't think it's conscious, but maybe I don't ask how you're doing because it will make me feel worse."

"I never brag about anything!"

Step out, step together, and fold.

"No, you don't have to. You're just good at life. Adulthood comes more easily to you."

"That's only because I had to grow up fast. My mom basically left me. It was sink or swim." Cher rests her hand on top of the stack of sheets.

I nod. "That's true. But do you know that you *never* come to me with your problems?" Cher juts out a bottom lip, nodding, and makes a confirming tone. I've struck on something.

"Either you don't have problems or you're talking them over with someone else. Or you think I really *am* such a bumbling idiot that I couldn't possibly help you."

"Oh, jeez, I don't think that at all." Cher presses the webbing of her hand between her thumb and pointer finger, an acupuncture point to relieve stress. "It just doesn't seem like you have room for my problems."

"Because I have so many, you mean."

"No. Because you *perceive* that you do. I could look at your life and see freedom and opportunity. I'm locked down by my mortgage, which, by the way, I scrape by to pay every month. My business is thriving, but can I take a paid sick day? Get away from work? My work is in my house! I'm praying my old dryer has another year left in her, or I'm going to be selling things on Facebook Marketplace, too."

Now it's my turn to really listen. I hadn't thought about it like that.

"And frankly, and I've never said this to you, but I envy the love you have for Samuel. I'm not sure I'll ever find my one great love." Her eyes begin to fill with tears.

I clasp her hand. "Oh, Cher!"

She shrugs. "I'm not sure I believe in 'one great love' anyway, but still, I'd like to settle down with someone for a bit. See what all the fuss is about."

I don't rush to reassure her that I know she'll find someone. If there's one thing I've learned over these last few years it's that nothing's a sure bet.

Instead, I say, "I peed a little, by the way, when I first got here. That's how scared I was of you."

"Shut up." Cher swats my arm. "But I *was* pissed." She chuckles.

"You were *pissed*!"

"I think this is a wake-up call for us both. A friendship reshuffling. I'll try to come to you with more of my problems, of which I have many."

"And I'll try not to be such a dickwrinkle when we talk about massage. I want to be supportive. I'm proud of what you're doing, what you've built for yourself."

"A dickwrinkle?!"

"I just made that up!" I do a self-congratulatory Cabbage Patch dance move with my arms.

"Oh my god, I've missed you." She hugs me to her.

"None of your new friends in Florida would have said 'dickwrinkle'?"

"None of them."

Against her neck, I say, "I do want you to know that I've been getting a life, just like you wanted me to do."

She releases me and arches an eyebrow, which is difficult to see because her eyebrows are as fair as a pair of chinos. "How's that?"

I tell Cher about joining the book club, about my new pals Deli and Quinn, and about my surprising affection for Lou. I tell her about Jamal and my budding interest in standing up for workplace rights. I tell her that I've been talking to Tony.

"And," I say, my eyes glittering with excitement, "I've started writing again."

"Whoa. Really? That's huge. I still remember all those stories you used to write. How much time you spent huddled over a notebook."

"You were right about choosing something. Journaling wasn't it for me. But this is different. I feel different."

I feel like I've had the floor for too long, so I don't get into what I've been writing about, or mention Quinn's business card, or the fact that I've been on Swooning Heart Press's website so many times reading the submission guidelines that I probably single-handedly drove up its web traffic. And I don't say anything about The Project or the fact that I'm going to be up against the rails yet again to meet my last deadline.

"You seem different. In a good way." Cher scoops up a pile of sheets to deposit in her therapy room. "I have to say, I'm impressed," she says from behind the stack. When she returns, I feel like I have Cher back. "And I'm glad. Relieved. I just want you to be happy, Joan, that's all I've ever wanted."

"I know." And I do. And I want the same for her—even if it makes me feel crummy by comparison, I want only good things for her. "Did you sign up for those online classes?"

She lights up. "I start in the fall. I hope it's not a waste of time and money..."

"I think it sounds very cool. Definitely worth trying." We talk for a while about how she's going to juggle her work with being back in school. As usual, Cher has a plan. But then she admits that she's not sure she can handle it all.

"All you can do is try," I offer, new at this. "You have to reach for what you want."

"Joan? That you?" Cher pretends not to recognize me.

I throw a dandelion at her but miss.

"When's your parents' big moving day?"

"Get this: They're staying put, after all that."

"*What?*"

"I know. I can't even."

Cher pulls out a bottle of chilled prosecco from her fridge. "I think this is a moment worth celebrating. For both of us. New ventures, new life paths, same great friendship."

I laugh as I retrieve two glass mason jars from her shelf, knowing she serves every drink in them, no matter how high-end. "You sound like a MasterCard ad, but I love you."

THIRTY-TWO

When I see the white van idling in the Apex employee parking lot the next morning, I make a mad dash for it. I'm still convinced, despite mounting evidence to the contrary, that it's Carmen.

It's broad daylight this time, and a spring breeze rustles my hair, bringing with it the fragrant, heady scent of the white viburnum bushes blooming on the edge of the lot. The sun's glare on the windows makes it hard to see who's inside the van. As I run, my tote bag clunking into my thigh, I can just make out the driver's silhouette, head angled down as if looking at her phone. Carmen hasn't noticed me yet.

Good, I'll have the element of surprise. Give her a scare. Serves her right.

I reach the driver's-side door and pound my palm urgently against the window. "I caught ya!" I yell, triumphant.

The driver visibly jumps, yelps in alarm, and covers her face like she's being attacked. When she lowers her hands and peeks at me, I gasp and recoil from the window, shaken. I blink and blink, trying to make sense of who I'm looking at.

It *isn't* Carmen. In the face peering at me, I see shades of Samuel—his eyes, the slope of his nose, the angle of his chin— and then the resemblance fades as quickly as it appeared, the features rearranging themselves, and I'm left staring into the eyes of a middle-aged woman as unnerved as I am.

"I don't understand," I say out loud. I take a step back as the woman unlocks the van and opens her door. The way she unfolds herself gingerly from the seat tells me she's been sitting here for a long time, possibly hours.

She steps out into the sunshine, steadying herself on thick legs. Her black capri pants reveal trails of varicose veins on her legs, leading to socked ankles. She wears a flowy, gathered-neck peasant top in a busy floral pattern that's likely too thin for the spring breeze. Her short, cropped hair curls around her ears. She looks like a woman who laughs with her entire body, shoulders heaving—but her face, for now, is serious. My heart is a startled bird, my hand springing to my chest as if to trap it, keep it safely ensconced in my rib cage where it belongs.

"Joan," she says softly. "I'm Patty, Samuel's mother." She reaches a shaking hand toward me. "Is there somewhere we can talk?"

———

I lead Patty to a stone slab bench that marks the start of the hiking trail up Mount Apex, directly behind the spa. In the summer and fall months, the trail is well traversed by tourists, many of whom start out vigorously but turn back after they realize the trail begins with a steep incline and doesn't let up.

We both sit, knees clamped together, bodies angled toward each other, the middle eighteen inches of the bench stretching between us like the board of a teeter-totter. The chill in the air seeps through my pants, and I wrap my arms around my body. I'm a collision of feelings, guarded and intrigued.

"Are you cold?" is the first thing I ask her.

"I run hot," she says, puffing out her blouse to let the cool air rush down her ample chest.

I nod, and we allow the birdsong in the trees up above to calm both of our nerves. Finally, I say, "So . . . it's been you all these months."

"Yes." Patty slides her wedding ring on and off her finger, over the knuckle and back again. "I've been building up the nerve to talk to you. I'm sorry if I scared you."

"I didn't recognize you just now. I mean, I did and I didn't." I gesture to her face. "I see Samuel, and then he's gone."

"My husband says it's the ears."

"It's the eyes, I think."

"Mmm," she says, agreeing. "I wasn't sure if you'd want to talk to me."

"I do. But why now? After all this time?" It comes out as more of an accusation than I intend, but truthfully, I needed her support then, not now.

"Well, I"—her voice cracks and she clears her throat—"I believe that I failed you."

"Oh." My eyes widen in surprise. I pluck and pluck at the side seam of my pants.

"After Samuel's . . . accident," she says, pursing her lips and steadying her breath, "I lost track of everything. I was despondent, depressed. I wasn't sure if I could go on. It's only been in the last, oh, maybe six months that I've begun to emerge from this fog. Yeah, I would describe it as a fog." Patty stares off, lost in thought, before returning to the two of us sitting on the bench. "I wasn't able to go through Samuel's things at first. His clothes, his shoes. It was all piled in his old bedroom at the house. Finally, finally, I've been doing it."

"Okay," I say.

"Joan." Patty angles her body so she's fully facing me. "What I found in those piles weren't just traces of Samuel." She suddenly grips my hand, and when she squeezes it, I move my intent gaze away from my pants to her face. We lock eyes. "I found traces of you. Everywhere."

My breath catches, and my eyes instantly brim with tears. "You did?" I manage to ask.

"I did," Patty confirms, and now she's crying, too. "It's clear my Sam was smitten with you."

One lone laugh, more like a guffaw, cuts through my tears. Relief flows through me, as if a long drought is over, the recognition I needed finally arriving. Our love had been real. And it had been as epic as I'd remembered it. I exist among Samuel's things. So much so that his mother came to find me, to tell me so.

"Looking back, I would have done a lot of things differently," Patty says. She releases my hand and fishes for tissues in her purse, handing one to me. She dabs at her eyes and I blow my nose noisily. "I'm told that you approached me at the funeral."

I nod, remembering how I had longed to hug her.

"You have to understand that I was not in my right mind." She rests her eyes closed. "Not acknowledging you—it wasn't a slight."

"It felt like one, to be honest," I admit, twisting the tissue. "I did take it personally."

"I'm so sorry, Joan. I'm sorry I wasn't there for you."

"It's okay," I say, and I mean it.

The birds increase their chatter, the afternoon dipping toward evening. After a pause, Patty speaks again. "I'm not sure if you're up for this—and I understand if it's too much— but I'd like to get to know you. Have you over for dinner every once in a while. I'm not sure if Samuel told you, but I'm a pretty good cook."

"He *did* tell me." I consider her offer, picture myself at Patty's table, a table where Samuel sat for so many years of his life, nourished by this woman. It's nice to imagine, but there's a part of me that wonders if, by stepping into Samuel's childhood home, taking his seat at the table, I'll be moving backward, away from the progress I've made.

"Maybe we can meet like this." I gesture to our surroundings. "Outside. A neutral space."

"That's a wonderful idea. I'd like that. Oh, and I brought you a few things." She pulls out an envelope from her purse and hands it to me. "There are so many photos of you and Samuel on his phone. I thought you might want some of them, so I had them printed."

Taking the envelope, I absorb her offering, brushing my hand over it with reverence. "Wow, thank you." I flip through the images, so many memories that I hadn't captured on my phone. "This one," I say, holding up an image for her to see. "We look happy here, but moments later, we got super-lost on a hike and didn't find the right trail for hours."

Patty giggles, her voice childlike, relishing stories about Samuel that she's never heard.

"And this one, we had just graduated from massage school. We were so pumped, so ready for the next stage."

"I'm glad to see that you're still working here. That you're doing all right."

My first instinct is to correct her, but as I think about my life over the last few months, I realize that I *am* doing all right. "Yeah. Me, too."

Patty reaches into the bag at her feet. "I also brought you this."

I gasp at the sight of it. It's Samuel's favorite book about super blooms. She passes it to me, and I rest the book on my knees, running my hands over the image on the cover, a desert mountainside in full bloom. "It's so beautiful," I say, slowly opening the book.

The next photo is a close-up of an orange California poppy tilting toward the sun. My fingers trace the outline of the petals.

"I dream of you," Patty says.

"What?"

"The meaning of the flower. 'I dream of you. I remember you.' It's fitting, isn't it?"

Fresh tears spring to my eyes. "It really is."

Walking back to our cars thirty minutes later, I say, "It's funny, I was just talking about you the other day to someone."

Patty stops and studies me, and a grin breaks out across her face, a Samuel grin. "You're dating someone!" she exclaims.

I toe the ground with my foot, instantly shy. "I . . . I guess I kind of am, yeah." Phone-dating for now, heading for something more.

"Oh, honey, I'm glad. And Samuel would be, too."

"Do you think?"

"Absolutely." And then, finally, nearly three years after I ached for it, Patty pulls me into a hug, and through her muscles and bones, through the squeeze of her arms and the thump of her heart against mine, I feel Samuel again, urging me on.

I fight the impulse to tell her about *Snow Globe*. I'll let that be a surprise. If I ever publish the book, the dedication page will say "For Samuel and Patty."

When Patty releases me, she says, "Let me grab your other things." She presses a button on her car key to unlatch the trunk of her van. Inside, along with a small box of my belongings, are boxes and boxes of holiday decorations—Christmas, Easter, Thanksgiving, Halloween.

Patty cringes, sheepish. "I might have what you could call a tag-sale problem."

I squeeze her arm. "Patty, I need to introduce you to my mother. I think the two of you are going to be great friends."

Snow Globe

The dirt under Evian's fingernails is a red clay, brick and spark and rubies, do-si-doing with sandstone and brown soil and blackened campfire embers. Visible from her windows, the mountains on the horizon are crocodile teeth rising up from the earth, glinting, ragged, undomesticated. The wind that whips her hair has traveled across prairies and deserts, is coming at her from both shores, sandwiching her in an oceanic embrace that leaves her feeling animalistic, capable. Where Vermont is a contented sigh, Colorado is a wolf's howl.

She hadn't expected to love living here as much as she does, sharing land with horses, tending to chores. Does she dare to call it home yet? It's been only two months, yet her path around the house feels worn and familiar, her touch to Cord's hand in passing a habit.

In her home office, she sits in a chair and adjusts her silver Yeti microphone, planted on her desk like a baby cactus. She presses her lips to the cold metal.

"Testing, testing," she says, watching a series of green lights unfurl on her computer screen. Today she's recording her first podcast episode, the next phase of her career along with the home massage practice she's opened on the ranch.

No one could have predicted that Evian's Week of Action at the Summit would garner national attention, and that her press release would tip off a Boston Globe *exposé about the current working conditions for massage therapists across the country. She's been fielding phone calls and emails ever since, other bodyworkers asking her for advice and support. No one else is leading the way, so Evian decides that she will.*

She pulls up the phone number for the woman she's interviewing about the successful union effort at the Hilton spa in New Jersey. Each week, her podcast will share stories from bodyworkers navigating the profession.

Outside her window, Cord walks down the long, dusty driveway, his head bent in deep conversation with a junior executive from Wrangler, one of his past rodeo sponsors. He's hoping they'll donate seed money to his rodeo school in exchange for publicity, their name next to his, Cord McCool & Wrangler teaching foster kids the ropes. Only Evian can detect the slight limp in Cord's gait from the accident.

As if sensing her, Cord shifts his gaze back to the house, finding Evian's green-leaf eyes, her face a full moon of light. He lifts his hat from his head as if it's rubber-banded to his ears, and she puts her hand over her heart.

Later, they take the horses for a ride through the valley, the sky ice-pop blue, the tips of the mountains dusted with snow. Cord lifts his arm to point to something on the horizon and Evian turns her head to look, marveling at this life, where it's taken her, where it's going.

The End

Summer

THIRTY-THREE

After the next book club meeting, I once again help Quinn put the chairs back while everyone else leaves and Deli checks out a manga.

I feel so much lighter since my reunion with Cher, and I'm still stunned that it was Patty in the van, working up the nerve to connect. When I told Tony what happened, he asked, "How do you feel?"

How did I feel? I pondered the question, finally landing on "Liberated. I feel liberated."

No closer to figuring out what to do about Carmen and my manuscript, however. Part of me still wants to take the easy out and keep Evian and Cord inside that purple notebook, safe in my drawer. But the other part of me can't shake the feeling that this is my chance to take a big, terrifying risk and maybe change my life.

Quinn's phone chimes, and she removes it from her back pocket, squinting at it. Then she whistles. "Look at this latest about the Bronzster."

"Huh?" I'm alarmed to hear Carmen's name as I was just thinking about her, and I try to keep the edginess out of my voice when I reply, "Do you mean her accident? And why are you getting notifications about her on your phone?"

"I have a Google alert pinned to her name. I told you I was a fan. And no, not the accident. Apparently the Bronzster is suing one of her past research assistants."

I gasp like a carp out of water and drop a chair.

"Are you okay?"

"I'm feeling a little faint. I didn't have dinner." It's easy to blame Martha, who, let's be real, could have brought more than fruit for her snack duty.

"I might have a protein bar in my bag." It's an offer Quinn doesn't think I'll take, but I do, and she rifles through her chevron-patterned purse for a Luna Bar.

I right the chair I dropped and sit on it, taking a bite out of the bar, making it two-thirds gone. Even in distress, I'm bummed about small portions.

"What were you saying?" I ask weakly.

"What? You mean about Carmen? Nothing, just that she's a serial suer."

"What do you mean?"

"She's infamous for suing everyone from her dry cleaners, to her dog walkers, to her research assistants. All for trivial things, too. Bizarre. I guess she has trust issues or something. I'm sure this research assistant didn't do anything much."

It's a good thing Quinn is turned away. She doesn't see me double over, my head hanging between my knees like I'm a flight attendant demonstrating in-flight instructions.

From the moment I met Carmen, I'd been aware that she could crush me with the smallest of efforts, like taking a thumb to a scrambling ant. Why had I never googled her for the details of what she'd done to others who'd crossed her?

Between my legs I see Deli come back with his book, and he gives me a searching look. I bolt upright and slice my hand across my neck, effectively silencing him. Bless him, he walks over asking no questions and changes the conversation.

"Anyone want to shoot some pool?" he asks.

Does he have no friends his own age? Wait, do I?

"I'm beat," I say, standing up on wobbly legs.

"I'll go," Quinn says, surprising us both.

Lucky for me, the pairing means I don't have to take Deli home—annoyingly, Deli doesn't drive, and he lives far enough from my house that a pizza would get cold had I been delivering one. I drive home gripping the steering wheel, the Luna Bar doing nothing to settle my stomach, Quinn's voice in my ear. *Carmen's a serial suer . . . I guess she has trust issues or something.*

———

At home, I'm already a ball of panic. I flip through my pilfered pages about the spa. If that's not fodder for a serial suer, I don't know what is. I might as well have poured a cup of coffee on Carmen's head, ruined her dry cleaning, and lost her dog. I'm not in hot water. I'm in liquid magma.

Worse, I find a fresh postcard from Carmen in the mailbox—declaring that she's moving up my deadline and is arriving in two days instead of two weeks. My breath shortens. I clutch the postcard, pacing from the kitchen into the living room like a dog on a yard leash wearing out a single path on the lawn.

Two days. Two days!

On my phone, I head to Google and type "Carmen Bronze." Images of Carmen's book covers pop up, muscled men clutching the hems of fair maidens, along with an article in *BookFair* magazine hinting that a new Carmen Bronze book is in the works. *If only they knew.*

I type "Carmen Bronze lawsuits." Pages upon pages load.

"Holy mother of god." My eyes bulge. I click on an article from *The New Yorker* titled "The Romance Queen's Love of Lawsuits." Carmen wasn't exaggerating about her army of lawyers. There's an image of her in a black suit ascending the stairs of a courthouse, flanked by four litigators.

The opening paragraph reads: "By night, she writes about love. By day, she sues anyone with a beating heart. No author has been as proprietary about her ideas as the famed, industrious, and increasingly mistrustful Carmen Bronze, or as petty about minute, non-malicious misdeeds, from shrunken sweaters at the dry cleaner or burning-hot coffee at a café. Besides reading her books, it's best not to cross her path for fear of losing your shirt."

When Carmen finds out what I've done, she'll smudge me out.

My breath has grown both shallow and loud, and the only thing I can think to do is blow into a paper bag like I've seen people do in movies. I race to the kitchen. All I can find is a large paper bag from the grocery store. I gather all four sides of the bag toward my mouth, but the bag is stiff and unwieldy and threatens to give me paper cuts around my lips.

My second idea: I'll bolt for Canada, notebooks clunking along in a satchel on my hip. Oh, right, I've never been out of the country and don't have a passport.

Eating sometimes helps. I pour a bowl of Frosted Mini Wheats, baby loofahs in a milk bath. The sickly-sweet white icing has a slightly calming effect.

"What am I worried about?" I ask Sweet Bird, who is now camped out on the rug, switching his tail back and forth like a naughty finger. "By the time she finds out about my little book—*if* she ever finds out about it—her own book will have topped the bestseller lists, and she won't really care anymore.

Besides, hers will be set in California now. A totally different milieu." Quinn had used the word in book club, and I felt smart and writerly saying it myself. "And no cowboys! Two very different stories."

I gravitate toward the couch, where I sit and balance the bowl on bent knees, my feet on the edge of the coffee table, as I chomp on the cereal. The sweetness gives way to a haylike consistency and then to mush.

Two days is plenty of time to finish, I tell Sweet Bird . . . and myself. I'll start tonight, and I have tomorrow off, so I can work on it all day. "This doesn't have to be a crisis," I say out loud. If anything, this new deadline frees me from Carmen sooner.

Either Sweet Bird is disgusted by me or it's time to go hunt something, because he suddenly shoots out the cat door. Watching the door swing back and forth with ever smaller undulations until it goes still, I look down at my phone, buzzing in my hand, and jump as if I've been electrocuted. Okay, so maybe I'm not totally calm yet.

It's Lou wondering if I can cover his morning shift tomorrow. I'm going to a Cuddle Party, he writes.

My first reaction: *Hell, no.* But then I remember how kind he was in my hour of need. What is a Cuddle Party and why is it in the morning?

You cuddle with strangers in a nonsexual way. Everybody needs to be touched, you know? It's self-care. And this one just happens to be before lunch.

It couldn't be easier to jeer him, but instead I text, Sounds interesting. I think I can move some stuff around. I look at my calendar.

Honestly, I'm not sure if there is enough window to create fake research *and* accommodate intimacy between strangers. But I did promise to be a better friend, and good friends certainly take inconvenient work shifts so a fellow body-worker can recharge—whatever bizarre form that takes. I watch my forty-eight hours dwindle as if I'd thwacked the top of an hourglass to speed up the sand.

But after two more bowls of Mini Wheats and a few hours of copying words into a notebook, I go to bed, feeling calm enough to sleep.

The next morning, I stride into the Apex ready to make quick work of Lou's shift. I've got four massages on deck: two Swedish, one hot stone, one deep tissue.

The last one is with Stanley, a middle-aged, thick-waisted man so committed to discussing the weather that he's either very nervous or a meteorologist. Everything is going fine—I'm counting down the minutes until I can get back home and work—until suddenly it's not.

My hand seizes up. A spasm curls the fingers of my right hand, gripping me in pain.

My right hand. My writing hand.

I walk out of the Apex with an Ace bandage wrapped around my hand.

THIRTY-FOUR

Between writing my book and giving massages daily, I've really done a number on my right hand. Carlie, who's seen it all when it comes to therapist injuries, wrapped my hand and armchair-prescribed anti-inflammatories, ice baths, and rest—none of which will be conducive to churning out half a composition notebook to appease Carmen Bronze.

I could switch to a laptop, but (a) she doesn't trust them, (b) she'd be able to sniff out the truth—that I'd crammed a two-month assignment into two days—and (c) I can't afford one. At home, I sit at my desk and try writing left-handed, but the scrawl is illegible. I think about calling Cher, but her handwriting won't work—it's all loops and hoops.

Who else could impersonate my handwriting?

I text Deli: Any chance you're good at forgery?

Deli, responding instantly: No, but my girlfriend is.

Girlfriend?

April and I got back together. T-Mobile girl.

Are you sure? I can't help asking. Something about April's glowering stare as we drove by makes me protective of him.

Why do you say that? Deli responds. She's really into me.

Who knows, maybe I got a misread. I'll meet you and April at the store in 20 min, I text back.

I grab my composition notebook for The Project off my desk, leaving *Snow Globe* behind.

Had I been paying attention and not fixating on how to fool Carmen, I might have noticed a familiar motorcycle parked on the side street next to mine, and a telltale scarf flapping in the breeze.

———

April is running late, so I'm impatiently pacing in front of the deli counter while Deli weighs a half-pound of roasted turkey for a woman cooing softly to a baby strapped to her chest in a long blue wrap. I've lied to Deli, telling him I started taking night classes and need April to write my assignment for me, and he buys this ludicrous story.

"What exactly happened to your hand?" Deli asks.

"It's just a strain," I say, waving him off.

When April finally materializes, forty-five minutes later, her energy is so repellent that I feel like a beaming Care Bear next to an ominous cloud, even in my foul mood. Her heavy, dark eyeliner and dog collar bark at me: Keep back.

So I do, taking a literal step backward as I say, "You must be April." My eyes dart over to Deli, who seems as wary of her as I am, and he's suddenly fixated on scrubbing a spot on the counter with a towel like he's scratching a lotto card with a penny.

"You're the one who gave him the dumb nickname," April accuses me.

"Oh, uh, guilty." I put my good hand up like I've been caught, and then try to break the tension with a forced chuckle.

Deli doesn't interject to defend the nickname or to move things along. I lean toward her—though not too far, in case she nips at me—and whisper, "I hear you're quite the forger."

"Huh?" April's pink hair inches toward her eyes as she furrows her brow.

"Forger? That you might be able to fake my handwriting. I'll tell you what to write. I'm prepared to pay you." No time for fine print: I can't pay her today, but after I get my payment from Carmen.

April narrows her eyes at Deli. "What's this lady talking about?"

Deli continues busying himself with the now-gleaming counter. "I texted you, 'Any good at forgery?'"

"No, you texted, 'Any good at forestry?'"

"No, I *didn't.*"

"Check your texts, moron. Why do you think I sent you back a tree emoji?"

Deli examines his phone. "*Oh.*"Then he looks up at me. "Oops."

"*Oops?*" I'm furious, wild-eyed, and I can't believe I pinned my Hail Mary on these two, who are now bickering about forgery versus forestry.

"Why would you be good at *forestry?*" Deli asks, trying to find his footing in the argument.

"Why would I be good at *forgery?*" April responds, affronted.

I leave, pronto. They're no help to me. If I don't figure out a plan soon, Carmen will sue me for everything I own. I race up and down the supermarket aisles to find a shopper who looks like a criminal and might be able to pull off my handwriting. I'm harried, desperate, surmising faces with crazed eyes, and causing people to leap out of my way. "What's wrong with that lady?" I hear a kid ask her father. I don't realize until I'm at the bakery, wheezing, that I'm also crying. I pick up a wrapped baguette and begin to tap my head with it, urging my brain to "think, think, think."

How, oh, how can I dupe Carmen Bronze?

I take a huge bite of the baguette, one hand bandaged, the other clutching the breadstick, my hair astray, and then I turn to the same kid who asked her dad if I was okay, who's been trailing me with curiosity since the pasta aisle.

I crouch down. "How's your handwriting, little girl?" I ask, my mouth full, crumbs snowing from my mouth. She runs away, screaming, and that's how I get escorted out of the Price Chopper.

I wiggle out of the security guard's grip just in time to run into Tony in the parking lot.

"Do you know this woman?" the guard asks Tony, as I stand there with my arms crossed over my chest.

Tony, confused, shifts his gaze back and forth from me to the uniformed man. I've never seen my almost boyfriend out in the wild before—aside from eating lunch together a few times at the Apex, we still haven't had our first date—and if I hadn't been so mortified, I might have noticed how adorable he looked clutching his reusable bag. I might have wrapped my arms around his waist and pressed my cheek against the warmth of his chest.

It's also the first time he's seen *me* out in the wild, and having a security guard as a chaperone isn't a good look. It's more like a warning bell, and it's clear from Tony's bewildered expression and his slow answer that it's ringing loudly.

"I do," he says, "yes."

"Can you make sure she gets home? She was having a . . . moment." The guard rolls his eyes.

I glare at him, but he's already retreating back into the store. I'm left shuffling my feet, avoiding Tony's eyes.

"Did you steal something?" He chuckles, but he's also a little unsure.

"Of course not," I respond. Then I notice the baguette in my hand, the end torn raggedly like a dog got ahold of it. "The guard said this was on the house."

"What's going on?" Tony's staring at the doors of the Price Chopper, likely wondering if he's missed something crucial about me during all those hours on the phone. Like that I'm a crazy person. Then he notices my bandage, and the concern on his face doubles. "What happened to your hand?"

"It's just a strain," I say, defeated. I sigh and brush my bangs out of my eyes. "The guard's actually right. I am having a moment." I hesitate, but only because the truth feels too ridiculous to say out loud. Not to mention complicated. And exhausting. Carmen would be here before I could explain everything to Tony. "It's a long story. Let me tell you later. Please."

We stand there silent for a few beats, as Tony winds and unwinds his reusable bag around his wrist. I want to make a bandage joke—*twinsies!*—but he's not in a playful mood.

"I don't like secrets, Joan. I'm confused why you won't just tell me what's going on."

"It's just—a lot to explain in this moment. Trust me."

"You said you were ready to date someone else. To meet Chelsea, which is a really big deal to me."

"I *am*," I say with all the reassurance I can muster.

His eyes search mine, and I'm hoping that in them he sees a woman with integrity. My heart has slunk to the heels of my feet, but now it's lifting a little, as if it's tethered to a bunch of helium balloons.

"I have to be honest," he says. "This makes me feel really nervous." His voice goes quiet. "Maybe you're not as ready as you think you are."

I reach for him, setting my fingers on his forearm, and he doesn't flinch at my touch. My smile is weak, a meager attempt to toss him a rope so I can swing across, back to him, over the divide between us that I've somehow created in the midst of this already shitty day. "Bite?" I offer the oversized breadstick, praying, hoping, that we'll begin to laugh. It's that or cry, for me.

"I'm good," he says, giving a curt nod. His frown is unbearably deep, his lips arcing downward, and his dark brown eyes are two pools of disappointment, wounded and sad. He rubs his forehead as if our encounter is giving him a migraine. I understand, then, that I've grossly miscalculated, and that revealing all of my cards—forgery and all—would have been a better bet. Tony's so honest he wouldn't steal a rogue almond from the bulk section, and suddenly I'm coming across as a liar who's toying with his heart.

Pop.

Pop.

Pop go the balloons that were buoying my own heart. It plummets back toward the ground ungracefully, the way a rock falls over a cavern, hitting and bumping every outcropping in its path.

"Tony," I plead, ready to spill the beans. But I open my mouth only to close it again, a frog without a ribbit, and Tony turns from me to enter the store, his shopping bag limp and deflated in the hand I never got to hold.

THIRTY-FIVE

There're no signs of a forced entry, no shattered glass in the windowpanes on the door, only Carmen Bronze sitting in my living room, her legs outstretched on the coffee table, sipping a glass of my old, fizzy orange juice.

"What's with the bandage?" she asks. "And is that a baguette?"

In a stupor, I inspect my hand as if I'm discovering the injury for the first time. "It's just a strain." I look to my other hand. "It's stale."

Then my brain erupts: Carmen's in my house!

My book!

My gaze darts to the desk. There's an empty expanse of cheap laminated wood where I had left the purple notebook. My pulse starts to sprint, and I look back at Carmen.

"Don't worry. I found it." Her smile is slow, taunting. She pats the notebook by her side on the couch as if she's petting a friendly lapdog.

But it's not a dog that's on Carmen's lap. It's Sweet Bird, the traitor, purring as if he's been neglected for weeks. She indulges him, stroking his fur from his head down to the tip of his tail and back again. He stretches, exposing his belly. *He has claws*, I would have warned anybody else. Instead, I'm hoping there's a telepathic bond between me and Sweet Bird, and that he can read my mind: *Attack!* I silently repeat.

His purr grows louder, a total "fuck you" aimed right at me.

"How did you get in here? The door was locked."

Carmen mimes picking a lock. "I learned a thing or two when I wrote *The Thief, the Baker, and the Candlestick Maker.* An instant classic, by the way."

"You broke in. *To my home.*" I slip on a menacing tone, jutting out my bottom jaw. "And you helped yourself to juice." It's been in the fridge for weeks, so joke's on her.

"Didn't think you'd mind." Carmen crosses one black biker boot over the other, and Sweet Bird jumps down, annoyed. She places her glass just to the left of a coaster.

"I *do* mind." I cross the room to plunk the glass back onto the coaster. It's a pet peeve.

"You know what I mind? Being screwed over. What's with this?" She holds Quinn's business card.

As I stand silent, reaching for an explanation, Carmen's right eyebrow arches in a caret, the symbol hovering above the number six on a keyboard. Above her eyebrow, I notice, is a fresh scar from her entanglement with the scarf. It looks worse than she'd let on, and a smidge of my irritation melts away as I imagine Carmen recuperating in a hospital room alone.

Carmen waves the card at me, and I blink myself back into the room.

"It's not what you think . . ." I begin, and then I falter. Being bluntly honest with the most bluntly honest woman I've ever met might be the only way to stop Carmen from sauntering out the door with my book. Really, it's the only hope I have.

Sinking into my desk chair, I fling up my hands, the bandaged one feeling like it's in an oven mitt, the wrapped baguette leaning against the desk. "Okay, yes, in the process of working on The Project, I ended up writing my own book."

Carmen glowers. "I *knew* it."

"How did you know?"

"You included a page of chapter seventeen of your book in the second notebook you gave me, you dolt."

"Oh my god!" *Did I really?*

"Just titillating material, by the way. Your main character—named after a bottled water, of all things—was teaching her man friend how to give a massage." Carmen sneers. "But what first ticked me off to your treachery were the missing pages you ripped out of your first installment."

I gasp. The pages about my pregnant client that I used for the first chapter about Evian. That I kept for myself. I didn't think she'd notice. But *of course* she had.

"Now why rip out three pages unless it was something you didn't want me to have?" She taps her lips with her pointer finger as if she's unlocking a mystery. "Then all of those questions about calling myself a writer. You were more transparent than my ex-husband when he used to ask if I wanted my feet rubbed. You and me"—she indicates the two of us—"we had ourselves a deal. Plus, I paid you good moolah."

Did Carmen's voice just turn Soprano-esque? I edge a little toward the door.

"It just . . ." My own voice is low. "It just took off."

"What do you mean it *took off*? It can't just *take off*. Airplanes take off. Boats, maybe. What are you talking about?"

"I was doing exactly what you said, making notes."

"Oh, this'll be good." Carmen clasps her hands on a knee, leaning forward. Sweet Bird tries to reclaim his perch, but she swats him down.

"And one day I started dabbling. I wrote my first chapter. Just for fun." But it was more than fun. It had been a way to save myself. I don't know how to explain this to Carmen.

"Uh-*huh*."

"And it kept snowballing. I couldn't stop. I started writing during all of my spare time." *All the time I should have been writing for you.* I breeze past it. "It was freeing, redeeming, exhilarating, healing." I turn to my desk and dramatically run my left forefinger over the top of it. "Remember that day in the diner when you said I would land somewhere? Well, I have landed. This is what I'm meant to be doing."

"You're meant to be checking for dust?"

I frown. "No, writing. I love it. As you must love it." I'm grasping for common ground with her.

Carmen steeples her fingers together and taps her lips, as if she's deciding how to explain something to me. "Is a midwife still awed by the miracle of life thirty years in?"

"I'm sorry?" The crease between my eyes is a deep gorge of worry.

"I'm saying, you watch enough babies get squeezed out and even that gets a little old. It's the same with writing. After thirty-four books, let's just say it's lost its luster." She shrugs. "Babies. Books. It's all a paycheck."

I'm shocked by this admission. "But surely you're still inspired."

She lolls her head in a slow circle, groaning from the back of her throat. "You 'emerging' writers kill me with your insistence on inspiration and meaning." She mock-asks herself a question like she's a fan at a book signing. "'What *inspired* you to write this particular book, Ms. Bronze?' And on and on and on." She circles her pointer finger in the air. "Then I have to make up some story, as if I've been hit by a bolt of creative lightning thirty-four times."

"I see," I say, picking at the fabric of my wrist wrap. "Um, well, for me, and I hate to use this word, but it's been a . . . a transformational—"

"Blech."

"—experience."

Carmen blinks.

"And I can't part with my book now." I step closer to the coffee table, the barrier between us. "See, I wrote this book as a way to deal with my grief over—"

"Oh, save the sob story," Carmen mutters. "We all have one." For the briefest of moments, Carmen's face pales. She reaches up a shaky hand to brush her fingers over a thin gold chain of a necklace I've never noticed before, the pendant hidden behind her black sweater. There's something about the reflex that feels familiar. I finally understand. Carmen Bronze is a card-carrying member of the grief society. She's lost someone she deeply loved.

"What's yours?" I ask.

She opens her mouth, nearly divulging something, but then closes it tight, the hurt in her eyes saying, *You've forfeited the privilege to get to know me.*

She flicks Quinn's business card. "It's one thing to dally a little on your own—but you're planning to publish this thing, right under my nose."

"That's just a pipe dream. No one else has even read it yet. I'm not even sure I'll send it to Quinn. She loves your work, by the way."

"Of course she does." She stares long and hard at me. "And where, exactly, is your third installment of research? The one due to me tomorrow?" Carmen plays it up, acting like she's looking in vain around the room. "I must have missed it on your teeny-tiny excuse for a desk."

The notebook for The Project is in my tote bag where I left it by the door, half-full of crappy research. I make a move to show it to her, fan the pages so she can see I've done *something,* but then I stop. Carmen's right to be mad. I *have* duped her, am in the process of duping her still. I feel like I'm awakening from a dream, and I see with startling clarity the lengths I'm going to to protect myself, to lie, to outwit someone who genuinely asked for my help—and is paying for it.

What kind of person am I? I was a subpar friend to Cher, almost refused to help Lou, pushed my body to the point of injury, hid the full truth from Tony and from Quinn, and moments ago lied to Deli and April so they would join me in my conniving ways.

"I don't have it," I admit.

"You don't have it. You *don't* have it." Carmen taps her fingers on the notebook, one by one, pinkie to thumb, her fingers doing the wave in a baseball stadium. "Let me get this straight. I hire you to do a simple task, you sign a contract to do this simple task, then you make it un-simple by writing your own romance novel in *the very setting* where mine is taking place, it just 'takes off,' you say, and now you not only want to keep the work that I've paid you for—but you're also taking *my idea,* you see, my idea of a down-and-out, sullen heroine working as a massage therapist at a spa who finds redemption and true love, and you're going to turn around and sell that book, publish it to the masses. Meanwhile my agent has parked a car up my ass, *honking the fucking horn* for chapters! So where does this leave me?"

I'm not sure if I'm supposed to answer, so I don't.

"Behind my deadline, looking like a fool with a car shoved up my ass, with another research assistant pulling the wool over my eyes, that's where it leaves me."

"I didn't mean to . . . shove a car up your ass." That didn't come out right. Also, why is Carmen's agent always literally or figuratively shoving things up her ass? I sink back into my chair and slump forward, hanging my head in my hands.

Sweet Bird tries one last time to finagle some chin scratches from Carmen, pressing his body against her leg, but his timing is terrible. She shoos him away with her boot. "This cat is worse than a mosquito," she says, making me want to defend him.

Carmen rubs her temples. She pulls a pill bottle out of her bag. "Is there any adultery in your book? Anybody cheat on anyone?" She deposits a single pill on her tongue and takes a slug of orange juice.

"No," I say, my answer almost muffled in the bandage of my palm.

"Backstabbing?"

"No." I lower my hands.

"Murder?"

Straightening up, I say, "No, none."

"Scandal?"

"Nope."

"Forgery? White-collar crimes?"

I gulp, thinking about my own forgery attempt. "No."

"Hot sex?"

I blush. "It's fairly vanilla."

Carmen looks perplexed. "So what happens?"

I bite a fingernail on my injured hand, my fingernails just free of the bandage. "Evian and Cord fall madly in love with each other and they run away together. To Colorado."

"Boring with a capital 'Boo,'" Carmen booms. Sweet Bird springs for the cat door.

"Exactly." I'm cheering up. "It also touches on workers' rights."

"Oh, for crying out loud. No one wants to read about that."

If hope is a rainbow after a storm, I think I glimpse it. Maybe Carmen will have no interest in my novel. I start to babble. "See, it doesn't have that much in common with your book. My male protagonist almost dies from being hit by a car. Your male protagonist has a disease that hardens his muscles, right?" I'm recalling our first diner meeting, when Carmen was riffing ideas. "And you even said that you're switching the setting of yours to the West Coast. Vermont spas versus L.A. spas—they're light-years apart. I mean, we're talking B celebrities versus Gwyneth Paltrow."

"I'm a B celebrity?"

"No. Uh . . . I mean, L.A. is Goop and we're . . . the Miracle Maple Body Accentuator. We're a bit more homegrown, is all. It's a different scene, I'm guessing, than the one you found while you were out there."

Carmen dabs at her scar again, considering. As kooky as she is, she's a reasonable lady, right? Maybe she gets it.

But then she picks up the notebook, shoves it into her bag, and I gasp.

If she leaves with my book, it will feel like losing myself and Samuel all over again. I'm afraid that, without it, the black clouds from before will block out the light again, ushering back in the darkness. "Please, Carmen," I say, my voice just above a whisper, my throat constricting. "I know what I did was wrong. It really did just get out of control, and I never meant to pull one over on you. I'm sorry."

Fat chance.

She begins to cackle, slapping her thigh at some joke I'm sure is at my expense. Only it's not a joke but a terrible truth bomb. "It doesn't actually matter how different your book is from mine. You signed a noncompete agreement."

"I don't even know what that is."

"In your contract. The one that you didn't read."

"You told me not to bother reading it!"

"I most certainly did not."

"You were tapping your foot to hurry me up. Whatever—what's a noncompete agreement?"

"The contract explicitly forbids you to write in the romance genre or anything about massage therapy for a period of ten years. It's standard. I put it in all of my contracts to avoid this very situation."

"What?" Tears prick my eyes. "Why didn't you tell me?"

"I didn't think I had anything to worry about. You said you weren't a writer." Carmen shrugs one shoulder. "Apparently, I was wrong. Now I legally own your book, and I can do with it as I please. Publish it as my own. Burn it like a PTA mom from Alabama using *Twilight* as kindling. Wipe my ass with it."

This is worse than I had imagined.

Carmen stands up, her eyes boring into me. "You listen to me, Margaret Atwood." She steps over the coffee table, almost taking out the juice glass. "I can sue your ass and take every cent you own, and I still might, since you basically shat on our contract like a pigeon taking a dump on a park bench. I have every lawyer in Manhattan on speed dial. You'll be on the streets with your massage table. 'Massages. Massages for fifty cents,' you'll crow. Except I'll take the table, too. So don't you mess with me."

I swallow hard. Carmen thrusts on her sunglasses, loops the scarf around her neck until it looks like a brace, snatches the baguette, and pulls the strap of the bag over her shoulder, my book caged inside. Then she lowers the sunglasses an inch down her nose and says, before sauntering out the door, "I'm surprised there's no backstabbing. You know it well."

THIRTY-SIX

After Carmen leaves, I sink to my knees and bawl my eyes out. Quickly, though, anger tags out sorrow, and I storm around the house grumbling and yelling. I push my desk chair over, and then I give my desk one ferocious kick, instantly collapsing it to the floor.

How dare Carmen break into my house, steal my book, insult me—my list of grievances trails on and on.

When I tire of that game, I rage at myself. I was such an idiot, dropping bread crumbs to my book like a dim-witted Gretel. And I can't believe that I didn't at least *skim* the contract. Who does that?

Most of all, I'm disappointed in myself that I've been cowed into submission. I know I've lost my book and that I won't fight for it. There's no way I want to go to battle with Carmen. But without my book as an anchor, will I slide back into a depression? And lose my job after all this?

There's also my wrist. Now that the ibuprofen is wearing off, it's aching, and "just a strain" is beginning to feel like an understatement. I'll have to take time off work to heal at my own expense, and it goes without saying that Carmen's not paying me the second two-and-a-half grand that I was counting on. Beyond this physical injury, I could be in for a world of financial hurt—all the more reason I wish I could sell my book.

Eventually, I pry myself up from the couch as if another person is pulling my heavy arm, my sodden body. I lumber to the kitchen to make a cup of tea, snap on the electric kettle, and turn on NPR as if it's any other afternoon and not an hour after my book was stolen by the person whose book idea inspired mine.

"Tourists are flocking to Chile's Atacama Desert to see a rare phenomenon," the reporter says. "Called a 'super bloom,' the once-barren desert is filled to the brim with wildflowers."

I fiddle with the dial, turning it up to make sure I'm hearing it right.

The reporter continues: "The Atacama Desert receives less than 0.6 inches of rain a year, but this year's above-average rainfall worked a sort of magic on the desert, waking up the millions of wildflower seeds lying dormant."

I grip the edge of the counter, my arms covered with goose bumps. A rush of wind seems to travel up my spine.

What are the chances that a super bloom would be erupting *right now* and that I just so happened to turn on the radio at the exact moment to hear about it?

The seeds are so patient, Samuel had said. *They know, without a doubt, they have greatness inside that they're waiting to release.*

And with this memory of Samuel whispering in my ear, with seeds blooming in a *goddamned* desert, claiming their full potential and knocking the world's socks off, with the echoes of my old professor telling me to "get serious," and with my teakettle whistling at full bore, I know, without a shadow of a doubt, that there's no way Carmen's keeping my book.

I'm a seed, baby, and I cannot be denied.

I'm also a seed that needs help. I call Cher. When she answers, I explain everything, the story tumbling out of me.

"Give me a second to think," she says, hanging up without a goodbye.

Fifteen minutes later, she texts: Meet me at my house at 5 tonight.

I breathe the first sigh of relief I've felt in hours. With Cher by my side, anything is possible. I'm just hoping dinner isn't involved. If she's planning to solve this problem by feeding me a bulgur-wheat burger, I'm screwed. I pick up my tea and go to the living room to survey the damage.

———

Cher's house is especially quiet, no humming, no gurgling pots, no Suzanne Vega blasting from the stereo. Also, no Cher. I clear my throat and step deeper into the kitchen. Only the Christmas lights above the sink are on, and I feel as though I've snuck down to unwrap the presents under the tree before everyone else is up.

A list is scrawled on the back of an envelope: *Rescue Squad.* And under that heading:

Pastrami.

Pet Lover.

Ram Dass.

Bookworm.

The list is baffling. Plus, Cher's never been a list person. But it's definitely her loopy, circular handwriting.

"Cher?" I call out.

There's ruffling in the living room, a loud thud, and then silence. I halt, unsure. "Cher, what the heck?"

After more shuffling and an audible "You're on my toe," Cher finally responds, "We're in here."

We? Who is 'we'? Why is *we?* I'm uneasy. "You're being weird," I yell, crossing the threshold into the living room. "And you're making lists now?"

As I round the corner, my jaw drops.

"Surprise!" five people shout, not at all in unison, so it sounds like music in a bungled round. They jump up from various chairs and the couch in the middle of the room. I look from face to face to face.

This is the list.

"Ram Dass" is Lou, his arm chummily around Cher's shoulder.

Jamal is "Pet Lover," hand on his hip, the bracelets around his wrist clinking together.

"Bookworm" is Quinn, looking quirky-chic as ever in a headband and a faded "Ithaca is Gorges" T-shirt tucked into high-waisted, wide-legged jeans. And "Pastrami" is Deli, of course. He looks up from his phone and nods a "What's up?"

I shoot Cher a beseeching look. She reaches out to me before I can say anything or turn and run.

"This," Cher says, sweeping her arm toward the motley crew, "is your Rescue Squad. Also, what happened to your hand?"

"It's just a strain," Deli answers for me.

"It could be more serious than that," I correct Deli, aiming my frustration at the wrong target. I turn to Cher. "What do you mean 'Rescue Squad'?" I'm touched that they all drove over here, but I have my doubts that this team could rescue a capsized toy boat in a bathtub.

Lou jumps in. "We heard there's a book needs liberatin'. I have it on good authority that Carmen's staying another night at the Apex." He's taken on a southern accent for no apparent reason.

"Which means we have tonight to get your book back," Cher says. "We're all in. Right, friends?"

"I've got a blue belt in karate," Deli says and shrugs, indifferent, now playing Angry Birds on his phone.

"I'm not entirely sure why I'm here," Jamal says, flicking a piece of lint from his jacket.

"I can't believe this is *the* Carmen Bronze," Quinn says.

"About that," I say. "I'm sorry I didn't say anything before."

Cher clasps me by the shoulders. "So now the question is, are you in, Joan of Author?"

"Like Joan of Arc!" Lou proclaims.

"Do you want to fight for this book?" Cher shakes me, conjuring up a drill sergeant. "I said"—Cher winds up again—"do you—"

I throw a hand in the air. A hush befalls them. I examine the group. Lou, his face earnest and endearing, so full of hope. Deli, improbably becoming a friend. Quinn, my book-loving companion, understanding full well why I need to reclaim the words I toiled over. And Jamal, my compatriot, considering putting his neck out there with me to better the lives of our coworkers—and now helping me.

Yes, this is my Rescue Squad. These are my people.

And yes, I want my book back.

"Let's do this," I say.

THIRTY-SEVEN

Across the coffee table, Lou unfolds a blueprint of the Apex Inn. When I ask him how he got it, he just says, "I have my ways." The six of us huddle over it, Carmen Bronze's hotel room on the second floor circled in red pen. The goal, which seems increasingly farfetched, is for me to break into Carmen's room and steal my book back.

"The way I figure it, you have two options. Number one: We airlift you in, but I don't think any of us has access to a chopper." Lou glances around the table as if someone might actually volunteer a helicopter. Cher laughs the way a baby bird chirps, sweet and needy. She beams at Lou and Lou winks back. I watch with fascination and horror.

Are they? No. Are they . . . flirting? I push the thought from my brain.

"Didn't think so. Had to ask," Lou continues. "Next option is to get Ms. Joan of Author to this window here, the window at the end of the hallway next to the suspect's suite." Lou's taken to calling Carmen Bronze "the suspect." He marks an X on the second-floor window, which abuts what the map says is Carmen's balcony. "All you have to do is climb out and shimmy along this sill to the suspect's balcony. She's the first room, so you won't have to contend with another guest's balcony. You open the sliding glass door . . . and voilà, you're inside."

I frown. "I don't want to be a downer here, but that doesn't exactly sound safe. Plus—" I wave my bandaged paw. Army-crawl over a windowsill with only one good hand? Aren't there any less dramatic options?

Lou dismisses me with a wave. "Don't worry, you won't be that high. Ten, twenty feet, give or take."

"Again, not to piss on the parade, but ten *or* twenty feet—that's a big difference."

Cher laughs again, throwing her head back to expose her naked neck. Lou stretches out his foot to graze Cher's leg. *No,* I think. *No.*

"Also, Carmen's door is probably locked," I say, stating the obvious.

"Nope," says Jamal. "I volunteer at the animal shelter with Darla from housekeeping, and I asked her to unlock the sliding glass door for you. Darla told Carmen she was there for turndown service, and Carmen bought it."

"Oh, wow," I say, touched that Jamal is using his connections to help me.

"One thing you should know about Darla—she says you *never* say hello, but she's gonna help because Carmen leaves her room messier than a group of frat bros, and she doesn't tip."

"I've never *not* said hello."

"You're not always the friendliest," Deli agrees. I shoot him a look, wanting to say, *What about your girlfriend, Little Miss Ray of Fucking Sunshine?*

I turn back to Jamal. "Can't Darla just slip me a key to Carmen's room?"

Jamal is affronted. "Do you want to get her fired? You get caught and they'll trace that back to her."

"Right," I say slowly, realizing that *I* could get fired if I'm caught. This is all so absurd. I mean, how do we know that Carmen will be out of her room while I'm scooting through her window?

"There's an elephant in the room," I say.

"I think I know what you're going to say." Lou intertwines Cher's hand with his, and my fears are confirmed. "We were waiting for the right time to announce the news. Cher and I"—he kisses her hand—"are soul mates."

"Ewwwww," groans Deli, squeamish, as if he's watching his mom and dad make out in the kitchen.

Cher and Lou take turns explaining that they rekindled something when they met at the Cuddle Party yesterday.

"It's all about timing, isn't it, babe?" Cher taps Lou's nose. *Babe?*

"Tick-*tock*," Lou says, as if the clock just struck hanky-panky.

"I thought it was supposed to be a nonsexual cuddle party," I say.

"It was," Lou defends.

"Until it wasn't," Cher purrs, and they both collapse over each other, laughing.

"Wow." I shake my head, totally thrown off, but I recover enough to raise an imaginary glass to toast them. Cher said she was looking for love, and maybe she's found it in Lou, who, I've come to realize, is one of the kindest of souls. He'll be good to her, even as he drives me crazy. "Congrats to the happy couple." Everyone clinks cups. "But that wasn't what I was going to say, about the obvious thing."

Five sets of eyes stare at me blankly.

I tap my bandaged hand on the X marking Carmen's room. "How do we know Carmen won't be in here?"

"Darla says Carmen always eats dinner at nine in the Apex

Tavern," Jamal says, fidgeting with his bangles. "And by 'always,' I mean that's what she did last night, so don't blame me if that's not right."

"That's your time frame," Lou says, stroking Cher's bare shoulder. "Get in her room by nine, out by nine-ten. You'll have just ten minutes to locate your book."

"I can do that," I say, clapping my hands together, wincing with pain. Damn strain.

"Here's your trouble spot." Lou marks a corner of the hall-way on the second floor and then points his finger. "Camera." Cher and Quinn nod in vigorous agreement.

I peer at the map. "What do I do?"

Unfolding his legs, Deli jumps up, hurries to the center of the room, removes his shoes, and demonstrates a martial-arts roll on the ground. "All you have to do is roll low enough to the ground and you won't get caught on camera," he says. "Near this side of the wall, where the camera angle won't catch you."

Lou whistles through his teeth. "Pretty sweet moves there, kid. Ever try capoeira?"

"Cappa—what?"

While Lou and Deli talk Brazilian dancing, Quinn leans over, pressing my ability to do the martial-arts move. "Joan, do you think you can stop, drop, and roll?"

"Sure," I say with fake confidence, as if this fixes the camera problem. I haven't really tucked and rolled since I was six.

The getaway plan: climb down a ladder that the Rescue Squad will put in place for me, timing it to avoid the security guards.

"Can't I just climb up the ladder in the first place?" I ask. Lou explains that they can't leave the ladder for long or secu-rity will see it.

As implausible as it all sounds, this seems to be the best chance to save my book. What do I have to lose? My job? That could be gone at any moment, given Tara's propensity to hand out strikes. My dignity? I lost that when I was escorted out of the supermarket by a security guard. My relationship with Tony if he finds out what I've done? I've already blown that.

"Fifteen minutes till go time," Lou says.

Everyone stands, and without speaking they crowd around me, as if they're bidding me farewell on a long journey from which I might not return.

Cher produces a suede backpack with yellow and orange stitching, a souvenir she picked up from a street vendor in Tulum. "You're going to need this," she says.

I take the backpack. "Thank you, Cher." Pulling her in for a hug, I whisper into her ear, "You're the best friend a person could have."

She squeezes me back. "I feel the exact same way."

Lou steps forward, putting his feather necklace over my head. "It's yours now. Maybe it's always been yours." The necklace is part of Lou's identity, and his chest looks bare without it. I run my thumb over the feathers, and truthfully, I do feel fortified.

Jamal steps forward. "*Someone* forgot to tell me to bring something." He leans in and whispers, "Carlie and I are in." Then he smiles at me, and my stomach flip-flops. One crusade at a time, but I'm excited by the idea of rallying together to make it easier to work at the Apex.

"I brought this." Deli holds his arm out stiffly. It's a tub of potato salad. "I know it's your favorite. Maybe you'll get hungry along the way."

I doubt that. I could puke with nerves. Nevertheless, I thank him.

Quinn is next and hands me a thick book.

I read the title aloud: "*How to Get What You Want from a Narcissist.*"

"Pretty sure Carmen is one," Quinn offers.

"So thoughtful."

"I know it's long . . . but maybe you can scan it for tips."

"I'll do that." I don't want Quinn to feel unhelpful, but the book is heavier than a filled teakettle.

I survey the goods. A backpack, a feather necklace, a tub of potato salad, and a self-help book—all likely to hinder me more than help me. It's the oddest assortment of warrior send-off gifts I've ever seen.

Lou's watch alarm beeps, startling the group. He clears his throat. "Enough dawdling. The time is now."

I put the book and the tub of potato salad into the back-pack. As I stand, the feather necklace dangles. When I toss the backpack over my shoulder, it violently thunks against my back, and I face the group.

Should I salute? Seems right. I salute with my bandaged hand. All five of them salute me back.

Outside, the light is dim. I give a final wave to the Rescue Squad crowded around the door, and I trot to my car, the book knocking into my back. My left brain is having a fit, yelling, "This is utterly insane." But the rest of me feels armed and ready. I am Joan of Author, and I'm headed into battle.

THIRTY-EIGHT

My Honda bumps over the gravel employee parking lot of the Apex Spa, and I'm careful to avoid the prying eyes of the valet working out front. The lot is empty, the spa closed. The whole vibe feels ghostly and abandoned.

The sun has set, passing the baton to a full moon concealed by a stretch of wispy clouds. I hurry past the employee entrance. My aim is the big house, the inn itself with its outstretched wings. Which room is Carmen's? I study the second floor, rows of lit-up curtained windows like gold-plated teeth in a smile, and then I toot a little. Just a thip. There's nothing like the thrill of passing gas outside when I think I'm alone.

I press on. A blue light shines from the indoor pool, bathing the garden along the path in an inky hue. The backpack thumps against me with every step, reminding me of the gifts inside, and I'm awash in bashful gratitude toward my friends.

A voice halts me.

"*Psst* . . . Joan!" I whip to my left and see Tara, of all people, sitting cross-legged in a crop of pink peonies and early summer irises, the ballerinas of flowers, with their perfectly erect posture.

Tara beckons me with a languid wave. What is she doing sitting in the dark like a garden gnome? How will I shake her? And did she hear me fart?

I look around to see if I've been spotted by anyone else and cross the footpath.

Tara's hair is ruffled and staticky, like she'd rubbed a balloon against it. She's holding the cheeks of a plucked peony with two fingers, tilting the flower toward me. "Isn't this the most exquisite thing you've ever seen?" She lowers her nose to the petals and inhales. "Have you ever smelled anything like this? I mean, *ever*?" Her eyes plead for an answer.

This is a woman who's never had a hair out of place, so it's baffling (and a little pleasing) to see her acting like a wacko. "Tara, are you okay?"

Tara throws her head back and cackles, and the flowers touching her shoulders shake, too. "You should see your face!" She points at me. "You're just so *worried*!"

I didn't come here to be heckled by Tara, who might be having some sort of nervous breakdown or a call to the wild. Plus, I've got a schedule to keep. "Sorry to show some concern," I mutter, pivoting for the path.

"Wait, please!" Tara yell-whispers. She reaches out a hand to me, waving it in distress. "I'm actually *not* okay." And just like that, she begins to ugly-cry.

I step back and crouch. "Hey, hey," I soothe.

Tara flaps her hand in front of her face. "I'm really fucked up. I've just been so stressed. The Miracle Maple Body Accentuator salt scrub didn't sell like I thought it would, so I ate a pot brownie. It wasn't kicking in, so I ate another. I'm never going to feel normal again!" She begins to wail. Now this is making sense.

"Shhhhhh," I whisper, groping for Tara's arm through the thick, woody stems of the irises. "It's going to pass soon."

"It won't," Tara insists, lolling her neck from side to side. "It will, it will."

Tara sees my bandage and screws up her face. "What happened to your hand?"

I wish I had this written on a button. "It's just a strain." For a nanosecond I'm tempted to lobby Tara on base pay. Launch into how even benign injuries like this could set us bodyworkers back for weeks, if not months. In her state, I might get her to agree to anything.

I let the moment sail past with the warm breeze. She'll hear from Jamal, Carlie, and me soon enough. I don't want to take advantage of her.

Tara knocks the limp peony against her forehead. "I'm an idiot."

"You're not," I say, stilling the flower. "We've all been there."

Tara sniffs. "You have?"

"Sure." Not true. I know how edibles work. You can't just eat *another* one because the first one hasn't kicked in yet. You'll be floored, as Tara is now. "Let's get you home, huh?" I pat Tara's hand, trying to urge things along.

"I can't drive like this."

Damn.

"I could call my husband to come pick me up?"

"Great idea!"

"But I left my phone inside, in my office."

Damn.

"Where in your office?" Tara's office keys have tumbled out of her pocket, and I pick them up off the ground.

"Next to my thingy that I type on."

"Your keyboard?"

"Joan, you are brilliant!"

As I dash for the door, I hear Tara chortling, saying, "You're *not* my worst employee after all!" I wonder if she'll still feel that way when she realizes I've burgled one of the inn's celebrity guests. Carmen's Yelp rating will plummet to negative five stars.

I'm back in two minutes with Tara's phone. She dials her husband and as I step away to give her privacy, it dawns on me: Without Tara's ultimatum forcing Carmen Bronze upon me like a hand-me-down prom dress, I would've never met Carmen. And if I hadn't met Carmen, I might not have found my way back to writing.

Tara, you're not my worst boss, after all.

"He's on his way," she yells to me.

"You're good?"

"I'm good! Thank you, Joan." And after a hesitation, Tara says, "And Joan, please don't tell anyone you saw me here."

Please don't tell anyone you saw me here, either. "Mum's the word."

Overhead, the shy moon is dipping a toe into visibility. I return to the path leading to the back entrance of the inn, the doors open to the outside courtyard for smokers until 10:00 p.m. Behind me, Tara talks to herself. "He loves me, he loves me not." Another peony bites the dust.

———————

I pad through the lobby like I'm an ordinary guest, my shoes squeaking on the shining tile floor's alternating dark blue and white squares. I turn left toward the elevators. At the end of the hall, the ensconced lights of the inn's tavern cast a rusty-orange glow. If Darla is right, Carmen should be in there now, berating a waiter, no doubt. The pot-brownie setback means I have just about eleven minutes to break into Carmen's room.

A sign propped up on an easel congratulates a couple, Laura and Ted, on their nuptials, and I can hear the rowdy wedding party laughing and whooping. Someone clinks a glass, causing a cascade of chants: "Kiss, kiss, kiss, kiss."

I slink past, careful not to be spotted.

The elevator is old and slow to close, so I *do* take the opportunity to crack the self-help book. Tip number twelve for dealing with a narcissist: "Use 'we' statements."

Moments later, the elevator chimes, announcing my arrival, and I step through the sliding doors, running smack into Darla and her housekeeping cart.

"Ooof, I'm so sorry," I say, knocking a miniature shampoo bottle to the ground. I stoop to pick it up, the contents in the backpack shifting forward and bonking me in the back of the head. Upright again, Lou's feather necklace swings like a pendulum, and I hold the shampoo out for Darla, who steadies the cart with one hand on her hip. She's wearing the Apex custodial uniform, black slacks and a button-down shirt with the teal embossing. Her entire body might fit into one of my pant legs, and she hasn't lost the affinity for teased '80s bangs. The gum she's chewing is getting a spin-cycle tumble in her mouth.

Darla snatches the bottle back without responding.

I lean toward her. "Thank you," I whisper, "for opening the sliding door."

"I don't know what you're talking about." She fiddles with her cart, shampoo bottles and mouthwash swapping places.

"Oh." I lean even closer. "You . . . You didn't unlock it?"

"Damn, lady, haven't you ever watched *CSI*? I said, 'I don't know what you're talking about.'" Darla gives me a pained look.

"Ohhhhh, right, gotcha, of course not."

She narrows her eyes at my arm. "What happened to your hand?"

I could scream. "It's just a strain."

Unconcerned, Darla continues, "Maybe I need a little something to . . ." She makes a gesture to lock her lips.

"Oh, yes, sure. Let me just . . ." I pad down my pants as if I have a hidden wallet in my pocket. "Gosh, I don't have anything on me."

Darla pulverizes her gum. "What about that?" She points at my chest like she's making a "made you look" joke. I tilt my head down and see that her finger is aiming at the feather.

"It's yours." I pull it over my head and string it around Darla's neck. Thank you, Lou. "Deal?"

"Deal. Besides, I'll take any excuse to get back at Carmen Bronze. Do you know how many times I've refolded that damn white scarf? Only to find it on the floor again? Toss it over the balcony if you get the chance."

The scarf. I suddenly realize why she wears it all the time, even in summer. I think it's to hide her necklace. The necklace her hand flew to when she talked about loss. The pain she doesn't want anyone to see. It's a buffer between the world and her broken heart.

In another life—a life where we aren't stealing books from each other—Carmen and I might be friends. I imagine my days without her. No more bizarre phone calls, no postcards. No more breakfasts at the diner, Carmen spouting just as much nonsense as wisdom.

I can't believe I'm thinking this, but I'll miss her. Maybe we already are friends, and I've ruined it.

"I will," I lie. "Well, thanks again." My hand is up as if I'm thanking my taxi driver. Darla rolls her cart away, her head bent as she takes in her new accessory.

I take a deep breath to regroup. There is serious ground to cover in less than six minutes. I sail down the carpeted hallway. It's the first time I've been in the bellows of the Apex hotel in years even though I work here, and I take in the beige carpet with brown swirling leaves, each leaf the size of my hand. I run my fingers along the raised grooves of the wallpaper, thick stripes of beige and brown. A framed image of Monet's *Water Lilies* offers soothing pastel relief from the prisonlike stripes. Poor Claude. Did he realize his work would become a staple of doctor's offices and hotels?

I stop in my tracks, tipping to my toes, as if I'm catching myself from falling into a ravine. There's the camera that Lou had warned about, blinking green and hanging in the upper corner. I imagine a security guard in the basement, legs on his desk, eating a donut as he halfheartedly watches the camera monitors and then turns back to a crossword puzzle. Given the camera angle, I can't avoid getting filmed, even with the martial-arts roll that I have no chance of pulling off.

I don't know what to do next. The plan hasn't worked. Should I call it a day? I gave it the ol' college try, which in my case doesn't mean I tried hard at all, given that I dropped out.

I saunter into view of the camera—I look like a guest here, after all, not some face-masked burglar with a black sack over my shoulder—and carry on down the hallway, past room 230, 232, and so on.

At room 248, I pause. Carmen's room is next. My heart is beating as fast as the wings on a bird that Sweet Bird chases. My breathing is rapid. My back aches, and I can smell the potato salad, making me both nauseated and hungry.

And then I do something that's not part of the plan. I plant myself in front of Carmen's door.

A roster of brave people filters through my brain: Tony, willing to be vulnerable again after his first marriage didn't last; Jamal, putting his job on the line to stick up for what he knows is right; Deli, thinking about taking a professional leap; Cher, forging her own path, answering to nobody but herself; Lou, being his true self in a world that mocks earnestness; Quinn, sticking with her novel for years; my parents, taking stock of what matters most to them; Patty, Samuel's mother, working up the nerve to talk to me and build a relationship; and Samuel, of course, with his magnetic smile, who lived boldly, fiercely, pushing the boundaries, and daring me to push them, too.

Then I raise up my fist and knock. No answer. I knock again, and I wait.

THIRTY-NINE

The door whips open, and there stands Carmen, tiny yet looming, her springy hair haloing her head, her beady eyes blazing, a long kimono wrapped around her like a sorcerer's robe, and a tray of room service in her arms, clearly heavy.

I had a hunch she wasn't eating in the tavern tonight. She loathes weddings.

"You're not room service. Or did you change jobs?" Carmen says, not at all surprised to see me, still handing me the tray.

I take it like an obedient servant, depositing it in front of her door, a welcome mat of untouched food. There's also a colorful plastic kid's cup with a lid, the bendy straw a submarine's periscope, and I can only deduce that Carmen ordered that for herself. Chocolate milk? The woman is a mystery.

"Can I come in?" I ask.

Carmen's sigh is fatigued, and she pushes the door open wider as an invitation, turning wordlessly back into the room. I follow, stepping high above her rejected meal.

The living room in Carmen's suite has a stone fireplace and two upholstered golden yellow chairs facing each other, fit for two women in colonial gowns drinking tea, stitching needlepoint, and talking about the menfolk. A crystal chandelier hangs overhead. Heavy maroon curtains are drawn over the sliding glass door leading to the balcony, where I would have made my grand theft entrance had I gone through with it.

I also scan the room, spotting my purple notebook on top of a grand piano, next to an empty tumbler glass with sweating ice cubes. My heart parachutes in my chest.

Carmen crosses the room to the piano.

"You've come for this." She picks it up, and motions for me to sit in the yellow chairs, which I do, my posture erect, making me look regal-meets-Kegel. It's all more formal that I had imagined, and my adrenaline is walloping along like I'm shimmying on the ledge.

Carmen tucks the notebook against the arm of the chair, clearly protecting it. She swirls her glass, and the ice cubes slide around each other. I wring my hands, smoothing the fabric on the chair, crossing and uncrossing my legs. The backpack rests near my feet.

Finally, I look up at Carmen, who is studying me, and I notice her eyes are puffy, her nose red.

"Did it—you look like you've been crying."

Carmen purses her lips. "I haven't cried about anything 'sad'"—she puts the word "sad" in air quotes, as if sadness is only questionably real—"since I watched *Free Willy*. Great film. I find the plight of whales exceedingly tragic."

"Oh," I say, wanting to crawl underneath the carpet. "Why were you crying?"

Carmen lets her eyes slide toward the notebook.

"Is it because Evian's mother dies?" Moving Carmen to tears feels like the best compliment I've ever gotten on my writing.

Abruptly, she springs up, waving my notebook in the air like a devout Bible-thumper about to eternally damn me, pacing in front of the unlit fireplace.

"You're going to grovel for your book, beg me not to sue you. And why should I? Just because you 'wrote your heart out'? Just because the whole process 'transformed' you? Oh, *wah, wah*. I saw a sunset once in Tangiers that turned my insides to mush. Did that mean I got to keep it? Ha." She turns and jabs a finger toward me. "We had a deal. Why would you betray me like this?"

The parachute in my chest deflates, the poor paratrooper careening toward a canyon.

"Carmen, it was never my intention to betray you."

"That's what they all say."

I try the book's advice. "We can see you've been hurt before."

Carmen glares at me. "Don't try to psychoanalyze me. You know, you should have told me in the beginning that you're a writer. I never would have hired you. From my vantage point, you've been duping me from the outset."

"In all honesty, I didn't know. I didn't think of myself as a writer. I hadn't written in years."

Carmen huffs. "I have the legal right to put your book in my name. You know that, right? I might just do that. My fans will think I've gone bonkers, because this is *so* not my style. I'll have to interject some scandal. Treason, maybe. Change the narrative arc. Keep Evian, though make some adjustments. I'm bored by the unionizing. And I've never had a thing for cowboys. Too stinky. Maybe Cord is a surgeon. A strapping surgeon whose name is Lucas. Oh, and they certainly won't end up in Colorado. I have a vendetta against that entire state."

I bow my head and curl over a sharp ache in my stomach. To hear Carmen talk about obliterating Evian and Cord pains me deeply. They feel so real to me, and in a way, they are, born from me and Samuel, as if we had both given them a rib, little parts of us woven into them.

But as I squeeze my eyes shut, I see a super bloom, the flowers exploding. Clearer than the photos in Samuel's book, the flowers surround me, blazing with life. Tears rush to my eyes. There is no other way to interpret this vision than as a gift from him, giving me strength and clarity when I need it most.

Evian and Cord don't need to be enshrined in ink and paper to live on in my mind. I'll always have them, just as I'll always have Samuel.

And my writing. If I wrote this novel, I can write another. This is just the beginning for me.

"Carmen," I say. "I'm not actually here for my book."

Her head snaps up. "What?"

"I was coming to take it back, but I changed my mind. I'm here for you."

"For me?" She raises an eyebrow acidly, but she leans forward, intrigued by my sudden shift.

I nod, all of my jumbled thoughts coming together. "Yes. You matter to me. I've grown . . . fond of you." My face reddens at the admission. In my thirty-four years of life, I've told my parents that I love them. I've gazed into Samuel's eyes, expressing my adoration. Notes passed between Cher and me in middle school stamped us as BFFs. In bed in the early-morning hours, when Sweet Bird nuzzles against me, I sweep my hand over his back, whispering sweet nothings.

I've never, until now, sat across from another grown person and declared my *like* of them. I feel clumsy, silly, but I'm also filled with conviction. I want Carmen to know that I care about her. I don't want to lose her from my life.

"This is some weird ploy to get me to let down my guard," she says.

"I swear it's not."

"I'll burn this notebook in the fireplace."

I swallow. "Okay, fine. If that's what you need to do to believe what I'm saying."

Carmen's mouth flaps open and then shuts. She presses back against her chair like she's been forced by a strong gale. "I . . . matter to you," she repeats, as if she's never uttered those words.

The Rescue Squad comes to mind, and I know how she feels. Mattering to people is a new concept I'm still getting used to myself.

"The book is yours. To do with as you please."

Carmen fiddles with the chain of her necklace, silent, likely batting back the caustic part of her brain that's chirping, *What's the catch?*

"What's on your chain?" I ask, pointing my chin in her direction.

She looks down, surprised to find herself touching it. Surprised someone noticed. Untucking it from her blouse, she chuckles once as she inspects the pendant. Then she holds it up to me.

I lean forward, squinting. It's a tiny, rose-gold-plated C. "It's lovely," I say. "For Carmen?" I ask.

She shakes her head. "My first love. Carlos. He died in a goating accident."

I think I've misheard her. "Boating accident?"

"*Goating* accident."

"Oh, my, that must have been . . ."

"Gruesome, yes. We met in the Desert Southwest." Carmen rubs her thumb over the C as if she's stroking someone's cheek, speaking quietly. Carlos was a farmhand on an eighteen-acre alfalfa farm in Taos populated with small cabins for writing residencies. Carmen was holed up in one of the cabins for three months working on her second novel, and every morning she found little tokens on her doorstep. A garnet heirloom tomato that she sliced and sprinkled with salt. Rigid, pale-green celery stalks that she smeared with peanut butter. A log of fresh goat cheese that she ate by the fingertip. Who was leaving these sumptuous gifts? It was a mystery until one morning she yanked opened the door to find the farmhand setting down a broccoli crown, his eyes the color of blue water flecked with green lily pads, his eyebrows and hair dark as the soil. And those strong hands, the way they cradled that broccoli.

She didn't get much writing done after that.

"Then what happened?" I ask.

"I lost him too soon—as you lost your Samuel."

Now I'm the shocked one. "How do you know about Samuel?"

Carmen looks at me like I'm crazy—or just plain slow on the uptake. "Are you kidding? The Apex spreads gossip faster than a head cold."

"True," I concede.

She drums her fingers on the armchair. "I *was* crying earlier."

"Okay," I say slowly, worried that if I speak any faster, I'll scare her off.

"Not just because you killed Evian's mother, the poor woman. I'm giving up writing. Retiring. Your book—I can't write with that kind of passion anymore. It's gone." She makes a *poof* gesture with her hands, tears seeping from her eyes. "Or maybe I never had it."

I scooch my chair closer. "Carmen, your books mean so much to so many people. You're the reason I started writing again. *You* were my inspiration."

"Oh, please." She dabs at her eyes before the tears have a chance to escape.

"It's true. I wouldn't have gotten started if it weren't for you."

"I can't write another book. And on such a grueling schedule. All alone."

"Okay, but don't you set your own schedule? And I thought you were a loner by choice? I mean, you created your dream scenario. No one to answer to—besides your agent. No one to breathe down your neck. No one to annoy you."

"My readers expect a book from me every year," she says and sniffs. "And I thought I wanted this, but guess what happened when my last book hit number one? I had no one to toast with. No one to call. I poured most of the bottle of champagne down the sink."

I chew on my lip, considering.

"Plus, I'm out of ideas. I don't really want to write about a massage therapist. Touching people all day? Gross." Her smile is sad, defeated.

"Well, knowing that a little earlier would have saved me a lot of heartache," I say, trying to lighten the mood.

Carmen doesn't answer, sweeping away invisible crumbs from her robe.

"Carmen, do you remember when you challenged me at the diner to be my true self?"

She shimmies her shoulders to indicate she sort of recalls what I'm saying.

"Now I'm going to do the same thing to you. What do you really want to write about?"

She stares at the floor. A minute passes, and I think she's just not going to answer me.

"Carlos," she finally says.

"Your lost love?" I ask.

"I've never had the nerve to write about him."

I nod, truly getting it. "You've written everyone else's love story. Maybe it's time you wrote your own."

The room is overly warm, and I uncross my legs, slick with sweat behind the knees. Carmen must be overheated, too, because instead of answering me, she strides across the floor, opening the sliding glass door four inches. A breeze filters in, ruffling the curtains and offering us sweet night-air relief.

She returns to her chair, the weary lines on her face giving away her exhaustion. She looks like a lost little child.

"Will you help me with it?" she asks, her voice a wafer-thin whisper.

I frown, uncertain about what she's suggesting. "As your research assistant?" That's the last thing I want to do. "You know your story better than anyone."

She shakes her head. "As a writing partner. A . . . A friend."

The great and formidable Carmen Bronze—a woman who's sold enough books in the last two decades to fill an entire floor at the library, whose next book is more anticipated than another *Star Wars* movie—wants *me* to help *her*? Not as her peon, but as her partner?

My smile is as wide as the piano keys. "Yes, of course. I'd be so honored."

Carmen looks visibly relieved, as if I might have turned her down. "I don't want to keep doing everything myself. That small press. The Swooning something—" She snaps her fingers, looking for the word.

"Heart. Swooning Heart."

She hesitates before asking, "What's their deal? Do you think they'd want to publish me?"

My eyes bulge with excitement. "Are you kidding? My friend Quinn will lose her mind."

Carmen claps her hands together, resolute, color coming back to her pale cheeks, her eyes filled with the intensity that

I'm used to. She shakes her foot, not nervously but excitedly. Her gears are spinning. "Okay, then. It's a deal. You can have your book back. In exchange for your help. Your friendship." She looks down at the ground while saying the last part.

I should be thrilled, but it's not hitting me right. "I'm your friend because I'm your friend," I say. "It's not a deal or a quid pro quo."

Carmen rolls her eyes, but with more affection than usual. "You Vermonters produce more sap than your trees." She sniffs the air. "Do I smell potato salad?"

"You can smell that? Sorry, yes. I guess it is a little overpowering." I unveil the potato salad from my backpack, thinking Carmen's going to tease me for hauling around a tub of spuds drenched in mayo and flecked with red onion.

Instead, she's thrilled. She stands up, my book sliding to the floor. "This place is so organic I've been shitting microgreens. Whole. I'm starving. Toss it here." She holds up her hands, football style.

When I hesitate, unsure if she truly wants me to chuck it at her, she wriggles her fingers and says, "Your book for the potato salad. Now, that's an equal trade."

Before I can ask more questions, Carmen nudges the notebook across the floor with her toe. "Hand it over," she says, as if we're swapping ransom victims. With my left hand, I make the toss. Then I reach down for my book, pulling it to my chest the way I had the night my dad left it for me on the desk. I didn't think I'd ever hold it again.

"I'll burn our contract in the fireplace tonight," Carmen says, using her fingers to feed herself potato morsels.

The dreaded contract, up in flames. I could whoop and holler. Instead, I eye the stone hearth. "Is that . . . a working fireplace?"

Carmen dismisses the question, diving for a potato.

Remembering the Rescue Squad, I slip my phone out of the backpack and text Cher: I'm not dead. Abort the mission. I'll fill you in tomorrow.

"I'm going to call it *The Countess and the Goat Herder*," Carmen says, her mouth full of food.

"Your new book?"

"Yes, the one about Carlos. Now, how often should we meet via FaceTime to discuss our work? Daily? Twice daily?" She sees my face fall and laughs at herself. "You're right, that's crazy. Daily. And as you start plotting your next book, keep in mind that I have no patience for maps at the beginning of books, or family trees I have to refer back to, or Jane Austen retellings, or modern-day takes on Shakespeare, or animals as protagonists and people who turn into animals, as well as time travel, dream sequences, alien invasions, main characters waking up in bed in the first paragraph . . ."

Not for the first time when it comes to Carmen Bronze, I think, *What have I gotten myself into?*

"More tomorrow," she says, stopping herself. "Now scoot. Oh, before you go, take my agent's card. I think you've got the moxie to take this author business all the way. Many people start out, but few people persist."

I let her words wash over me. "Thank you, Carmen." She hands me a white card with raised black type, the name Carlotta Reedsalot standing at attention. I narrow my eyes and thumb the card.

"I'm guessing this is . . ."

"Me." She winks.

"All that time you said your agent was going to be 'up your ass,' you were talking about yourself?"

Carmen shrugs. "More or less."

I groan.

"What? I can't trust someone *else* to represent me."

"You're the worst in the best sort of way."

She beams. I pocket the card. At the door, I glance back at Carmen standing in her robe, her scarf draped over the chair, the near-empty tub of potato salad balancing on her fingertips like a fortune-teller's ball. Maybe she is a wizard.

Carmen nods. I nod back.

And then I slip out the door, back down the hallway, past the Monet, past the camera and its sleeping guard, past Darla's resting cart, down two floors in the elevator, past the closed tavern and the silent lobby with its revolving gold door, and out into the chill of the night and the light of a full moon, standing tall for all to see.

All the while, my book is nestled next to my beating heart. A heart that had slowed but never stopped. A heart that had been biding its time, just like the seeds, readying itself to awe the world.

Was it the writing?

Or was it simply that the forces of nature couldn't destroy me? That nothing could stop me from pushing up to the surface, because something innate in me wanted to survive. Not only survive but transform, so that I was a better copy of my original self. Not Evian. Not Cord. Me.

I take a deep breath, and on the exhale, a fire alarm rings out on a wing on the second floor, likely Carmen's room, my contract up in flames in a fireplace with no flue. From across the Apex campus, a figure runs in the dark toward the alarm, flashlight in hand, speaking low into a walkie-talkie.

It's Tony. He doesn't see me, but I'm aware that my pulse has quickened at the sight of him. My bosom heaves.

EPILOGUE
ONE YEAR LATER

Swooning Heart Press sends Carmen and me on a ten-stop book tour. I'm promoting *Snow Globe*, and Carmen, the real draw, is promoting *The Countess and the Goat Herder*, a tour de force that's been holding strong on the *New York Times* bestseller list for twelve straight weeks, polishing her Queen of Romance crown.

Only Quinn and I know she didn't write this one for the sales numbers. She wrote it for herself, and it's evident in how passionately she talks about the book, the way she answers that dreaded question from all of her fans: What was the inspiration?

"It's based on my first love," she says, and fans eat it up. But it's true. Carmen inspired my writing, and I returned the favor.

It's been the privilege of a lifetime working with her on it and having her help on my novels. My next book is a rom-com called *Cuddle Party*. We FaceTime every two weeks to spur each other on, and I look forward to each conversation. She's ruthless with her feedback—crossing out entire passages and scrawling *I'm snoring*—but she's fair, and when she does offer praise, it feels like it's raining Snickers.

I sent a copy of my first book to that English professor, and on the inside cover I wrote: *I got serious.*

When it came time to record Carmen's audiobook, I suggested Deli read the role of the goat herder. He nailed the audition, sounding exactly like a strapping young man who knew his way around a pasture and could dip a woman for a long kiss even as he kept an eye out for wolves.

For our author photos, Jamal did our hair and makeup. I looked less Glamazon and more "Joan actually showered," but I like that the image resembles me. The last thing I want to hear from readers is "Are you sure this is really you?" Jamal's house-sitting for me while I'm gone, and by the updates he's sending, he and Sweet Bird are having their own romance. I'm not sure Sweet Bird will want to be with me when I return.

With my next book now in the works and a larger advance from Swooning Heart (thanks to Carmen's astronomical book sales), I gave my notice to Tara, who wasn't sorry to see me go. I had become a rabble-rouser agitating all the other employees for better everything. But if Tara thinks I was causing her stress, she's going to need to commit to a steady meditation practice or more pot brownies, because Carlie's just getting started. It really sounds like the tide will turn soon.

To boost my income, I rent a table at Cher's boutique spa in Newchester, where I see a handful of repeat clients each week, including Nancy, the lovely woman who wept on my table but has turned out to be one of the funniest people I've ever met.

Speaking of past clients, at my book launch party for *Snow Globe*, a woman approached me. Something about her face looked familiar. She thrust a business card at me: Sybil Campbell, CEO, Melp.

My mouth dropped open and I gaped at her. Melp? My awful fake website to review mothers? Not so fake anymore, apparently.

"I sold it to Google for millions. Mill-*yuns*." She hefted a Prada bag onto her shoulder and danced her fingers at me. "Toodle-oo!"

So *that's* why she never reported me. She took that idea and ran with it.

Now, in Las Vegas after a morning book reading, I autograph six books (Carmen's line is fifty people long), pack up my tote bag, and check my phone. I have three texts.

The first is from Mom, and it's a photo. Not of a giveaway item. It's a selfie of Mom and Patty, Samuel's mom, out for a hike. They're walking buddies now. At least, I think it's them. The image is of their foreheads, and the text says Saved a cop. By which I think she means "Made it to the top."

The second is from Lou. We're co-throwing a surprise birthday party for Cher, and he's wondering if I think a piñata in the shape of a lit joint is a good idea. Or does it look like a penis? he asks. I don't have the heart to tell him that it *is* a penis. Buy it! I respond.

And the third text is from Dad. A book about a little boy whose best friend is a dog. That's got legs, no?

I reply, That's called Old Yeller. Love you, Dad.

I slide my phone into my bag and wave bye to Carmen—I'll catch her at the airport in a few days.

It takes over three hours to get to Death Valley, even with a long line of traffic from folks rubbernecking at the splendor.

A super bloom timed perfectly with my visit. Thank you, Samuel.

Parking, I walk a few paces from the rental car, forgetting to close my door, my mouth forming an O shape as I take in the sight of entire mountainsides, once brown and barren, now carpeted in flowers: vibrant orange poppies tittering in the breeze; tall violet lupines; deep purple bluebells; crayon-yellow desert sunflowers; evening primrose, as bright white as a pressed wedding dress.

I've never seen anything more spectacular, not fireworks displays or sunsets or the glorious fall foliage in the golden hour of October in my home state all the way across the country.

If I were to step into the field and sink down to sit on the dirt, the tattoo on my upper arm—one single California poppy, its four petals as bright orange as marmalade, a wisp of green for its hearty stem—would blend right in, another flower hardwired to soak up every minute, aware its time is fleeting. A flower that says, "I'll never stop dreaming of you."

"It looks like rainbow sherbet," someone near me says.

"It reminds me of a Dennis Rodman hairstyle," I hear another tourist say, and I chuckle before the tears well up, my own joy colliding with sorrow. I teeter, off-balance, but then Tony's hand slides into mine, five fingers curling toward me the way the flower stems curl toward the light, and I regain my footing, squeezing his hand in return as we gaze, side by side, at one of nature's rarest phenomena.

ACKNOWLEDGMENTS

Thank you to Zibby Owens and Leigh Newman for founding Zibby Books and daring to shake things up. And for your willingness to say, "Yes, send us your manuscript." Receiving your book offer was the best shock of my life, and I have the photo to prove it.

To Bridie Loverro, a debt of gratitude that you saw the potential in my zany manuscript and decided to acquire it as your first novel with Zibby Books. Your editorial guidance was brilliant, and your compassion and kindness have made you a true friend.

Zibby Books has the most nurturing, warmhearted, and badass team of people who worked incredible magic behind the scenes. Thank you to Anne Messitte, Jeanne Emanuel, Kathleen Harris, and all of the team members. I'm eternally grateful for support.

To my agent, Hannah Brattesani, thank you for first passing on my manuscript yet sending me the loveliest rejection email with actual feedback that truly helped me elevate the book. I'm so thankful that, ten months later, you were willing to take another look. And I've been so lucky to have your wisdom and insight as I navigate this journey.

Thank you also to Lucy Carson and the rest of the team at

the Friedrich Agency, as well as Jill Gillett and Carolina Beltran at WME.

A long embrace to Claire Bidwell Smith for making the introductions and for your consistent support over the years. To Bianca Marais, the champion of emerging writers, thank you for reading first chapters, answering my frantic publishing questions, and urging me (and so many others) on.

To Allison Saltzman, thank you for the phenomenal cover. We all loved it from the moment we saw those cucumber eyes.

Thank you to all the talented bodyworkers I interviewed to better understand the industry and profession, including Jodie Allegar, Patty Brown, Sarah Knox, Brittany Purdy, and Stephanie Rodriguez and Tobie Schuerfeld—both of whom reviewed drafts for accuracy. What you offer the world is a true gift, and I hope you get the respect (financially and otherwise) that you deserve.

Writing a book is hard, and sticking with it for years is even harder. I couldn't have done it without the support of dear friends and early readers who pumped me up with their enthusiasm for this project, including Kathryn Donahue, Marion Jordan, Sarah Marcus, Wendy Sweetser, and Caeli Widger. Thank you to the Lunas—Christine Eck, Hope Gaurdenier, Jane Sarouhan, and Danielle Tait—for holding my dream with me. Rob Stewart, thank you for sharing your knowledge of all things Vermont.

To Zoe Pappenheimer, the first person to read my full manuscript, thank you for your support and willingness to endlessly discuss plot holes and all things bookish. Alexandra Russell, I cherish you for your enthusiastic praise yelled on my voice mail and for getting brave in the big waves with me. There are not enough flowers in the world to send to Carly Wahl, who knows this book as well as I do and gave me the crucial feedback I needed to hear. You're next.

A heartfelt thank-you to my writing group members (kudos to Bianca's matchmaking), including Sharon Doering, Melissa Griswold, Hanna Rynkiewicz, Jamye Shelleby, and Isabel Tallysha-Soares.

Pages of this book have received editorial feedback from several key players, including Dori Ostermiller at Writers in Progress, Janice Obuchowski at the Threepenny Editor, Kate Senecal at Pioneer Valley Writers' Workshop, and Andrea Robinson. Special thanks to Debra Jo Immergut for her nuggets of wisdom.

I'm indebted to all of the booksellers, bookstagrammers, and Zibby Books Ambassadors for supporting this book.

Love and thanks to my late grandmother Susie Shephard for gifting me a typewriter when I was eight; to my parents, Cathy DeVoe and Tim Tady, for nurturing my love of reading and writing; and to my siblings, Sara Pascal and Joseph Tady, for agreeing that I'm the funniest in the family. I agree!

And finally, a million kisses to my husband, Alex Bartlett, who took me on a surprise birthday trip to a spa all those years ago, which planted the idea for this book in my brain. You've been endlessly patient and endlessly encouraging. My children, Lisle and Satchel, got in the habit of chanting, "We're going to kick anyone's head in who doesn't like Mom's book." So if you don't like this book, watch out.

ABOUT THE AUTHOR

Megan Tady is a writer and editor who runs the company Word-Lift. When she's not scrutinizing copy, she can be found stocking her free neighborhood library, challenging anyone to a dance-off, or stewing over how *Portlandia* stole all of her jokes. She's a corn-fed Nebraska girl who now lives in a quaint New England town with her husband and two kids. Her next novel, *Champions for Breakfast*, also to be published by Zibby Books, is the story of estranged mother-daughter skiing champs whose lives go off-piste when an avalanche in a Swiss village forces their reunion.

[○] @megtady
[🐦] @megtady
www.megantady.com